RUSSELL JAMES

THE PORTAL

This is a **FLAME TREE PRESS** book

Text copyright © 2020 Russell James

FLAME TREE PRESS
6 Melbray Mews, London, SW6 3NS, UK
flametreepress.com

US sales, distribution and warehouse:
Simon & Schuster
simonandschuster.biz

UK distribution and warehouse:
Marston Book Services Ltd
marston.co.uk

Thanks to the Flame Tree Press team, including:
Taylor Bentley, Frances Bodiam, Federica Ciaravella, Don D'Auria,
Chris Herbert, Josie Karani, Molly Rosevear, Mike Spender,
Cat Taylor, Maria Tissot, Nick Wells, Gillian Whitaker.

The cover is created by Flame Tree Studio with
thanks to Nik Keevil and Shutterstock.com.
The font families used are Avenir and Bembo.

Flame Tree Press is an imprint of Flame Tree Publishing Ltd
flametreepublishing.com

A copy of the CIP data for this book is available from the British Library
and the Library of Congress.

HB ISBN: 978-1-78758-481-5
US PB ISBN: 978-1-78758-479-2
UK PB ISBN: 978-1-78758-480-8
ebook ISBN: 978-1-78758-483-9

Printed and bound in Great Britain by Clays Ltd, Elcograf S.p.A.

RUSSELL JAMES

THE PORTAL

FLAME TREE PRESS
London & New York

For Christy,

For putting up with all that being married to a writer entails.

CHAPTER ONE

1720

At minutes before midnight, five matches flared in the darkness, and then five tallow candles flickered to life.

The dim yellow flames illuminated a large circle etched into the drafty barn's dirt floor. The circle encompassed two triangles, one inverted upon the other, all six sides radically concave. An upside-down wooden cross impaled the ground at the star's center. The musty air smelled of dried dung.

Five girls carried their candles to their designated points on the circle. Providence Neely's wick's amber glow lit her face, which brimmed with anticipation. In moments, Mr. Blackwell, agent from the East India Company, would fulfill his promise and whisk her and the others on a journey to a place far away, where sermons did not fill each Sunday, where drink and dance were not forbidden. They would exercise control over all creatures that walked the Earth, and they would be forever young.

Beside her, Sarah Rogers giggled. Providence stopped herself from slapping the stupid girl. If Sarah's barn had not been the place the East India man had selected for the ritual, Providence would have never let the silly, freckled girl into the group. One of the other girls shushed Sarah.

Thoughts of Mr. Blackwell swirled in Providence's head. Though stout and bald, he was somehow captivating. His presence set a fire between her legs she'd never felt before, a fire he promised in private to quench, after the girls opened the Portal to the magic place beyond.

"This is the time," Providence began, "and this is the place Mr. Blackwell chose. Are you ready to commit yourselves to his service?"

"Yes, we are ready," the girls answered together.

"Are you prepared for the Cleansing," she asked, "to strip away the impurities heaped upon you by the church and your families?"

"Yes, we are."

"Then clear your minds."

Providence went to a stall in the rear of the barn. On the ground lay a burlap sack adorned with the gold twin-lion crest of the East India Company. She knelt, opened it, and pulled out the Portal, a disk three feet across, carved in thick, polished cherry. The symbol from the barn floor covered the center, inlaid in actual gold. Each triangle point hosted a picture of a strange, unrecognizable creature. Mr. Blackwell had taken her to find it, washed up on the shore outside Stone Harbor. Its arrival was a mystery, Mr. Blackwell's refusal to touch it even more so. He explained this was the door to his kingdom, and the girls were the key to unlock it.

The far doors to the barn flew open. A mob of men with blazing torches charged in. The girls screamed. The torches' flames overpowered the candles' dim light and the girls squinted against the sudden brightness.

Providence gritted her teeth at the sight of the Stone Harbor elders. The men were armed, two with muskets, the rest with knives, pitchforks, one a rusty whaling spear. Reverend Snow, the aged, scrawny windbag, led the pack, ever-present Bible clasped against his chest. His eyes burned with his usual self-righteous fire.

"There!" He pointed his bony finger at the cowering girls and their flickering candles. "Just as I warned you! Witchcraft afoot in Stone Harbor!"

Providence doused her candle and ducked into the stall's shadow. She shoved the Portal back into the burlap sack and dragged it over to her feet.

Sarah's father muscled his way to the front of the group. His hard, angry face melted into shocked disbelief as he recognized his daughter at the strange symbol in the dirt.

"Sarah? How…how could you…?"

Sarah dropped her candle and scrambled over to her father's feet. She wrapped her arms around his legs. Her face, white with fear, turned up to face his.

"Father, it wasn't me!" she implored. "'Twas the East India man. He bewitched us."

"Did I not warn you all?" Reverend Snow said. "That man's promises to make us a great seaport were falsehoods."

"We are but his pawns," Sarah said. "Surely compelled we are, by him and by Providence."

Providence wanted to beat the whiny weakling with the Portal. Sarah had never been worthy of following Mr. Blackwell.

"Providence is here?" Reverend Snow said.

"She's the full witch," Sarah said. "Not me. She rides a broomstick and speaks black magic to cats."

Providence knew that pack of lies would earn her a perfunctory trial and a death by pressing. She needed to get out of here now. She hoisted the heavy sack, grasped it to her chest and stole out the rear door and into the night.

A blast of cold wind off the harbor whipped her long skirt around her legs. She clenched the ponderous sack tight and ran for the sheep pasture. Behind her, torches lit the night as some of the elders left the barn.

In spite of her pounding heart, she tried to think clearly. Above the other four girls, Mr. Blackwell had entrusted *her* with the Portal, and with special instructions for its care. Should the Cleansing be unfinished, she had to hide it, to keep it out of the hands of the reverend and the others. Mr. Blackwell promised to keep her under his protection forever if she would protect the Portal.

She crossed the pasture at a run. The sack seemed to gain weight with each step as her arms grew tired. Bleating sheep scattered ahead of her. As the sheep's cries rolled down toward the barn, the clamor of men's voices echoed back in reply.

"She's up there!"

"Grab her, brother! Use care for her spells!"

She cut right and entered the forest. The autumn's bare branches reached for her like goblin hands from the darkness, each revealing itself a split second before ensnaring her. She ducked and weaved, but one branch snagged her skirt at the knee, and ripped it all the way down to the hem. Then another branch whipped against her cheek and drew blood. From behind her came the sound of men charging across the pasture. Their voices grew louder as they closed on the forest.

Her heart seemed about to burst, her leg muscles burned. The Portal felt like it weighed a hundred pounds. She sagged against a tree and scanned the forest for a hiding place.

Moonlight lit a large, flat piece of shale amongst the fallen oak leaves. She stumbled over, dropped the sack beside the rock, and fell to her knees. Her hands shook as she grabbed the stone's sharp corner and pulled with all her strength. The stone yielded and revealed a patch of soft, dark earth. With her bare hands, she attacked the ground. Her nails split and tore as she dug through roots and rocks. She scraped a shallow grave for the Portal.

Sheep again bleated a warning. Torches flickered at the forest's edge. She tossed the sack in the hole. It was just deep enough. She grabbed the rock and heaved it back over the exposed earth. It landed with a sharp crack. The edge of the stone shattered, leaving a jagged border along one side. She kicked the soggy leaves back over the rock. Trickles of icy sweat ran down her face. She stood and raised her chin in triumph.

I did it, she thought. *I saved the Portal. Its resting place shall never pass my lips. My East India man will shield me from their torments. Even if they capture me, no stones will crush my chest. Mr. Blackwell will rescue me. I know he will.*

Leaves rustled at her feet. A flash of tan and copper lunged at her exposed leg. Twin spikes of pain lanced her calf as a copperhead snake clamped onto her leg. She dropped to one knee with a scream. The snake released her, slithered off, and coiled a few feet away.

Her leg went numb. Panic surged within her. She knew that many had died of copperhead snakebite. But didn't snakes slumber this late in the fall?

The heavy shuffle of a dozen feet through the detritus of the forest floor came closer. Torches bobbed between the thick tree trunks. The voices grew louder, but the words less distinct as the poison made Providence's head spin.

What grievous fate befalls me? Providence thought. *How can this happen? All he asked, I have done.*

She collapsed to the ground. All around her went dark. Her last breath passed her lips, and she wondered why her East India man had not protected her.

*   *   *

A little higher on the hill, Mr. Blackwell, as he called himself this time, stood in the shadow of a great glacial boulder. A broad black hat shielded the stocky man's face from the cold; only his chin and black goatee poked out from its shadow.

With a sweeping hand gesture, he sent the copperhead retreating into the woods to return to its interrupted hibernation. Blackwell was indeed there to protect, just not to protect Providence.

This window of opportunity had closed. But the Portal lay safe. He'd be back in a few hundred years. Immortality bred amazing patience.

CHAPTER TWO

2020

A persistent fog still blanketed Stone Harbor, though by 9 a.m. it should have long burned off. It suited dockmaster Charlie Cauble just fine. As far as he was concerned, the fog's embrace brought comfort, not the eerie unease mainlanders associated with it.

It also slowed down the boat traffic, and that was fine with him as well. He pumped gas from the dock house at the pier's end, but he didn't work on commission, so less work didn't bother him at all. Not that there was much work after fall rolled in anyway. The thrice-a-day ferry service to the island cut down to twice a week after Labor Day. The pleasure boats from Long Island and New England that made the thirty-mile run either way had all nestled in boatyard cradles for the winter. Commercial fishing, like he used to do, collapsed in the mid-1960s with the crash of the cod. Some winter days, he happily spent eight hours without interruption. His old bones didn't mind the respite.

With hands long gnarled by life on the sea, he pulled his heavy corduroy coat tighter against the still-chilly air inside the dock house. He flipped on the radio to the AM station out of Rhode Island that carried daily rants about government conspiracies and a damn accurate weather forecast. A tinny voice fought its way through the static to announce the market prices for a lengthy list of fish. Charlie clicked on the coffee maker for the first pot of the day.

The radio announcer's voice suddenly sounded like it got twisted sideways. A burst of static obliterated the signal. A high-pitched whine faded in, then out. The announcer's voice returned with a Bruins hockey score.

An engine rumbled off in the fog. Charlie raised an eyebrow. He'd memorized the burble of every local boat in the harbor. This one wasn't one of them.

He listened harder, past the gurgle of the coffeepot. The low, loping rumble meant twin engines, idling in the fog with a tiger's bass growl. The unseen ship had massive power lurking one stab of the throttle away, big V8s, over four hundred cubes. Big *thirsty* V8s, he thought. He flipped on the power to the pumps, stepped outside, and peered into the swirling mist.

The boat materialized just to the right of the dock. A sharp black bow, only a few feet above the waves, nosed out of the gray. Then the long, sleek twin hull of a glossy speedboat appeared out of the gloom. A low mid-ship cabin, wrapped in blacked-out windows, tapered back into an open rear cockpit.

She idled up at dead slow, left no wake. The boat slid past him. Each sharp pop of the exhaust spit an angry, oily slug of cooling water back into the harbor. The name on the transom in gold script letters read:

Killin' Time

Charlie's skin crawled. It was the same feeling he had when he was out on the Atlantic, and the advancing line of clouds loomed large and dark.

The ship's engines roared in reverse for a second, and then shut down. The boat did not stop and drift. It froze, perfectly aligned with two pier pilings. Water lapped the hull, but the ship did not move. Goose bumps rose along his arms. In a lifetime near the sea, Charlie had never seen the likes of that.

The door at the back of the cabin popped open. A squat but beefy man stepped out. He was bald, with a black moustache and goatee. Despite the fog's dim light, he had on a pair of round, rimless dark glasses. He wore black pants and a black long-sleeve shirt, the polar opposite of the usual tourist-faux-nautical attire. His shirt's open neck exposed a ropy gold chain.

The man went to the bow and picked up a black nylon line. He walked to the stern and picked up a second line secured there. He stepped up onto the dock. Every other boat on the sea would have bobbed when someone with this visitor's girth stepped off it. The *Killin' Time* remained deathly still.

The man in black whipped the lines around cleats on the dock. The lines hung limp. He started toward Charlie. Charlie swallowed hard and his palms began to sweat.

"Charlie, how ya doin'?" asked the stranger. The hairs on the back of Charlie's neck stood straight up at the unnerving familiarity.

The man's voice rumbled and scraped like rocks on an iron plate. His accent hailed from deep within Brooklyn. He grinned as he held out his hand, a grin somehow completely uninviting, devoid of warmth, more rictus than smile.

Charlie shook the man's hand in vacant reflex. The visitor's hand was cold, normal coming off the water this early. But this hand was *lifeless* cold, like a fish on ice. He dropped it immediately. The man in black's grin grew slightly wider, as if they'd just shared a secret.

"Joey Oates," the man said, introducing himself. "You top her off for me while I visit a pal, okay?"

"Yeah, s-sure," Charlie stammered. A rising tide of black dread threatened to drown him.

Joey tapped his fish-hand against Charlie's cheek.

"That's good," he said with condescending approval. "We're gonna have a good relationship while I'm here. I can sense these things."

Joey Oates turned and headed down the dock toward Main Street. The fog enveloped him and he vanished. Charlie shivered.

He quickly topped off the *Killin' Time* and headed back into his small office. He already decided he wasn't asking Oates to pay. If he volunteered it, Charlie would take it, of course. He got the feeling that asking Oates for anything would be a bad idea. He looked out the window. An isolating wall of gray obscured the view of the town.

"Jesus, why doesn't the damn fog burn off?" he said to himself. "Who needs all this fog?"

A ferry full of tourists sounded pretty good to him right now.

CHAPTER THREE

Allie Layton woke up feeling all right. Not great, but all right, and all right was a major achievement.

She pulled open the curtains on her bedroom's sliding glass door. Fog masked the rest of the world. The muffled, soothing whoosh of breaking waves drifted up from the unseen rocky beach at her property's edge. She sighed at the fog's comforting insulation. The rest of the world was at least thirty miles away from the island. The fog made it seem even farther, as if the world ended just beyond her back patio. Right now, that was as much world as she needed.

She'd felt just the opposite growing up in Stone Harbor. The island bred claustrophobia. The small town, virtually unchanged since the 1960s, scared her, made her fear that she too was destined to remain small. The ocean she saw now as protection then had been a barrier, a living creature intent on constricting her dreams until they suffocated.

Ten years made a difference. Now the relaxing, repetitive pounding of the surf all night and waking to the fresh, tangy smell of the Atlantic made each day fresher, cleaner than the hazy daybreak over the Los Angeles foothills had ever been. It didn't hurt that this furnished summer house she leased from a mainlander was only six years old and sparked no memories. Nothing in the place reminded her of anything. She could be someplace new while being someplace old.

She padded into the bathroom and flicked on the light. The wrinkles around her brown eyes were a few years early, the dark circles underneath still more pronounced than she wanted to admit. But she looked better than she did before rehab at Santa Linda Valley, and way better than she did in her infamous LAPD mug shot, an internet favorite when anyone searched *celebrity arrests*.

She twirled her long dark hair into a knot and clipped it in place. It had grown in thick and full after she'd shaved her head into a Mohawk that last crazy night. And then dyed it green. Santa Linda Valley had shaved the rest as a courtesy when her agent checked her in. Her hair had helped make her famous, but she liked it in spite of that.

Allie had the misfortune of fulfilling her dreams. After moving from the island to attend her freshman year studying drama at UCLA, she landed some small parts in cheesy commercials. Her long, silky black hair and soft brown eyes made for a great headshot, and a curvy body sealed the deal for a number of small roles. The break came months later when she landed a supporting, then starring, role in the afternoon soap *Malibu Beach*. She dropped out of college. Millions tuned in each day to see Allison Layton play good girl Britney Daniels and her battle against the revolving cast of two-dimensional villains bent on turning her life upside-down.

Money, fame, and fans poured in. She acquired all the trappings of Hollywood success: a mansion in the hills, a personal trainer, a Jag convertible, a romance with a high-profile actor, and finally, slavery to a very expensive, illegal habit.

She told Santa Linda counselors many reasons why she started using cocaine. She was always tired, it helped her keep off the weight, and in Hollywood, it was as easy to find as a Starbucks. She told her agent she tried it first on a whim, like grabbing a cookie when passing through the kitchen. All through rehab, she kept to that lie. At any rate, deep addiction soon supplanted her true initial reason, escape.

Within a year, each white line she inhaled from her glass tabletop took something with it. She lost the looks that helped make her famous as she began to snort breakfast and lunch. Bizarre behavior and tabloid headlines made a joke of her goody-two-shoes role on *Malibu Beach*. Lines like 'Mr. Jones, I know what you are thinking and I'm not that kind of girl' evoked nothing but laughter when spoken by the out-of-control addict from the cover of the *National Instigator*. The writers put her character into a coma, and she was fired.

Powdered expenses grew, income dwindled, and the descending financial spiral accelerated. She hit rock bottom in an arrest for drunken shoplifting at Neiman Marcus. That night, her former agent found her before she put the razor she'd used on her scalp to work on her wrists. He checked her into rehab. That had been twelve steps and six months ago.

She left her bedroom and entered the kitchen. The flick of a switch started up a pot of coffee, lest she shed all vices and become a saint. She flipped on the radio to a classical music station. For now, that was more than enough. To the shock of her leased home's owner, she hadn't restarted cable service and was happy to keep the television dark. She hadn't even acquired a phone. No land line, no cell, no internet. She'd grow strong in the peace, quiet, and solitude.

Of course, the island grapevine had spread word of her return. Her parents had retired to Arizona, but she saw plenty of other familiar faces when she went into town to fill the refrigerator. Each person gave her a forced reacquainting conversation when they met. They were not rude people, they were just unsure of the etiquette used when speaking to a washed-up Hollywood actress. She forgave them. They hadn't spent any time in LA practicing.

Most of her high school class had never returned after college, though a few non-college bounders like Howie Whitman and Janice Rice (now Van Cleve) had filled some of the adult spaces in town. She had not sought them out. She was feeling *all right*, not great. She was still sorting some things out, and answering repetitive questions from old friends was not how she wanted to do it. She hadn't even looked up Scottie Tackett, who was the only one she wanted to see. She'd call him when she was ready.

This morning's plan was to brave the fog and creep into town on the weekly supply run. Residual checks for overseas distribution of *Malibu Beach* provided a small income, and she felt liberated to live within it. Today she would part with some of it for edible basics such as bread and milk, and a therapeutic necessity, sheet music.

In high school, she had played the clarinet, even been in the band. She enjoyed it, but it fell by the wayside at UCLA. While some considered acting an art, she had stopped viewing it as such. Playing music certainly was, and she wanted to draw strength from one of her roots she still loved.

Allie dressed down in jeans, white running shoes, and a faded sweatshirt this morning. It was hard to imagine how primped and coiffed she always had to be in the Unreal Times, as she called her Hollywood stint. Casual felt better. Casual felt like Allie. She was even enjoying the old Toyota she had driven here from California, a happy simplifying step down from the Jag she snorted away. She called the little blue four-door Stewie and it had not only crossed the continent, but it conquered the hill down into Stone Harbor each week without a miss.

At some point today, Allie planned to head out to Blue Jay Market, with a side trip to Mercer's Music. She'd go midday, when she figured she could get in and out without seeing anyone important.

CHAPTER FOUR

Carl Krieger's cramped dive wasn't much of an apartment. At some point years ago, the rambling old house on Sand Street had been capriciously subdivided into an asymmetrical warren of minimal living spaces. Walls and floors drooped and wandered over sagging beams and joists. Even light seemed to abhor entering the place. One small dirty window gave some meager illumination. Two bare forty-watt bulbs offered some glum assistance.

Apartment 2B consisted of one room, a tiny kitchen, and a closet converted into a shower stall and toilet. Combinations of used clothes and leftover food littered the place in piles Carl thought qualified as housekeeping. Dingy, decades-old wallpaper covered each wall, edges peeling as if even it wanted to escape the place. A few sticks of previously abandoned furniture, indifferently placed, just added to the clutter. The stained sink and its insect inhabitants testified to Carl's 'wipe and reuse' theory of utensil sanitation. Unbelievably, the foul-smelling dump still exceeded Carl Krieger's low standards.

The apartment's low price made up for all the shortcomings. Scraping barnacles at Captain Nate's Boatyard did not pay much. Carl might have expected more of himself by age forty-seven, but no one else had, and so he followed the conventional wisdom. He made enough to keep him in beer and internet porn, so prepping boat hulls and odd job day labor got him over the low bar he set for his life.

Carl was up and stirring by 9 a.m., an abnormal accomplishment. He didn't have to be at the boatyard until ten, and with personal hygiene optional, another forty minutes of sleep wouldn't have cramped his style. He threw on a wife-beater shirt that was only historically white and a pair of stained boxers. The shirt trumpeted all his worst features, as it covered neither his thick mat of back hair, nor his protruding belly. Several days of pure silver growth speckled his pudgy face. He popped himself open a Budweiser breakfast.

A knock sounded at the door.

"What the hell?" Carl said. If it was the goddamn landlady again, he'd have to kick some ass. His rent was paid. He didn't want to hear any more of the old shrew's bitching about the building's roach problem. Like it was his fault that they infested the place.

He plodded over to the front door. One bare foot squished something gooey into the carpet. He paused at the door.

Something felt wrong. Icy. Dead. The door seemed to radiate cold, the way frosty mist rolled off a block of dry ice. He touched the door with his fingertips. Room temperature. Something inside him still felt a chill. He shrugged.

"Who the hell is it?" he asked through the door.

"Flower delivery for Mr. Krieger," a raspy voice with a Brooklyn accent said.

Before Carl could absorb the response's stupidity, the solid wood door burst open. The door handle didn't move. The deadbolt didn't spin. The doorframe didn't explode into pieces. The door just flew open, fast and hard. It nailed Carl in the face.

His Liquid Breakfast of Champions flew from his hand. Carl staggered backward. He dropped ass-first onto his ratty couch. Blood streamed from his nose. He pinched it to stop the bleeding, which only started him coughing as the blood ran down his throat instead.

"Son of a bitch!" He looked up at the doorway. "Who the f —"

His first sight of the stout stranger in black cut his sentence short. A chill shivered up Carl's spine. Dark power surged from the man like sparks from a live wire. For the first time in forever, Carl felt afraid. His pulse pounded with the bone-deep terror previously reserved for his father's belt-assisted beatings.

"Mr. Krieger," Joey said. "I'm Joey Oates. There is the matter of this small debt you owe me. I'm here to collect."

"W-who are you?" Carl squeaked. "What debt?"

Oates grabbed a straight-back chair, spun it around backward, and sat facing Carl. The darkness in Oates' eyes stretched on into eternity.

"Last summer, we made a deal," Oates said. His eyes narrowed. "The deal over the Dickey girl."

Enough blood drained from Carl's face that his nose stopped bleeding. No one knew about the Dickey girl.

"W-what Dickey girl?" he said.

Oates pointed an index finger at Carl. Fresh blood burst from his nostrils.

"Oh, shit!" Carl grabbed a shirt from the couch and crushed it over his nose and mouth.

"We save time and pain when you don't act stupider than you already are," Oates said. "And mind the foul language when we talk business. It offends me.

"We had a deal with the Dickey girl," he continued. "I'll jog your memory. She was a day-tripper with her church group. You kidnapped her, and took her down to the boatyard in your van."

Oates made a circle with his hand. A hologram popped into existence. Krieger and a teenage girl were in the unfinished cargo area of an old van. The girl lay naked and bound on the stained, threadbare carpet. Carl stood over her, a hunting knife in one hand, a dildo in the other.

"You finally indulged one of your fantasies," Oates said. "She didn't survive it, but hey, you're an amateur at these things. When you took her, you signed our deal. Now I get to take possession."

"Possession?" Carl said, muffled by the damp, bloody shirt.

"Of the soul, Mr. Krieger," Oates said.

Only one creature in the world harvested the souls of the damned, could make all this supernatural shit happen. Carl sagged at how real the surreal implication felt.

"You knew right from wrong." Oates pointed upward. "He had his shot at you." Oates pointed to his chest. "And now I have mine. I can call you to repay your debt anytime. In my magnanimity, so far, I've let you live. In addition, you've been under my protection. That adds some juice to what you owe."

Carl looked around at his disgusting apartment. "You been taking care of me?"

"Do you think first-timers ever get away with murder, Mr. Krieger?" Oates asked. "Who do you think kept Miss Dickey's body under the rocks in the harbor? Who convinced the deckhand on the ferry (another debtor of mine) to swear that he saw her on board that day? Who keeps your kiddie porn –"

The cheap smartphone on the table beside Carl buzzed. It flashed through two dozen sick examples of child pornography, and then went dark.

"– out from the cops' watchful eye?" Oates finished. "You're deeply in my debt."

No one knew those details of his crime, or of his twisted personal obsessions. There had been a lot of coincidences that allowed him to get away with murder. But he didn't need that proof to know who Oates was. He could feel it, that paralyzing terror deep in his bones.

"W–what do you want from me?" Carl asked, not really wanting to hear the answer.

"A small favor, really," Oates said. "Just an interest payment. I need a repeat performance. I'll select the girl, the time, and the place. The rest is up to you."

Carl's jaw dropped. Oates could order him to rob a bank or something. Instead, he asked for the second round Carl had longed for since a month after the Dickey girl. Oates was even going to do the legwork for him.

The idea of consequences dawned in Carl's dim mind. This island got real small after tourist season. The suspect list would get short fast. Pedophiles didn't last long in prison.

"Supposing I don't want to do it?" Carl asked with a show of false bravado.

Oates scowled. Carl's asshole tightened.

"That would be a shame," Oates said. His index finger pointed at Carl again. "I may have to ask for more than an interest payment."

Like turning on a faucet, blood gushed from Carl's nose. The force of it sprayed through the wadded shirt and his interlaced fingers. He went lightheaded. The sticky liquid drenched Carl's shorts.

"Of course," Oates continued in the same measured tone, "I can always call in the debt if you can't make the payments."

Carl's heart stopped like it had been clamped in an icy vice. His eyes bulged. His lungs screamed for air. The edges of the room went dark.

"I'll do it!" he gasped.

Oates dropped his index finger. Carl's heart restarted. His nose dried in an instant.

"A wise move, Mr. Krieger," Oates said, rising from his chair. "Meet me at the dock at noon. Bring whatever your fantasy may require." He looked Carl over with bemused disgust. "Make yourself presentable first. Bad bait doesn't catch fish."

Carl stared at Oates wide-eyed. He nodded like a bobblehead. Drying blood coated his mouth and chin.

"And here's a commemorative gift I give all my truly devoted." Oates raised one hand over Carl's left shoulder.

Carl's shoulder went white-hot in an instant. Burning pain like he'd never felt before seared through his skin and deep into his bones. He shrieked and grabbed his shoulder.

"A pleasure doing business, Mr. Krieger."

The fire in his shoulder died. Oates turned away and passed through the doorway. The door shut itself behind him.

Carl slapped at his shirt, assuming it had to be on fire. It wasn't. He pulled the shirt away and inspected it. Not even singed. He tore it away and exposed a red circular scar, a brand with two inverted triangles inside. He touched it. At least it didn't hurt.

He sighed, and then went a bit jittery at the receding adrenaline surge. The idea of another rape and kill excited him, a thrill heavily tempered by the ominous presence of Joey Oates in the fantasy. He wondered why Oates would go to all this effort for Carl to enjoy himself. What would Oates get out of it?

But reasoning about the long term had never been Carl's strong suit.

He's looked out for me so far, Carl thought. *With Oates in my corner, maybe this is the start of something big for me.*

CHAPTER FIVE

A tiny bell tinkled as the front door to Stone Harbor Hardware swung open for the first time that morning. Modern technology offered generations of improvements on the tarnished brass bell Scott Tackett's grandfather had hung on the door. But it wouldn't be right. The bell was supposed to alert the owner to a customer, but over generations had become the equivalent of the Walmart greeter, though with more heart. The bell said welcome, it said take a step back in time to before big box hardware took the soul out of fixing the gate to your picket fence.

Stone Harbor Hardware was nearly frozen in time. Millions of footfalls had worn wavy its polished hardwood floors. Long fluorescent lights tried in vain to dispel the shadows in the narrow aisles between the tall shelves. The scents of varnish and stamped steel filled the air, overlaid with just a hint of mustiness for credibility. Sure, the shelves now held wireless alarm systems and programmable thermostats, but one aisle over from those, a dozen different nails still sold by the ounce, ready to hand-fill into brown paper bags.

Scott Tackett looked up from behind the counter, though he knew that 9 a.m. meant octogenarian Len Andrews was the customer. He'd been the go-to handyman in town in his younger days, dropping in every morning for whatever he'd need for that day's projects. Now people tossed him small jobs he could still handle, replace a hinge here, mount a new mailbox there.

Len shuffled up to the counter. Scott had never seen him in anything but denim overalls. The world's oldest hammer, with a scarred black oak handle, hung from a side loop. Today's cap advertised Charleston Tools, though scoliosis angled it down and away from any audience but children. The stale aura of spent tobacco enshrouded the old man.

"Len! What's on today's worksheet?" Scott asked with a big grin. Almost six feet tall and broad-shouldered, Scott had learned early on that a disarming smile minimized his sometimes-intimidating size.

"Well, gotta mend a porch step at the Blue Fin Bed-and-Breakfast."

Len's voice had an accent from southern Maine and the rasp born of a million smoked Camels. "Best to bring some eight-penny."

Scott led Len down the adjacent aisle. He counted twelve nails into a bag and went through the ceremony of weighing it and marking it with the microscopic price.

"Did I ever tell you your grandfather sold me the first nails I ever bought?" Len said.

Only a few hundred times, Scott thought. "You don't say."

"Darn fine that you took the reins here."

Scott never let on to anyone that he took the reins by default. A Rensselaer engineering degree had been his ticket off the island, and he'd become a junior partner at a firm. He and his wife, Anita, visited Stone Harbor for holidays (summer ones mostly), but Scott had no desire for a permanent return. His mother had died of a particularly aggressive cancer years earlier, and when his father, Gary, had a heart attack, Scott took a leave of absence. He and Anita moved into the family's big old Gothic house on Scudder Lane. Scott planned to cover for his father as he regained his health.

His father got worse instead of better. Scott's turn as daytime assistant became full-time employee, with his exhausted father watching from behind the counter. After his father's death, he'd just kept coming to the store, his own slightly more positive version of Jimmy Stewart at the Bailey Building and Loan in *It's a Wonderful Life*. He resigned his mainland job.

Len paid for his purchase with linty pocket change. "This here's damn near the last real business left on Main Street. Bunch of tourist nonsense everywhere else."

Indeed all the façades of a working, seafaring New England village still lined the streets, but behind the masks, the butcher shop sold candles, the apothecary sold clothes, the weekly *Stone Harbor Crier* had gone belly-up and had become an antique store, prominently featuring the old printing press. The inconvenience of a ferry ride to the mainland had been Scott's store's saving grace. A few thousand island residents were just enough demand to keep one hardware store in the black.

"Len," Scott said, "if I wasn't here to keep you supplied, the whole town would slowly fall into ruin."

"You betcha," Len said. He gave a little smile with his crooked, yellowed teeth and patted Scott's arm with a quavering hand. "You give my regards to the missus."

Scott tensed, but Len didn't notice. He shuffled out and the little bell rang him goodbye. Scott ran his fingers through his longer dark hair. Sadness shaded his blue eyes.

Scott hadn't spoken to Anita in several years. Anita, who had always lived in some metropolis, began to fall into the 'claustrophobic' camp during her stay on the island. She'd put her life on hold when she agreed to the temporary move to Stone Harbor and she missed it. She compensated for her sense of social isolation by taking first weekends, then weeks, on the mainland. Just as his father really needed help, Scott found himself doing most of it alone. He was not surprised when one Thursday the ferry delivered a set of divorce papers in place of his returning wife. They had never discussed it, but both knew it was coming. He signed and mailed them to her lawyer without even calling her. The final decree arrived two weeks after he buried his father. Too many losses, too close together to process at once. Len might have forgotten about it, but Scott certainly hadn't.

The front door had barely swung shut when Deborah Deering marched through it. She carried her ever-present miniature white poodle, Precious, against her shoulder. The doughy old woman with the gray pageboy haircut had her lips pursed and chin raised, a look that made Scott sigh. She was here to complain.

"Selectman Tackett!"

"Deborah, don't call me that."

"Well, you *are* a selectman, aren't you?"

He was. His regular customers had convinced him to run last year when old Darrin Pierce hung it up after a decade. Scott liked the idea of giving back to Stone Harbor.

"I'm one of three," he said, knowing Deborah would miss the attempt to direct her to another.

Deborah tucked Precious up under her breasts as if about to defend her. The dog had taken the place of immediate family in widow Deborah's life. Watching the two of them made Scott understand why her grandchildren never visited.

"Well, someone needs to do something about the Harrimans' vicious dog! It chased poor Precious and nearly gave her a heart attack."

She pointed the panting little dog at Scott. Its eyes wept something black onto its curly white fur. The dog shuddered in her grip. The nervous little thing looked like it was always on the verge of a heart attack, with or without the Harrimans' German shepherd going after it.

"Deborah, the Board of Selectmen doesn't take care of that kind of thing. We keep the dock repaired and get the village green grass cut. You need to contact Chief Scaravelli."

"That worthless sack? Lot of good he'll do me."

In a more combative mood, Scott would have agreed with her. Scott regularly went head to head with the police chief over some lax law enforcement. The other two selectmen saw things differently and thought the world of the retired New York City cop. Leaving Scott a steaming, frustrated minority.

"Deborah, there's nothing I can do."

"Well…can't you make the Harrimans buy a muzzle for that wolf of theirs? You sell those things here, don't you?"

"Seriously. Go right down the street to the police station and fill out a complaint. Ask for Milo to take care of it if that makes you feel better."

Deborah's face screwed up in disgust at the mention of young officer Milo Mimms. "Like that child's any better!" She gripped Precious so tightly that the dog squeaked. She turned on her heel and tromped to the door. "If my Precious ends up dead, it's on your head." The bell tinkled as the door slammed behind her.

Scott couldn't shake the mental image of her dead dog draped across his head and laughed. His dislike of Scaravelli made him kind of glad to wind Deborah up like a clock spring before sending her his way.

But aggravation like Deborah Deering and Chief Scaravelli weren't anywhere near enough to turn him off about Stone Harbor. Anxious as he had been to leave at seventeen, it was comforting to be back at twenty-nine. He belonged here now. The town grapevine still ran through the hardware store as it always had. He knew every detail of the harbor oil spill last March and the Dickey girl who drowned falling off the ferry last summer, not to mention the lesser news of new mainland grandchildren. He was part of the fabric of this little society, and that meant a lot to a man stripped of his roles as son and husband.

He headed to the back of the store to unwrap a shipment of new snow shovels. Today would end up sunny after the fog burned off. But winter was just around the corner, bringing with it the threat of an old-fashioned nor'easter blizzard on the island. Stone Harbor Hardware was still the 'go to' place for the practical necessities, and it was Scott's responsibility to be ready. Even if that meant unpacking snow shovels in the warmth of September, and roofing tar during a January freeze.

CHAPTER SIX

Business was slow through the morning. Just before noon, Scott took a broom to the hardwood floors near the entrance. A cold tingle sparked in his feet.

He stopped sweeping. The odd sensation felt like something between the prickle of pins and needles and a vibration from the floor. He reached down and touched the hardwood slats. He felt the same thing, a line of cold energy that made his fingertips pulse, like there was a refrigeration line running under the boards. He swept his hand in a semicircle. The charge was stronger near the register.

He stood and walked to the counter. The tingling grew stronger with each step. So did a weighty sense of dread. Whatever energy he felt beneath him was more black hole than bright star. He stepped behind the counter. The sensation peaked.

The bell rang the arrival of a customer and broke Scott's concentration on the phenomenon. A squat, bald man with a goatee stepped in, dressed in black head to toe, with a ropy gold chain around his neck.

Scott caught his breath. A sensation of evil radiated from the man like heat from a sunlamp. So powerful was the feeling that Scott completely forgot his search. Instead, he had to fight to keep from running out the back door. Everything about the man's appearance screamed Mafia hit man, but Scott felt something even darker than that about him.

"How ya doin'? I'm Joey Oates." Oates' face betrayed no emotion. He surveyed the store and locked his eyes back on Scott. "This was Gary Tackett's place."

"I run it now," Scott said. "I'm his son. He passed away."

Oates gave him a no-shit-Sherlock look. "No foolin', huh?"

Oates stepped closer. The air seemed to thicken. The boards under Scott's feet nearly buzzed with power.

"I'm an old pal," Oates said. "We done some business a while back."

Scott's father, Gary Tackett, had been as straight-arrow as they came, a deacon in the church, an honest businessman, Scott's idol. Scott knew the store's financials inside and out. Oates wasn't in them. He couldn't think what business his father might have had with someone this creepy. Scott stepped back until his butt hit the counter.

"No, can't say that he mentioned you," Scott said.

"Yeah, most of my business partners don't." Oates looked Scott up and down the way a butcher appraises a side of beef. "Good to meet ya. We may do some business ourselves. I'll be in touch."

Oates left the store and it felt like a suffocating cloud left with him. Scott sighed and realized how tense every muscle in his body had become. He sagged against the countertop.

Whoever that guy was, and whatever business that guy did, Scott wasn't about to have any part in it. He couldn't imagine that his father ever had.

★　　★　　★

The weak, waning sun dipped down over the harbor. Closing time was hours away, but Scott had a delivery of shingles to make outside town. So he made the executive decision as Stone Harbor Hardware's CEO to call it a day early. He flipped the deadbolt on the front door and switched off the neon open sign in the window.

As he turned back to the counter, he remembered the strange sensation he'd felt that morning, that near-electric hum through the floorboards that sent a terrifying chill through his system. He'd tracked it back to behind the counter, then Oates' disconcerting arrival derailed his investigation. He hadn't thought about it again because whatever he felt had disappeared after Oates left the store.

The rational side of him made a list of practical reasons to resume his investigation, ranging from damaged water pipes to faulty wiring, any of which would be bad news for the store. Emotionally, he needed to find the source of the sensation that had filled him with dread, a darkness only bested by Oates' unwelcome appearance.

He moved to the same spot where the tingling had been the strongest. The stillness of the closed, empty store eliminated all distractions, but he still felt nothing.

As a kid, he'd been the one to shimmy into the crawl space under the store whenever little emergencies demanded, so he knew every wire and pipe under the floor. None ran under here.

He knelt and traced his fingers along the seams in the uneven hardwood floor. He flashed back to being fifteen and having his winter chore be refinishing the surface, a tedious hands-and-knees task that consumed a lot of sandpaper, varnish, and sweat. His father told him that his grandfather had pounded many of those nails in with his own hands. At the time, Scott hadn't cared. As he ran his finger over the countersunk nail heads now, the image made him proud.

No missing nails, no loose boards, no weak seams. Nothing looked out of place and he was sure that there was nothing underneath the boards but gravel and dirt.

But something looked wrong with the lower trim of the display case to his left. The battered, two-inch-high painted trim ran uniformly from one end to the other, except for the two-foot-long piece next to him, where the chipped edges exposed bare wood and two crooked Phillips head screws replaced the finishing nails that held the other pieces in place. The trim hadn't looked like this when he'd slaved over the floor around it.

Scott raised an eyebrow. Crooked screws were his father's hallmark. He might have run a hardware store, but his personal home improvement skills had been meager at best. He'd never seen the man cut a board's edge straight. And he sure wouldn't use screws when he could use nails, unless he was going to unscrew them later.

Scott grabbed the powered screwdriver from the drawer under the register. He fit the tip into the screw's head. The right side of the screw slots were damaged, but not the left. The screws had gone in, but perhaps never come out. He switched the driver to reverse and backed out both screws almost all the way. He grabbed the screwheads and pulled the panel free.

Inside lay a flat, hexagonal granite slab, the same dark gray so commonplace on the island. Scott slid it out. An odd design was etched in the stone's unpolished surface. Two isosceles triangles lay superimposed on each other, one pointed up, one down, but the three sides of each were radically concave. A circle circumscribed the resulting six-pointed design. In the dead center were two recessed handprints, like a grade school kid would make in plaster.

Scott had never seen anything like it before. But in the same way that a biohazard symbol or a swastika carried an inherent, ominous evil in it, so did this simple collection of three shapes. Upon closer inspection, he saw that strange words edged the circle, some with letters outside the English alphabet. He bit his lower lip.

Whatever this thing was that his father found, he'd thought he had to hide it from everyone, including Scott. The stone was old, but the engraving wasn't. The carving's edges flickered with the sparkle of fresh-chiseled rock. Scott leaned back with the granite slab between his feet.

Confusion swirled inside him. He would have sworn upon a stack of Bibles that he knew his father better than anyone else did. After Scott's return to Stone Harbor, they'd spent most of every day together, whether it was at the store or at some time-consuming medical treatment. They didn't ignore that his father's end was near. They went over the hardware store's books, the family finances, the family history. His father told him hundreds of stories about Scott's grandparents, about growing up on the island, about meeting and marrying Scott's mother. In all of that, how could a secret like this never have come up?

Oates' cryptic comments grew even more disturbing. If this secret stone existed, what secret business had Gary Tackett and Oates contracted? How much more of his father's life was out there for Scott to discover? All he'd unearthed today hinted at a man far darker than Scott ever thought possible.

Scott slid the stone back under the counter and screwed the panel back in place, as if he could just reverse all he'd done, and make the disturbing discovery dissolve from his memory. His world was sure a lot simpler about eight hours ago.

CHAPTER SEVEN

Scott drove back toward town after delivering the load of shingles to a contractor's site. Sometimes running the store all by himself made him feel like a one-man band. But he was happy for this end of day diversion. Oates' visit and the strange object under the counter had changed the whole sense of being in the store. He'd always been more than comfortable there. He'd felt at home. Now he didn't know how to feel. He drove back into town on some kind of internal autopilot, all conscious thought consumed with conflicting thoughts about his father.

About a mile out of town, an unfamiliar sun-faded blue Toyota sat parked askew along the side of the road. Scott let off the accelerator. He pulled in behind it and popped on his emergency flashers. The window tint made the interior indistinct, but he could see a dark-haired woman inside, looking back between the front seats, her hand shielding her eyes from the low sun.

An out-of-towner with a broken car was a regular island thing. Given the low miles the locals drove, Willet's Automotive downtown made most of its revenues off visitors' rolling rust piles. Scott got out to do his civic duty for the visitor. After all, he was, as Deborah had reminded him, a selectman.

He walked alongside the car.

"Do you need a hand?" he asked, a bit louder than usual to get through the raised window.

"Scottie?" replied a muffled voice.

The window rolled down. Scott caught his breath and his heart did a little sprint as he recognized the woman at the wheel. Unlike the rest of the world, he didn't see the famous Allison Layton, star of *Malibu Beach*. He saw Allie, his date to the senior prom. He'd heard that she was renting a place on the far side of the island.

"Allie Cat," he said. Her old nickname slipped out before he realized he'd even thought it.

Allie hopped out of the car and gave him a quick little hug, more a crush of two coats than anything else.

"I should have known when I had car trouble, you'd be the one to arrive on the scene. Always the white knight."

He had to force himself to stop staring at her and answer. "Well, once a Boy Scout, blah, blah, blah. What's the problem?"

"I don't know. Stewie just revved really high, and died."

"Stewie? You still name your cars?"

"They name themselves. They just share it with me."

Scott leaned into the car and twisted the key in the ignition. The dash lit up. The gas gauge needle lay on dead empty.

"I hate to ask," he said, "but could you be out of gas?"

"Maybe? I've driven so little I haven't paid attention."

"Hop in. I have a can up at the house. We'll gas him up and go from there."

Indecision crossed her face. "Yeah, okay. Good plan."

They got into Scott's truck and he headed up the road. Allie had been the center of Scott's life the last time he lived on the island. Now, seeing her, he felt a strange combination of familiarity and raging discomfort. This was the person he grew up with, but she couldn't possibly be the same Allie from so long ago. Allie had become a Hollywood star, then a national personal train wreck. What did he say after so many years?

"I guess you heard that I'd come back," Allie said.

"You know Stone Harbor. The grapevine buzzed with it before you drove off the ferry. Hollywood star comes home isn't everyday news here."

"More like prodigal daughter, I'll bet. You can tell me the truth."

He had no intention of doing that. "No, not really."

"I still love it when you lie to me," she said.

Scott turned right into his driveway.

"No way!" she said. "You live in the same house?"

"Inherited it from my parents. It came with the family business and I didn't want to break up the set. Be right back."

Scott left the truck idling and went to the garage. He returned with a two-gallon gas can and tucked it into the truck's bed. Allie looked wistfully at the front of the house.

"This house always had the best porch," she said. "What happened to the swing?"

Back in high school, a canvas-backed porch swing faced the street. At night, the shadow of the overhang put it in darkness. The two of them used to sit there on summer evenings and dream of the future.

"Sun and salt air did it in," Scott said. He pulled out of the driveway. "I haven't gotten around to replacing it, I guess."

"You should so you can sit outside and just breathe. Living in LA gave me a whole new appreciation for Stone Harbor's fresh air."

"If you came back for fresh air, you botched your timing. We're about two weeks away from locking ourselves indoors until May." He dropped into a fake Maine accent. "You remember we got winter up in these parts."

"Yeah," she said with realization. "I'll need to buy a heavier coat, won't I?"

That admission relieved Scott of having to pry into her personal schedule. She planned on staying awhile. He liked that.

They returned to her car. He gassed it up. Two long starter cranks later, the car revved to life. Allie smiled in the front seat. Scott knelt down and looked in the open window beside her.

"And remember," he said. "The *E* on the gauge doesn't stand for *enough*."

"I'll keep that in mind."

The moment was about to pass. Good deed complete, they were about to part ways. Scott didn't want that to happen. A surge of adrenaline hit his system. He bit his lower lip.

This was crazy. He was an adult now, married, divorced, a business owner and selectman. Yet he felt as nervous as he did the first time he asked her out, certain that rejection awaited at the other end of his question.

"You free for dinner tonight?" he said. "The chowder is still good at Mackey's."

Her face fell. He held his breath. What had he been thinking? She'd dated Hollywood stars. He was her high school boyfriend. He prayed her refusal would be polite.

A hint of a smile crossed her lips. "Sure. That would be great."

Scott had to stop himself from pounding the roof of her car in jubilation. "Okay. I'll pick you up at six."

"I'm staying in a house near Goose Point."

"I know. We all know. It's Stone Harbor."

"Well, duh. Then I'll see you at six."

Scott returned to his truck as Allie drove off. He wondered what kind of strange circle life was completing for him.

Scott had secretly fallen in love with her at first sight in eighth grade, and by tenth grade had mustered the courage to ask her out. They became classic high school sweethearts, culminating in a dual graduation party and the senior prom.

But after their senior summer, she went to UCLA and Scott to RPI. Somehow, he thought that the separation wouldn't change a thing. But the drift apart was inevitable. They were both home for Christmas break, and it seemed a little strained. Allie looked subtly different. Her hairstyle, makeup, and clothes were a little more West Coast. (Scott had to admit some of it was an improvement.)

But she also acted differently. Her eyes no longer reflected the magic Scott still felt. She wasn't unhappy to see him, or cruel or anything. She just didn't seem to be Allie Cat anymore. She had come back as Allison. By the end of the year, her calls and emails had stopped, and that summer, only Scott returned to Stone Harbor. The harsh reality that romance could end hit him pretty hard.

Later, Scott had been aware of her success, but only peripherally. He knew that she was on a soap opera, but wasn't home during the day to watch that stuff. Sure, she had been tabloid fodder the last year or so, but he didn't read that checkout line trash. At least those were his excuses. In reality, he went out of his way to stay in the dark about her. Since age 13, there had only been one person that made his heart race and his breath come up short (yes, including Anita). He wanted to remember Allie that way. He wanted to remember his Allie Cat. Not whoever that was in the tabloid headlines.

He wondered which of those two he was going to have dinner with tonight.

CHAPTER EIGHT

All the way home, Allie muttered to herself, dumbfounded. Just this morning she had been content to be on her own, sorting things out in her head. Now she had a dinner date with her high school boyfriend. What the hell?

While the weeks on the island had calmed her down, something still didn't sit right. She *was* feeling more in touch with Stone Harbor's real Allie, and further from California's artificial Allison. But all of the good things: the sea, her music, and her growing insight about herself; all these things still felt peripheral.

When Scottie peeked into her car window, he released a flood of memories and emotions for which she was unprepared. It might have been nostalgia, maybe just wishful thinking, but she felt that same spark from years ago, that unique flash only first love delivered. She remembered how feeling unconditionally and completely loved gave her strength and self-assurance. She also remembered how giving love unconditionally and completely gave her a sense of being whole. That was the part of being Allie Layton she missed the most, and it had felt better than anything cocaine had ever done for her. So she said yes to Scott's invitation on total impulse.

Now driving home, she felt like an idiot. She thought about how stupid she must have looked running out of gas. She was twenty-eight, for Christ's sake. She had been on network TV and nominated for a Daytime Emmy. Scott must have thought she'd gone California ditz.

He was being polite to ask me to dinner, she thought. Probably feeling sorry for the tabloid disaster who limped home from rehab. Either way, she should never have accepted. An evening of being treated like a mended piece of china would be unbearable, not to mention being on public display in a restaurant. She'd barely left the house since her return, but every time she'd been the subject of the pitying stares or the whispered innuendo.

She pulled up in front of her house. She grabbed her bags, two of food and one envelope of sheet music from Mercer's Music, and got out of the car.

Maybe dinner would be okay, she thought. Maybe Scottie was the bit of normal that would help the rest of her come together.

Not after a month, the reasoning half of her brain responded. *You've barely got yourself together. Scottie's just some symbol of youth enhanced by hormone-shaded teenage memories. And you have some significant baggage, girl. Unemployed addicts are not in high demand. And what if he finds out about the Dark Thing? The Dark Thing is more than baggage. It's an anchor.*

The Dark Thing chilled her. Always lurking in an unseen corner, never quite out of mind. There was no sharing that with anyone. She was looking at Scottie with the simplicity of a sixteen-year-old. That girl disappeared on the West Coast a long time ago.

She put away her groceries and went out to the patio overlooking the sea. In the moonlight she could see the breeze lick the waves' tips into whitecaps. The crisp wind through her hair and scent of the sea felt good. She had always done her best meditation like this. Just her and the ocean to iron out life's wrinkles.

She thought about how many times through high school Scottie had rescued her on the side of the road, a victim of her woefully unreliable Mustang. Today was just déjà vu. Her life was way beyond needing a flat tire changed. Her life had a blown engine.

She'd call Scott and cancel. No good was going to come of this dinner. Better to dash this dream here in private instead of elsewhere with an audience.

Only one problem. She had no phone.

"Dammit," she said as she slapped the deck railing. Looked like she was going to have dinner after all. She'd make it quick and casual. No big deal.

CHAPTER NINE

Responsibility weighed heavy on the little shoulders of Natalie Olsen. For the first time, her mother had trusted her with something very important to do on her own. Dinner hung in the balance. She had to bring home rolls.

She and her mother had gotten home late from the Brownies meeting. Two traffic lights seemed to never to turn green, then a stalled truck blocked one street. During the rush to get dinner together, her mother discovered the rolls were hard as a rock. Natalie volunteered to go get some more. Instead of the usual, immediate no, after a pause, her harried mother had said yes.

At a month shy of eight years old, she'd never been allowed to walk to the corner market alone. It was only a few blocks away, where West Street met Main. She walked there with her mother every morning to her school bus stop. But this evening, she got to do it alone.

Her mother had handed her money. Real cash money. Five dollars with President Lincoln looking all solemn at her. More than a month's worth of her allowance. A fortune.

Natalie hadn't let her mother down. In the plastic bag on her wrist were the three things she had to bring home: rolls, receipt, and change. She stood outside the corner market, still wearing the brown beret and Brownie vest that made her feel so official. Her long blond hair reached her skinny waist and her green eyes blazed with pride. Natalie got a little chill at the responsibility of it all, the *grown-up* feeling of buying something on her own, something her family needed.

She set off on the uphill sidewalk for home. She thought about the things that might happen to the rolls on the way, like birds flying off with them, dropping the bag in a puddle, the bag splitting open and spilling everything onto the ground to be run over by a car. She whipped the bag around and clutched it to her chest. She reached the intersection of Spyglass Street, one block away from home.

"Hey, Natalie!"

She looked to her left. Spyglass Street was just a block long and ended at a steep, wooded cut into the hill. The businesses on either side were closed for the day. A windowless primer-gray van parked across the dead end. The back doors hung open. A man knelt behind the van, bent over a storm drain in the curb.

"Hey, Natalie!" He smiled and motioned her forward. "C'mon and give me a hand!"

The man wore blue jeans and a button-down Western-style shirt, like the ones she saw men wear on old TV reruns. A stripe of white skin ran along the border between his fresh haircut and the rest of his tanned face. His ratty shoes carried a liberal sprinkling of thick blue paint, like the paint on the bottom of Mr. Greeley's boat next door. The man smiled, but Natalie thought it was a fake smile, like the one the dentist gave before he stuck that big needle in your mouth.

"Natalie," the man called again, "I'm a friend of your mother. You have to help me get Mr. Boots. He's stuck down here. The poor kitty can't get out."

Natalie caught her breath. She had a cat, Whiskers, a good cat who sat on her lap all the time. Once he got stuck in a tree, and the neighbor had to help get him down. If there was a poor kitty like Whiskers in trouble, she should help him. If she was old enough to go shopping, wasn't she was old enough to help a kitty like her neighbor did?

A danger signal flashed through her mind. Her mother said not to talk to strangers. Anywhere or anytime.

But he must not be a stranger, Natalie thought. *He knows my name. Strangers don't know people's names. Only friends know each other's name, and he said he knows my mom.*

She took a few cautious steps forward. The man's smile widened. His teeth were kind of yellow.

"That's it, Natalie," he said. "I need someone to help Mr. Boots. He sounds so scared."

A faint noise came up from the storm drain. She listened harder.

A cat's cry. Just like Whiskers cried when he was up that tree. But the storm drain was a worse place, dark and wet. What if it rained? Would Mr. Boots drown in there?

"Can't you hear him, Natalie?" The man had the saddest look on his face. "He's very afraid. Can you be a big girl and help him out?"

Natalie gave the rolls in her arms a squeeze.

I got the rolls, didn't I? she thought. *I can help the kitty, and then go right home. Mom would want me to help this man get the kitty.*

She thought again about his yellow teeth.

But he must be a nice man if he has a kitty.

Natalie ran to the storm drain. Mr. Boots' echoing cries from below grew louder. The man in the painted shoes smiled, a tighter, edgy grin. The muscles in his arms tensed.

Natalie dropped to her knees at the drain's edge. She bent and peered into the dark opening. The man leaned closer.

"He's right down there," the man whispered.

He smelled strange, like a lot of perfume, like when she dropped her mom's bottle in the bathroom and it broke. Another smell poked through the perfume's heavy cover, a sour smell, like something rotten in the woods. A tremor of fear raced up her spine and out to her fingertips.

Mr. Boots cried again. Between her knees, a misshapen coat hanger hung on the grate. Duct tape held a digital recorder to the wire. A cat's meow wailed out of the tiny speaker. Natalie sucked in a breath to shriek.

The man's right hand shot out and crushed her throat, stifling her scream. She choked. The dinner rolls hit the grate. Her beret flew from her head as he pinned her to the cold, rough pavement. She transformed into a panicked whirlwind of arms and legs.

His left hand whipped a dirty cloth from his pocket. He clamped it over her mouth and nose. The sharp, tangy smell of the damp rag overwhelmed her.

"It's all right, little Natalie," he cooed. "Relax. Uncle Carl will make everything okay. We are going to play lots of fun games."

Natalie's pulse raced faster than she'd ever felt. She beat at his arms, kicked at his chest. He didn't flinch. Each blow she landed came weaker than the last. She started to unwind. Her head twirled, and she felt like she was floating. Her eyes closed, and the bad man and the drain without a cat all went away.

Carl Krieger scooped Natalie's limp little body into his arms. He stepped on the dropped bag of rolls and crushed it into the storm grating. He slid Natalie into the back of the van.

"Good girl, Natalie," Krieger said. "Uncle Carl's going to make a big girl of you tonight."

He slammed the van doors shut. The street was clear, just like Joey Oates had promised. Oates' instructions had been perfect. The stupid cat recording was a touch of gold Carl would have never come up with. He climbed into the driver's seat. He pounded the steering wheel with excitement about the upcoming night, when more of his fantasies would come true.

CHAPTER TEN

Chief of police Greg Scaravelli sat alone in the three-room station on Main Street, feet propped up on his desk. His wrinkled uniform stretched out a bit over the belly earned through twenty years of Nathan's Famous lunches. His graying hair was longer than he'd ever worn it as one of New York's Finest. His bushy moustache covered both upper and lower lips, making him look a bit like a walrus.

The station had a main lobby, an office with two desks for himself and his officer, and one cell. The whole dump could have fit in one corner of one floor of an NYPD precinct. Still more than enough space for a town where nothing happened. Retiring here from the force last year was a great move.

The clock hit 5 p.m. His sole officer, Milo Mimms, walked in through the front door. Scaravelli sighed. Only Milo would show up early for a twelve-hour shift. Scaravelli was the only person to impress in the department, and Mimms had failed that task on the first day.

The scrawny little guy couldn't get a uniform that fit, and he always reminded Scaravelli of a kid in a Halloween cop costume. Hell, at nineteen years old, he *was* a kid. The NYPD wouldn't have touched him for three more years. If then.

The weight of Milo's gun belt always seemed moments away from buckling his knees. His heavy, outsized peaked cap always looked ready to snap his neck at any second. Scaravelli knew tougher preteen gang members.

"Milo." Scaravelli tried to contain his disgust. "You know you don't have to be in this early."

"I want to make sure you have time to summarize today's events."

"Zero events, Milo. Stone Harbor was quiet and peaceful. Not even a stray dog call."

"That's good news, Chief." Milo broke into one of his idiotic smiles that made Scaravelli want to punch him.

Scaravelli waved him off like shooing a fly. "Check your equipment and get out of here, then. Keep an eye on the boatyard. Now that everything's up out of the water, kids have a bunch of new places to make out."

"Got it, Chief." Milo came to attention and departed.

Scaravelli sighed. Chief of police with a department of one. The upside to having Milo was that employing a real cop instead might have made Scaravelli actually work.

He couldn't complain though. Seven months per year, he didn't do squat. The infestation of tourists subsided, and the place lay cemetery-quiet. He and Officer Mimms took twelve-hour coverage to answer any calls and show a presence around town. Having Mimms on the opposite twelve reduced the time he had to spend in the moron's presence. The five summer months, a few mainland part-timers helped keep the tourists in line. The worst crime was a bit of drunkenness every now and then. He was pretty sure that he and Mimms had the only guns on the island. This wasn't policing. This was babysitting.

That left Scaravelli with no respect for Stone Harbor's inhabitants. He was used to New York City, where there was real crime. People there knew to suck up the small stuff, and just call the cops for the major malefactions like murder and arson. These people's worst complaints were unscooped dog shit and double-parking. But his moustache hid his grimace and he pretended to take their concerns seriously. This was just an easy paycheck. He'd had enough of earning the difficult ones.

Scaravelli heard the door to the police station open. He cursed under his breath. Who the hell was coming by after 6 p.m.?

He pulled his feet off the desk and went to his office door. A man met him at the threshold. Scaravelli didn't recognize him, but he did feel familiar. The bald, stocky man sported a goatee. He was dressed all in black, with a thick gold chain around his neck. He radiated cold, like an open freezer door. Scaravelli suddenly felt out of breath. The man was more than just unnerving, he was...viscerally frightening.

"Chief Scaravelli," the man said. "How ya doin'? I'm Joey Oates."

Scaravelli could not think of anything to say. There was something very disturbing about this guy, something that said getting on his bad side might be fatal, or worse. He had seen guys with this aura in the maximum-security side of Riker's Island. Scaravelli might have thought that he was lord of the manor at Stone Harbor, but the king had arrived. All hail the king. Scaravelli stepped back behind his desk as an excuse to put some distance between himself and Oates.

"We've done business before," Oates continued, following Scaravelli and ending up in front of his desk. "Back in the day in the city."

"We have?" Scaravelli said, trying and failing to exude the confidence of a chief of police.

"Lots of times. I got records of many transactions. We been partners a long time. A very profitable relationship it's been. Our transactions always paid me dividends."

Scaravelli thought hard, trying to remember this guy. He smelled a setup. He'd retired a few steps ahead of Internal Affairs flipping over some rocks he'd hidden things under. The IA bastards would hound you well into retirement if they had something they could stick their teeth into and tear.

"What are you talking about?" he said, looking as blank as he could.

Oates looked irate for just an instant, and then masked the emotion.

"Remember our deal with the platinum-blond whore on your first beat? She'd polish your knob twice a week, and you'd let her work. There was a dividend there for me, since it left her free to let others indulge their weaknesses."

Scaravelli frowned. That was decades ago. He absolutely never told anyone about that.

"When you resold the heroin you skimmed from the Quintaro bust in '08," Oates continued, "it fired off a host of crimes, addicts committed to buy the brown dust. Again, nice dividends."

Scaravelli went ashen. These were Scaravelli's most sordid moments. No way Oates could know all that shit.

Oates snapped his fingers. Scaravelli's desk chair zipped forward, caught Scaravelli in the back of the legs, and he dropped into it. Oates snapped his fingers again and some invisible force pinned Scaravelli to the chair. The massive, unseen weight on his chest threatened suffocation. The color drained from Scaravelli's face. Oates winked.

"But, my friend," Oates continued, "the best was when you flipped Orasco over to the Gambino family."

Scaravelli's jaw dropped. Detective Danny Orasco had been deep undercover in the Gambino family for several years, with the evidence to bring the family's top tier to justice. For seven grand to clear his bookie's marker, Scaravelli had blown Orasco's cover to a Gambino contact. That night, cops found Orasco beaten to death, tongue ripped out, all his fingers and toes amputated. Oates couldn't possibly have known about Scaravelli's betrayal.

Oates approached Scaravelli's side of the desk. With each step, Scaravelli's panic rose. Oates patted Scaravelli on the cheek. His hand had all the warmth of a slab of rotten meat. "So like you're thinking, who could know all this stuff? Who might be listening, might be encouraging you to take that darker, easier path?"

Oates' face elongated and reddened. A bony crest swelled on his forehead. He smiled and his teeth had turned to sharpened points. Fear paralyzed Scaravelli. Satan morphed back into Oates.

"Yeah, surprise!" Oates chuckled a scratchy, forced little excuse for a laugh. "All that Sunday sermon stuff was right.

"But lately, Chief, I'm greatly aggrieved to say, our business, it hasn't been so good. You been hiding out here on this island, and I get nothing from you. It's disappointing. If our relationship withers like this, I'll have to call my marker."

Scaravelli did not like the sound of that. "What marker?"

"Your soul, Chief," Oates said. "You sold it many times over. I get it at my convenience. You don't deliver for me, it becomes more convenient for me to collect."

A sharp pain lanced Scaravelli's upper jaw and shot straight into the center of his brain. Something wiggled against his gums. A gush of warm, coppery liquid swelled his cheeks. He coughed out a spray of blood. A bright red, sticky mess splattered the distended belly of his shirt and the wide legs of his pants. A white molar teetered on one of his shirt buttons.

Scaravelli shrieked. Oates buffed the edge of his fingernails against his shirtsleeve and held them up to the light.

"See? I mean business," Oates said, still checking his nails. "So let me tell you how you can make up for lost time."

Scaravelli couldn't take his eyes off his extracted tooth.

"Whaaat doo you want?" he gurgled through a mouthful of blood.

Oates passed his hand in front of Scaravelli. The blood flow stopped. The last of it dribbled down the chief's chin.

"There's gonna be a heinous crime here in Stone Harbor," Oates said. "At 7 p.m., you'll get a call at home from Colleen Olsen. Her daughter will be missing. You'll listen compassionately and say you'll look for her. You're gonna head alone to the woods north of Canale Road. You'll see Carl

Krieger's broken-down excuse for a van parked along the old dirt road. He and the girl will be inside. By the time you get there, the girl will be dead. You'll confront Krieger about his crime, he'll be armed –"

Oates pulled a snub-nosed .38 revolver from his pocket and put in on Scaravelli's desk. The serial number had been gouged away.

"– and he'll resist," Oates continued. "You'll have to shoot him. Fatally, I'm afraid. Then you'll close off the crime scene. The whole five acres from the road to the hilltop. At 9 a.m., you'll start your investigation there. I'll take care of the rest."

Scaravelli's jaw quivered. He'd done some shit in his life, but he hadn't killed anyone. It was going to be cold-blooded too. Scoring some dope or leaning on a whore was one thing. But murder….

"C'mon, Scaravelli. Don't go all holier-than-thou on me. Don't tell me you haven't thought about killing someone."

"Well, yeah, but…."

"I've been in your head. Seen the envy when other cops talked about wasting some perp. You've wanted this excuse for years."

Oates knew him better than he knew himself. That realization sent a shudder down his spine.

"Have no qualms, Chief," Oates continued. "Remember the Dickey girl's disappearance last year? She didn't fall overboard. She was murdered here in Stone Harbor, never made it to the boat. Krieger was responsible for that too. When you search the disgusting rat hole he infests, you'll find a souvenir he kept."

Oates reached over and spun around the wooden nameplate on the desk to show the gold letters saying CHIEF OF POLICE.

"You, Chief, will be the hero. You never believed that Dickey girl drowned, and you had suspected Krieger all along, right?"

"Uh, now that you mention it…."

"Of course," Oates said. "A top cop like you can sniff these things out." Scaravelli flinched at the sarcastic tone.

"So you save the island from a child-molesting serial killer. No one's gonna push for an investigation. They'll be too happy Krieger's gone. You'll end up with a lifetime contract protecting this island of sheep from nothing. Above all…."

A tooth on the other side of Scaravelli's jaw wiggled. Scaravelli quivered, eyes wide. His heart pounded faster.

"Your co-operation means I don't have to call my marker. *Capisce*?"

Scaravelli nodded so fast it made him dizzy. "Deal."

"That's good," Oates said. "Now you go home, you wait for Mrs. Olsen's call. Then out to Canale Road. Don't forget to bring the evidence." Oates pointed at the .38.

He walked toward the door, paused, and turned. "Consider our arrangement sealed."

He raised a hand in Scaravelli's direction. Suddenly Scaravelli felt like someone took a blowtorch to his shoulder. A wide lance of excruciating pain ripped through him all the way to his shoulder blade.

"Son of a bitch!"

Oates dropped his hand. The pain disappeared. Oates managed a grim little smile. "And put the tooth under your pillow, and you'll get a quarter," he said.

Oates left Scaravelli's office. The force that bound Scaravelli to the chair vanished and he nearly collapsed on the floor.

Scaravelli's heart slowed down. It ached from the jump into overdrive. He plucked the tooth from his shirt. Then he pulled his shirt open. A circular brand containing two inverted triangles was burned into his skin.

"Holy shit." He sagged back in the chair.

He rationalized that that encounter could have gone a hell of a lot worse. All in all, Scaravelli figured he'd come out way ahead. Krieger's the only loser as he grabs a few feet of well-deserved turf. The guy's a scumbag anyway. And if Scaravelli decided to actually play cop and arrest him instead, some liberal asshole judge would let him walk with some crybaby defense. In retrospect, the whole setup was looking too good to be true.

Scaravelli was not in the habit of looking too closely at things that were too good to be true. When the card said BANK ERROR IN YOUR FAVOR – COLLECT $200, he just collected the money and rolled the dice again. He did wonder what Oates meant when he said he'd 'take care of the rest' after Scaravelli secured the crime scene.

Screw it. He'd figure that out later, still having a jaw full of teeth.

CHAPTER ELEVEN

The apartment's intercom to the security desk buzzed. Camille's black stilettos clicked as she crossed the white marble kitchen floor. She pressed the response button with a long onyx fingernail. The tiny screen beside it popped to life. Luis, the night shift doorman, smiled at her. Like everyone else Camille spoke to, he flashed one of those nervous smiles that poorly masked fear.

"Uh. Ms. Camille, you've got a visitor, but he's not on the log."

The view switched to a man standing in the lobby in front of the doorman's post. He wore a suit but no tie, and his blue shirt was open at the neck. He was tall and muscular; his short-cropped dark hair screamed soldier or cop. He looked around the lobby as if sizing it up.

"Says he's Mr. Rene Kyler," Luis continued. "Says he represents a Mr. Oates?"

Camille's pulse spiked. Years of waiting, years of preparation. All for this. She swept her long black hair back and over one shoulder. "Send him up."

It was only fitting that she be the first of the five to know. After all, Oates had selected her first, before she became Camille, before she became free.

*   *   *

Back then, Camille was twelve going on twenty-one and had already overdosed on being a ward of the state. She was then named Consuela. Her mother had abandoned her at birth in the hospital. She shuttled through a string of foster homes, always the Hispanic kid in a non-Hispanic household. Each place hosted a horror all its own. First, there was the filthy house where rats scurried in the halls under empty fast food wrappers, and the blackened toilet had no seat. Then there were the crystal meth heads, who financed their habits with her state support check while she starved in the garage. And who could forget the Muellers, that lovely couple who shared a penchant for cheap booze and the belief that a lit cigarette against young skin was the highest form of entertainment? Each family was a different nightmare, with one common thread: indulging their sicknesses was more important than a borrowed little girl.

Finally, after another screaming session with the glowing red tips of a pack of Salem Lights (the box said *cool and refreshing*), Consuela climbed through a window and into the night. She carried everything she had with her, which amounted to the clothes on her back and a desire for self-preservation.

Life on the road meant hiding, scavenging, and starving. Theft became a survival skill. She avoided becoming a victim by shunning human contact. Whoever they were, they were out to hurt her for their own gain. Or worse, they might be some religious do-gooders who would 'save' her and return her to a foster home. Thanks, but no thanks.

One night about 3 a.m., in an alley behind an upscale steakhouse (they tossed the best trash if you needed a meal), Joey Oates first appeared. Consuela sat invisible in the shadow of a dumpster. Oates walked down the alley like he owned it. He warded off the night's chill with the plushest camel's hair coat the girl had ever seen. He shed the coat, revealing a black pinstripe suit, and left the coat on the steakhouse steps. He backed away, then turned to face exactly where she hid.

"Ain't no point in being so cold," he said. "The coat's yours."

He retreated a few more steps, but Consuela was wary. It spooked her that the man knew where she was hiding, when she was certain he could not see her. In addition, everyone was after something. No way this guy wasn't.

But she sensed no danger. God knows she had developed a nose for it over the years. She crept forward from the shadows.

"Go ahead, try it on."

Consuela sidestepped to the coat. Her eyes never left Oates. She picked up the coat. The thick, clean, plush wool held the promise of warmth. She slid an arm inside to the smooth caress of the silk inner lining. She inserted her other arm and shrugged the coat up onto her shoulders. It reached past her calves. She pulled the front closed and the coat almost wrapped around her twice. She'd never worn such luxury.

The pockets brushed heavy against her knees. She reached into her right and extracted one of several paper packs. Her eyes widened. Cash. The band read *$100*. She thumbed through the corners. All hundreds. If she added up every dollar she'd touched her whole life, she wouldn't have a fraction of this amount, and her left pocket felt as full as her right.

"You know what's overrated?" Oates asked. "Freedom. You got total freedom now, how's it feel?"

"Cold."

Oates gave the air an exaggerated sniff. "And it stinks. What defines true freedom? Cash. Piles of it. There's more for you where that came from if you want it."

A warning bell rang for Consuela. "I'm not screwing you. Or anyone else." She hadn't made it this far without being molested to give it up for a decent coat.

"No fears there," Oates said. "In fact, just the opposite. Part of the deal is that you don't have sex."

Consuela tugged the coat tighter. This was the kind of deal she wanted to hear more about.

The back door of the steakhouse swung open. A scrawny cook in a white apron walked out with a bulging black bag of trash. He took one look over Consuela's head at Oates, and froze. Oates stared at him. The bag slipped through the cook's hand and hit the ground with a splat. He backed through the door, and it closed behind him.

"Now that there is real freedom, the freedom of power. That's the freedom I'm gonna give you."

The idea of being able to protect herself with a look that inspired terror was pretty appealing. "I'll be able to do that?"

"No, sweetheart. I'll turn you into someone who draws power over men from the other end of the spectrum. Same end result though. You ask. They do."

"In return for…?"

"Very little. Next to nothing."

And Oates told her the deal. He would have some of his followers instruct her in the Dark Arts, give her a place to stay, meet all her needs. The word *witchcraft* never came up, but she wasn't stupid enough to think that what this man was talking about was anything else. She had to practice, stay chaste, and remain silent about it all. In the end, he'd give her dominion over others and eternal life by his side.

A long list of people were due her revenge. She took the deal.

He didn't say he was the Devil. He didn't need to. From the second he appeared, Consuela just understood he was, as if she and all humans had a sensor inside to detect the Prince of Darkness. But she felt none of the abject terror he inspired in the cook. Instead she felt a sense of something mesmerizing and unique. She felt family. She'd been alone and abandoned all her life. The key to her happiness, to her being complete, was to be with Oates.

Oates kept his word and delivered her to an Upper West Side New York penthouse. After the Cleansing, she shed the trappings of her previous life. She also dropped her given name, taking Camille at Oates' insistence. Then she learned the spells and mastered the potions that drew her vast power. Soon her mere presence could enthrall any man.

But what Oates had her practice the most was the Incantation of the Portal. Each day, she recited the Latin prayer until she could chant it without thinking, producing every tone and inflection to perfection. Oates explained that when the time was right, she would use that spell to open the door to his kingdom, and then pass through it to reign with him forever.

Over the years, other girls had joined Camille in the swank penthouse. One by one, Oates scooped other lost lasses from the city's human flotsam and cloistered them in the upscale refuge. Ivana, Donna, Andrea, and Katrina all joined the coven by the time Camille turned fifteen. Society never missed these girls as they slipped through the cracks and entered Oates' underworld. The girls never missed society, or as they called it, the mortal world. Pain and emptiness had primed them to embrace all that Oates offered.

He gave them great freedom with a few restrictions. No one could leave the penthouse without two others. No one entered the penthouse except the five. Most critically, no one had sex. Within these boundaries, they could practice their witchcraft, indulging any whims they might have. They all chose to tattoo a thin necklace of thorns around the base of their necks to symbolize their bond to each other. It was a wonderfully hedonistic life for all of them. All they had to do was await Oates' call.

*　　*　　*

Rene Kyler stepped out of the elevator and knocked on the penthouse door. He could have done this with a phone call or an email. But a decade of being Oates' right-hand man taught Kyler to do all business in person, and that the man's orders needed to be followed, not questioned.

He'd taken his own path to end up in service to Oates, as voluntary as Camille's, but as tied to murder as Carl Krieger's.

At an early age, Kyler had discovered that inflicting suffering and death was a lot of fun. He'd started with animals, learning that flies lived briefly without wings and that ants popped in a puff of smoke under a magnifying glass. By the time neighborhood pets began to disappear, Kyler had realized two things.

First, oddly, the population viewed his acts with abhorrence. Nothing in his head even hinted that his little torture experiments were wrong. Kyler's switch that fired up the guilt circuits was grounded out. In fact, he experienced little emotion at all. Sure, he had a pleasurable feeling when at age six he lit the Burnses' dog on fire (he relished the pun, it was why he chose the victim dog), but even that fleeting sensation felt shallow. The remorse, the love, the compassion people went on and on about were alien concepts. A girlfriend told him that was his loss; he replied that it was his liberation. Let the rest of the world act constrained by emotions. He could follow whatever path he chose.

His second realization was that he must hide the first realization from the rest of the world. Others sensed the power and freedom he had, and it scared them. They didn't understand him any more than gorillas understood humans. To be safe, he'd need to pass as one of the gorillas. He watched television, saw what it was that people expected to see, and mastered the pantomime. Concern, fear, empathy, disappointment. He could hold them like a hand of cards, then play them as needed with the cool precision of a Vegas pro. The process worked like a charm.

At eighteen, he chose the career of a Navy SEAL, where the controlled application of violence was part of the job. Weapons qualification and hand-to-hand training were good outlets for his growing fixation, while his animal experiments became an enthusiastic off-duty hobby. His job offer from Hell came during an insertion years ago into the hills of Afghanistan.

His unit was sweeping a village that had harbored some Taliban snipers. The place was the usual dun-colored collection of mud-brick and concrete-block buildings. The dirt streets of the village were deserted. With each step, Kyler's adrenaline level surged until he just itched to start a firefight. He paused outside the locked door on a rundown, one-room shack trying to pass as a home. He kicked in the door and rushed in.

To his disappointment, no militiamen filled his rifle sights. Useless, threadbare curtains hung like the executed on either side of a large broken window. Two small beds flanked a table made of discarded pallet boards. In the corner stood a woman in her mid-forties in a long dark skirt and a white head covering that left just a swath of her face exposed. Two small girls cowered behind her as if she was an impenetrable shield from the intruder at the door. The sun had bronzed the woman's face to leather and dirt streaked her cheeks. Her dark eyes danced in terror.

There were no weapons in the room. These three were no threat.

He lowered the barrel of his M4, and shot from the hip. A single shot tore the woman's left kneecap away. With a shriek, she collapsed on the floor. She gripped her shattered leg with one hand and pointed with the other to the two girls, now frozen with fear behind her. Tears rolled down her face as she implored him for mercy in Pashto.

Without a thought, Kyler threw the M4 selector switch from single to burst. One jerk of the trigger sent three rounds into the terrified little girls. Their tiny chests exploded as the impact plastered them against the wall. They fell to the floor by their mother's side.

With the last valuable things in her life stripped away, the mother's screams hit a higher octave. The pleading cries vanished, replaced with rage. She pulled herself toward Kyler, lips curled back in a vengeful snarl.

Kyler flipped the selector switch back to single and sent one bullet through her forehead.

Kyler stepped outside and closed the door, like a hotel maid who had just finished cleaning the room. He paused. The street was still empty. No one peered out at him through any windows. He moved to rejoin his unit.

When he caught up to the rest of the patrol, the NCO asked him if he had found anything back there.

"Nah, nothing," he replied.

About 2 a.m. that night, Kyler stood watch on the team's perimeter. A supernatural stillness blanketed the moonless countryside. The baying of wolves broke the quiet, and then they too went silent. He flipped up his night-vision goggles to give his eyes a rest from the fuzzy blue image. A cold chill settled around him, not a breeze so much as a...presence.

"Nice work today," a gravelly voice behind him said.

He spun and swung his weapon to bear on the voice. A stout man in a long black trench coat stood behind him. A fedora shaded his pale, round face and neatly trimmed black goatee. The man raised two fingers and Kyler's rifle flew from his hands. The man caught it with his fingertips.

Even in the darkness, his eyes seemed to look through Kyler. Kyler's stomach dropped a few inches. The intruder's presence triggered some sort of warning from deep in the shared human consciousness. In a country where evil had run unchecked for centuries, this guy emanated a malevolence above all others.

Two wolves came loping in. They sat obediently, one on each side of Oates. They stared down Kyler with piercing intensity.

"This weapon won't be necessary," Oates said, "or effective." He dropped the rifle to the ground.

Kyler looked around to his team. They all slept like the dead, without even the usual stray snore.

"Who are you?" he asked.

"I'm the mentor you always wanted," the man in black said. His thick New York accent reminded Kyler of the *Godfather* movies. "Lately I've been going by Mr. Oates. Been watching you, Mr. Kyler. You started out right when you torched the Burnses' dog at age six, and took another good step at age seven when you dragged Freddie Cohen out behind the bleachers, and taught him what the thick end of a baseball bat felt like."

Kyler hadn't ever told anyone about those incidents. How could this guy know these things? How could he just materialize out of nowhere? How could he put the rest of the team into a comatose sleep?

Like an anxious elementary school kid raising his hand in class, his subconscious kept trying to answer these questions. Kyler didn't need to call on it. When you finally meet the Devil, you know.

Oates grinned. "The light dawns."

More interesting was the fact that Kyler felt something shared between them, a connection, like long-lost brothers finally reunited. In a lifetime of being different from everyone else, he found someone who was the same. The fear that gripped him earlier dissipated.

"I got a career opportunity you can't pass up," Oates said.

*   *   *

And Oates had not lied. Oates usually had to use the carrot and the stick approach with those who signed his contracts, but he just buried Kyler in carrots. Unlimited impunity in return for unlimited service. Kyler agreed and Oates burned the brand of his contract onto Kyler's chest, a circle with two concave triangles within.

Over time, Kyler realized that Oates needed him to some extent. Even the Devil had limitations placed on him, probably a parting gift when God had stripped the rebel angel of his wings. God granted Satan the power to rule Hell, then condemned him to forever walk the Earth, unable to enter the domain to which Satan sent sinners' souls. Eons before man would mythologize Tantalus, God had already told that tale.

Then, Oates' interactions with the mortal had specific limits. Initially, Kyler thought Oates' penchant for selective human contact was born of a disdain for anything mortal. Kyler seemed to do the lion's share of the dirty work. As time went on, he realized that Oates could not randomly kill, rape, steal, or commit any of the sins from which he derived so much pleasure. He owned the body of those who had lost their souls to him, but he was powerless against the rest. He had to savor their pain vicariously, through the work of his disciples. And he could not gain a disciple by deceit; no contract could ever be signed through force or trickery. The rule seemed to never be a real limitation. People sold their souls to Oates cheap.

Oates *could* control members of the animal kingdom, as he controlled the wolves that first night. Their minds were simple and they lacked the strength a soul conferred. But people? Those he could only influence, tempt, and induce. Until they signed.

From the moment the transaction took place, Oates could call the damned one's soul southward any time, with great latitude in methods, all at once or piece by piece. Kyler had seen Oates snatch people in an instant with a heart attack, and torture others for days by slowly bursting one blood vessel at a time, until their body was a fleshy balloon of red liquid. The threat of a painful death induced the future eternally damned to do whatever Oates asked.

When Oates couldn't risk the vagaries of human weakness, he used Kyler, his sole full-time employee. The rest were just temps working one final job before a last permanent change of address. Kyler considered his solo position on Hell's corporate payroll another part of his and Oates' special bond.

Oates could travel in a flash from one place to another, but with another divinely delivered limitation that gave Kyler a kick. Oates could not teleport himself across water. God's inside joke seemed to be that his Son could walk on water, but Lucifer would have to swim. So while Oates could go from Los Angeles to Boston in a millisecond, he still needed a boat for the last leg to Stone Harbor. That was why Kyler drew this mainland assignment to summon the coven.

The apartment door swung open to reveal a knockout of a woman. Dark-haired, dark-skinned, and voluptuous. Perfect eyebrows arched over captivating brown eyes lined in thick cobalt eyeliner. Her sly smile dazzled. She wore a black dress, slit high up one side and cut low in the front. The string of thorns inked around the base of her neck caught his eye.

Oates had warned him that whoever answered the door would be male kryptonite. He was right. The woman hadn't said a word, and he was already enthralled.

He remembered Oates' second warning. So much as touch anyone in the apartment, or let anyone else, and there would literally be Hell to pay. Oates was a man of his word about things like that. Kyler forced his mind back on track.

"Camille?"

"Absolutely."

"Mr. Oates sent me."

"He couldn't come himself?"

"He's a busy man. But he says it's time for you to join him."

Camille gripped the doorknob. She closed her eyes in almost orgasmic joy, sighed and reopened them. "We'll be ready in minutes."

"Not yet. Forty-eight hours."

He pulled a long envelope from inside his suit coat. He extended it to Camille lengthwise so he could safely keep at least eight inches between them. The woman had some kind of magnetism within her that he feared he'd discharge if he got too close. She pinched the envelope's end with her fingertips. He released it like it had caught fire.

"A boat will pick you up at the dock at this location at the time listed." At least that's what Oates told him was in the envelope. "Don't be late."

"Wouldn't dream of it."

Kyler stepped back, nodded a goodbye, and headed for the elevator. The penthouse door closed behind him and he sighed in relief. He pressed the elevator call button.

One mission down, one to go. Doing his part for Oates' Stone Harbor event. The next one involved a group of real scumbags. After experiencing Camille's excruciating attraction, he was surprised to now look forward to meeting with thugs.

*   *   *

Camille ripped the envelope open with her fingernail. She extracted the paper within with reverence. The note listed an early morning time and a location out east of Orient Point on Long Island. She crushed the page against her pounding chest.

She opened the hall closet. From the corner she pulled a gnarled ebony walking stick, topped with the golden head of a goat with rubies for eyes. Oates had entrusted only her with this most powerful conduit to dark magic, and only to use at the appointed time, now finally here.

She walked down the hall to the master bedroom and opened the door. Like petals on a flower, five twin beds with red satin sheets radiated from a center circle on the floor. The center circle contained two superimposed triangles with concave sides, one triangle pointed up, one down. Camille's twin bed was empty, but her four fellow witches, her coven, slept in the others.

"Sisters!" she said. Forms stirred under the sheets. "It's finally time."

They would soon fulfill their destiny, and open the way for all of them to join the Master at his side forever.

CHAPTER TWELVE

That night, Scott rolled into the driveway of Allie's rented house. The mainlander had spared no expense, starting with the ocean-view lot. On an island where sandy beaches were nonexistent, ocean view was the next best thing. Exquisite landscaping surrounded the modern ranch, which was painted a pleasant robin's egg blue. He remembered selling supplies to the builders and visiting the site when the home was half-finished. He never met the owner, par for the course for the summer-shift residents. Scott shut off the truck and took a deep breath.

The dissolution of their relationship had been a decade ago. And it had been a dissolution, there had been no official termination, no Dear John letter, email, message, text. He wasn't beneath admitting that at the time, the sense of abandonment had been pretty crushing, the lack of any closure frustrating.

But that water had long passed under the bridge; they were both older, both different now. Would he ask any of his unanswered questions tonight? Should he? At this point in life, did a teenage romance really matter, anyway?

The front door opened before he even left the truck. Allie stepped out, her long hair bouncing around her shoulders. Scott flashed back to an identical scene, him pulling up to Allie's house in high school and watching her walk out for a ride to school. He never had to knock on the door then either.

But that Allie Cat always had a smile. This Allie looked pensive, nervous. The idea that he'd set her up to be uncomfortable made him cringe. She got in the passenger side and slammed the door. He looked over. She smiled. He remembered she was an actress.

"Ready for a whirlwind night on the town?" he said.

"I took a nap so I'd be able to handle it."

"Then away we go."

Scott pulled out and headed into town. He forced some small talk to break the silence. "Is your place nice?"

"Perfect. I opened the windows one night to fall asleep to the crash of the waves. Got a bit chilly though, about 2 a.m. It's so funny. The whole area was nothing but trees when I left."

"But for everything that changes in Stone Harbor, a hundred things stay the same. Mackey's clam chowder being high on that list."

She didn't answer. The silence felt ominous. From the corner of his eye, Scott saw Allie wring her hands. The truck approached Main Street.

"Scottie, can I ask something, and you not take it the wrong way?"

Here it comes, he thought. "Go for it."

"Can we not go to Mackey's? I'm not going to be comfortable sitting out on display in there. People staring, whispering."

"In this town? We take celebrities in stride. We have TV stars around all the time. Mick Jagger has a house two doors down from yours. Last summer, the Queen of England "

"Scottie, I'm serious."

He pulled the truck into an empty parking lot. "I understand. You know, a lot of cats have been disappearing in that neighborhood anyhow. Probably isn't safe to eat there. Second choice?"

The corners of her mouth sagged in distress.

"Tell you what," Scott said. "Dinner at my house then."

Her face brightened. "Yes! You can cook?"

"No guarantee there's any food in the fridge," he said. "I can at least order pizza from Angelo's."

"Angelo's it is. Can't wait. The only thing worse than LA air is LA pizza."

Scott ordered the pizza on the way to the house. He hung up and Allie laughed.

"That's so funny," she said. "I'd forgotten that here you don't need to give an address for delivery."

"Depending on who answers, I don't even have to give my name."

He pulled up in front of the house. They left the truck and he led her up the porch steps. As he unlocked the front door, Allie stared along the porch.

"Remember the year we made jack-o'-lanterns out here?" she sighed.

"We spread pumpkin guts all over, and next spring there were vines growing through the porch slats. My father made me crawl under there and pull them all out. How could I forget?"

He pushed open the door and gestured Allie in. She gave him a fleeting smile as she passed. He rushed a panicked sweep of excess everything from the living room: old mail, a set of socks, two paperbacks. "Make yourself at home."

Allie plopped down on the couch in the same spot she used to sit when they stayed up late to watch *Saturday Night Live*. She gave the room a once-over.

"Nothing's changed," she said.

"A little, but not much. After Mom died, Dad didn't change a thing, mostly out of inertia more than sentimentality, I think. After he died, I kind of continued the tradition."

Scott dumped the crap he'd collected in the laundry room. He returned in time to answer the door and accept a hot pizza. He carried it into the dining room. Allie followed him in.

"The dining room?" Allie said.

Scott thought a moment. "We're more pizza in the kitchen people, aren't we?"

"At least we used to be," Allie said.

"Then we must still be. Nothing changes in this house."

They transferred everything to the kitchen table, and ate the pizza straight from the box, with two sodas straight from the cans.

"I'm sorry I wasn't your first dinner invitation," Scott said.

"Oh, but you are."

"You're kidding," he said. "In these weeks, no one's asked you over for dinner? Not even Reverend Snow's adult Bible study group? They shanghai everyone they can."

"Reverend Snow still runs All Souls? How old is he now?"

"I think he knew Moses personally."

Allie laughed. "No, no one's invited me anywhere. They're not sure how to deal with me. It's like they think I returned from LA a fragile mess, one raw comment from a meltdown."

"Everyone saw you go through the wringer last year," he said. "After all that, what brought you back to Stone Harbor?"

"I had to ditch LA," she said. "I couldn't feel myself anymore. I'd spent so much time being someone else, on screen and off, that I'd lost Allie Layton. So I bought Stewie for nine hundred dollars and drove him here to find old Allie. Now he's my cross-country knight in faded blue armor. After three thousand miles, we're fast friends."

"Like the Mustang?" Scott asked.

Allie almost choked on a pepperoni.

"Oh, my God! My old Mustang! Has a car ever left anyone high and dry so often in the history of the world?"

"Luckily it's a small island, and you could walk home from most strandings."

"I seem to remember you doing the white-knight thing and rescuing me more often than me walking home."

"Since the statute of limitations has run out –" Scott's tone descended into mock seriousness, "– I'll admit that I used to sabotage your car just to save you."

They both laughed.

"So that's my story," Allie said. "Why are you here? I mean I know that you came here to help your dad, but after that, what kept you in Stone Harbor?"

Scott ran his finger across the lip of the pizza box.

"It's home," he said. Then he looked up at her. "I moved, but roots don't leave. It felt good to have my feet back on the island."

"I'd heard you got married."

"Momentarily. Her name was Anita. Allie, Anita. I guess I've never worked my way out of the *A*s. Well, island life didn't agree with her. There were too few places to go, too little to do. With the strain of caring for Dad…it was all too much."

He paused. More words came in a rush.

"We really shouldn't have married anyway. The more time we spent together, the more obvious our different needs became. Looking back, I can't tell you why I got married at all. It just seemed like the thing you did after graduation."

His face flushed. He'd never even said that to himself, let alone someone else.

"Well, there's a moment better suited for a therapist's couch," he said. "Sorry. That's the wrong whine to serve with pizza."

Allie touched his arm. "Don't worry," she said. "I have my own long list of inexplicable decisions. We'll go through them when we have a longer night."

They finished dinner and Scott caught her up on current island life, though a lot of it remained unchanged. Downtown rolled up the sidewalks at 5 p.m. Winter season still made watching paint dry seem exciting. The town still lacked a movie theater, but with satellite TV and Netflix, no one complained about it anymore.

Scott shut the empty pizza box. He relished how warm, how comfortable he felt with Allie. Since his divorce, dating never made his to do list, partially due to the inconvenience of meeting people on the mainland, but mostly from the dread of enduring that awkward, artificial time when both parties tried so hard to be someone they really weren't. There was none of that here.

Allie rose to leave. "I'd better get home. Thanks for dinner," she said. "Next time I'll cook."

"You cook?"

"It beats starving."

"I'll be the judge of that."

She thumped him on the chest and smiled. They went to the truck. Scott drove well under the speed limit, in no hurry to end the night.

CHAPTER THIRTEEN

The instant his home phone rang at 7 p.m., Scaravelli knew three things: Mrs. Olsen was on the other end, her daughter was dead, and all Oates had said was for real. Scaravelli grinned, then winced at the pain the grin engendered where his tooth was now missing.

"Hello?" The wad of gauze in his tooth socket made him mumble it a bit.

"Chief Scaravelli? This is Colleen Olsen, Natalie's mom?" Her voice was tight as a harp string, overwhelming panic barely held at bay.

"Colleen, what's wrong?" Scaravelli's mock concern bordered on sarcastic.

She didn't notice. "I know Milo's on duty, but I had to call you. Natalie didn't come home. I sent her to the market for rolls." Her words accelerated as maternal terror took control. "I know she's only seven, but it was just a few blocks away, and it's *daylight* for Christ's sake. That was over two hours ago, and we looked everywhere. She wouldn't just wander off. She's a good girl. You've gotta—"

"Slow down, Colleen," Scaravelli cut in. "Take a deep breath."

He had found that while making people take a deep breath rarely calmed them down, it at least shut them the hell up.

"Have you checked her friends' houses?" he continued, working hard to fake a reassuring tone. "She could be there."

"We've called everyone," Colleen said. "No one has seen her since 5 p.m. when she left the store."

Scaravelli asked the standard questions about height, weight, and clothing. He pretended to be writing it all down, repeating it back as Mrs. Olsen told him each detail. He checked his watch.

"I'll get right on it, Colleen," he said. "I'm sure that I'll bring your daughter home to you tonight." He realized only he got that hilarious joke.

Scaravelli hung up, strapped on his pistol belt, and headed out to his cruiser. He'd changed into a clean uniform, better to complete this show in costume. He unholstered the 9mm Beretta and chambered the round with Krieger's name on it. He double-checked that the safety was still on.

No point in blowing my goddamn foot off tonight, he thought.

He got in the car and headed out through the empty streets. After five, the town closed except for the Rusty Nail off Main Street. He headed up the hill and out of town along Canale Road.

Scaravelli's pulse climbed as he thought about the next thirty minutes. He pounded a little beat out on the steering wheel. He'd become a lot more comfortable with his role as executioner. Oates had made him a regular 007 with a license to kill. He'd off this scumbag Krieger, and completely get away with it. Even better, he'd be *rewarded* for doing it. Sweet deal.

He'd talked to other cops who'd wasted a perp in the line of duty. They either didn't want to talk about it, or wanted to talk about it way too much. Like he was some TV shrink, and they had to share their burden of guilt. Bunch of wimps. He didn't know how, or why, those guys stayed cops.

He imagined how he'd handle it. It would be nothing but a thing. Draw down, pop Krieger, and get on with life. Just like swatting a mosquito. The bug had it coming, living off the blood of others.

With Scaravelli's initial reluctance gone, Colleen's call had banished his second thoughts about Oates. Everything the man had said was coming true. He psyched himself up for the exercise of ultimate power, burning down Krieger. He flipped on the high beams and punched the cruiser up another ten miles per hour.

CHAPTER FOURTEEN

Drying sweat cooled Carl Krieger's skin and left a saline, oily sheen. The forest's darkness enveloped the van, a black, comforting curtain between his world and everyone else. He'd finished with Natalie and sat sideways in the driver's seat, his back against the window and his feet across the console. He exhaled deep, steady breaths. He felt good. He felt whole.

He'd parked a thousand yards into the woods, down a rutted dirt road scarcely wider than the van. Three hundred years ago, men had cleared this acreage for pasture by sheer physical strength and force of will. Sheep had grazed near the hilltop. Through neglect, their accomplishment disappeared as the relentless forest reclaimed the hard-won acres. Only the twin tracks of dirt and stone resisted nature's repossession.

He twisted the headlight switch. The van's dim interior lights tinged the rear compartment a pale yellow. He'd pulled all the seats out that afternoon to make room for his date. She lay white and still atop a dirty wool blanket, arms and legs tied spread-eagle to the stripped-out van walls. Her lifeless eyes stared at the ceiling. The fringe of her panties stuck out of her mouth between bulging cheeks.

This second time had been so much better. Right after doing the Dickey girl, he felt a huge emotional release, followed by overwhelming guilt. For days he struggled with the idea of turning himself in. But the impulse for absolution faded more each day, and by the second week, it disappeared.

Just now, after killing Natalie, he got that same wonderful feeling, a long mental orgasm to complement the short physical one. But this time, he harbored no guilt, not even a hint of remorse. He'd read in chat rooms about how society programmed the guilt about his sexual needs into him, how everyone wanted to repress him.

Guilt was for losers. If only he could get his dates to last longer. With more practice...next time....

Natalie's Brownie uniform shirt lay in his lap, this evening's souvenir, soon to join the Dickey girl's necklace in his apartment. He put the shirt up to his nose. He inhaled deeply, his mouth slightly open the way a lion checks the wind for prey. He smelled something soft and girlish, like baby powder, but tainted with the strong scent of fear. He treasured that fragrance. It smelled like love. He began to get aroused again. He reached down into his open pants.

The clock in the dash warned he was out of time. Oates' instructions were to stay here until 8 p.m., and then Oates would come help him get rid of the body. Carl turned off the interior light and rested back against the van door. All he had to do was wait.

The slow, low crunch of rubber tires on rocks sounded outside the van. Carl looked in the big side view mirror. A car was pulling up from behind, headlights off.

Must be Oates, he thought, *lights out to avoid attention. Smooth.*

The van interior exploded in a rhythm of blue flashes.

"What the hell?" Carl said.

He sat bolt upright and looked back between the seats. A patrol car's light bar blazed through the van's tiny back windows. Fresh sweat stippled his upper lip. The cruiser's front door opened.

He cast a terrified look down at Natalie's corpse, bound and spread in full display. With each strobe of the blue lights over her profile, shadows advanced and retreated across her cheekbones. Each flash seemed to paint an intermittent vengeful smile on her face. Carl spun around in the driver's seat and zipped up his pants.

There's two damn cops on the whole island, he thought, *and one of them is here now? How the hell can that happen?*

He grabbed the brittle old dashboard so tightly his fingernails punctured it. The curtain that separated his little fantasy world from reality pulled wide open. Some cop's flashlight was about to hit the cargo area, and the result of Carl's acts wouldn't look like the beautiful symbol of his passion he knew it was. Instead, it would look like the back of a sleazy van with a raped and tortured little girl on the floor, a sick crime scene. Others wouldn't understand. A flood of fear washed over him.

He popped open the driver's door. If he could intercept the cop, stall him until Oates arrived, then Oates would save him. This whole thing was Oates' idea anyway.

Carl got out of the van and tried to smooth his hair into place. He squinted with each blinding blue flash from the dark. He managed a fake, welcoming smile, and took a tentative step forward.

"Hello?" He shielded his eyes with his hand.

Carl shuffled forward to the van's rear bumper. A bulky shadow rose from the cruiser.

Scaravelli, he thought. *Goddamn it. Why couldn't I get the stupider cop?*

"Hey there, Chief? What's with all the light show?"

Scaravelli stood behind the shield of the open cruiser door, one hand on the door, the other down at his side, his pistol side.

"Stay right there, Carl," Scaravelli ordered. "I want your hands on top of your head."

Dread filled Carl like oil sludge. His hands began to shake.

Scaravelli got tipped off. No other way he'd be back in the woods this time of night. Except that no one knows where I am.

Except Oates.

Denial flashed through his mind for a split second, but with no staying power.

There is the matter of a small debt, he heard Oates say in his head.

"The bastard tricked me," Carl said under his breath. Then, louder, "H-hey Chief, let me explain—"

Scaravelli raised his 9mm from behind the car door. The barrel flickered blue then black in the revolving lights.

"No, no, no. Chief! Wait! This ain't my fault!"

The Beretta flashed in the night. The bullet exploded Carl's brain before he heard the gun's report. His debt to Oates was paid in full.

CHAPTER FIFTEEN

The acrid smoke of spent gunpowder drifted past Scaravelli like unholy incense. He had to suppress a laugh as he gazed down at the shocked look on Krieger's fresh corpse. What did the child-molesting shit bag expect?

Scaravelli nearly bubbled with a new sense of power. He'd been judge, jury, and executioner, all rolled into one. The last role had been the best. He'd waited just long enough to see that pathetic look of terror cross Krieger's face, to hear him plead for his useless life. How sweet to end his existence with one pull of the trigger.

Much as he wanted to savor every nuance of the end of Carl Krieger, he had to finish the show.

He slid his weapon back in its holster. He pulled the .38 pistol Oates had given him from his pocket. He walked over to Krieger and, straddling his chest, faced the cruiser. He leveled the .38 at the car.

No point in messing up my side of the windshield, he thought.

He aimed left and fired. A bullet smacked into the passenger side of the glass and left a hole encircled by a spiderweb of cracks.

Then he knelt down and grabbed Krieger's right hand. He put the .38 in it and wrapped Carl's finger through the trigger guard. He pointed the pistol in the air and squeezed Carl's finger against the trigger. The pistol popped again.

A little gunpowder residue in case someone did do an investigation. Scumbag the Child Molester fires twice; valiant cop returns fire and kills him. Tragically, just minutes too late to save the girl. A simple, unshakable story.

He peeked inside the van's back window. The blue lights lit Natalie's pale little nude body. No need to check that for a pulse. Oates had told him she'd be dead. So far, he'd been right about everything.

Scaravelli returned to his car. He picked up the radio mic.

"Milo," he said. "Come in."

"This is Milo in Unit 2, Chief, down at the harbor." Scaravelli shook his head. Why did Milo always tell him he was in Unit 2? Where the hell else would he be?

"Milo, head to the office and get every roll of crime scene tape we have. Then meet me on the dirt road that runs north off Canale. Oh, and call the clinic. I need an ambulance to the same location. Two DOAs."

"Really?" Milo said.

"Yes, really," Scaravelli snapped. "Now get off the radio and do what I told you to do."

"Right, Chief," Milo answered.

Scaravelli fell into the front seat of his cruiser. He flipped off the blue lights.

The darkness was near-absolute, save a few stars in the hazy sky. He realized he was in the company of two corpses. No big deal, he'd done that before. But he owned these corpses, one by his own hand, the younger one by his inaction. He'd known Krieger's plan and done nothing to stop him.

The thought gave him a chill. He pulled the door shut and waited for Milo and the ambulance.

*   *   *

Milo was sitting across town in Stone Harbor's other police cruiser, his racing pulse making his hand shake. He could barely get the mic back into its dashboard clip. The advent of real police work gave him a rush. Not parking tickets or stray dogs or loud music this time. Murder.

Frustration rolled in over Milo's initial excitement. His shift had started hours ago. Real, big-city crime happened, and Chief Scaravelli handled it alone. His heart sank under the weight of insecurity.

Every day on the job had been an emotional roller coaster since Chief Anderson retired and Scaravelli took charge. From day one, Scaravelli had treated Milo with contempt, at best concealed. He never had duties of any significance. The chief never put him in charge of even the temporary summer cops. Milo's cruiser was a used taxi and didn't even have a cage between the front and back seats.

Milo understood why. Any NYPD veteran would resent having a kind of green nineteen-year-old cop. As the only full-time officer on the force, and the only Stone Harbor native, Scaravelli couldn't just outright sack him off the bat, but Milo felt he was always one mistake away from a final paycheck.

He'd wanted to be a cop since he was four years old, and he wanted to do it in his hometown. His peers itched to escape after graduation, but for him, the cozy confines of the island were the picket fence of home, not prison walls. Others had ridiculed his dream, asking how a kid built like a matchstick would keep from being snapped in half by the first crook he cornered. But his father, who managed the Fisherman's Bank in town, had encouraged him all the way. Chief Anderson wouldn't have hired him at 18 if he hadn't shown so much 'promise and aptitude' as the old chief had said. He was sure that Chief Anderson's friendship with his father wasn't a factor in the decision, no matter what the town gossip reported. No, he hadn't been to the police academy *in person,* but he had taken all the online courses, and gotten A grades.

So Milo sucked up the all-night shift, even in the summer when the part-timers could have covered it, and Milo could have moved to days with the chief. Milo knew why the chief kept him there. At best, the chief wanted to avoid him. At worst, he was trying to make him quit.

Milo wasn't going to let the chief push him out of this job. Once he'd proven himself, Scaravelli would have to admit he made the grade, even if he continued to dislike him. A murder, no, a *double* murder, was just the chance he needed.

Guilt smacked him between the eyes. He hadn't even asked who was dead. On an island this size, it had to be someone he knew. He remembered reading about a police officer's need for professional detachment. He took a deep breath and pushed the worry to the back of his mind.

Milo fingered the rarely used switch for the roof rack of blue lights, the magic button that when pushed, transported him into the world of real-life law enforcement. He flipped them on and the lights strobed the harbor and docks. He noticed a black speedboat at the town dock, so low to the water he'd missed it as he drove into the parking lot. Definitely not a townie boat.

He dropped the cruiser into drive and hit the gas. Satisfying his curiosity on that would have to wait. He had to call the clinic. He had to secure a crime scene. He had to collect evidence.

He had to be a cop.

CHAPTER SIXTEEN

Scott smiled, awash in déjà vu. Driving with Allie in the passenger seat of his truck was a major flashback. Different car, different time, but the same sense of wonder as he watched her profile lighten and darken in the passing streetlights.

A few miles down Canale Road, blue flashing lights parted the night. Scott slowed down. He stopped behind a police cruiser parked along the shoulder, headlights blazing. Beside it, an ambulance's red lights sparkled a counterpoint to the blue police orbs. The ambulance doors hung open, the interior empty. A waist-high band of bright yellow crime scene tape stretched across the woods' edge, like some misplaced runner's finish line. A hundred yards down the dirt road, the headlights of a second police car illuminated a dull gray van through the skeletons of the denuded trees.

"I thought you said Stone Harbor was still dead dull after summer," Allie said.

"It is. Or should be." Scott slipped the truck into park. His role as town selectman came to the forefront. "I should go check this out."

Allie clicked off her seatbelt. "I'm game."

"No, you stay here."

"Ooh, look at me and my bad listening skills."

She opened the door and left the truck. Scott shook his head and remembered how headstrong his girlfriend had been, and how it was one of her better traits. He joined her on the passenger side of the truck just as Milo Mimms walked up from the cruiser by the road.

Milo stopped between them and the dirt road, his thumbs hitched into his oversized gun belt, shallow chest as puffed up as he could manage. It made Scott smile. Scaravelli was a grade A jackass, but Milo was a good kid, idealistic about law enforcement, committed to the community.

"You need to stay back, sir," Milo said, like some TV cop, even though he'd always been on a first-name basis with Scott. "We can't have anyone contaminating the crime scene."

Two paramedics struggled to pilot a gurney down the bumpy dirt road. A white sheet hung loose over a tiny body in the gurney's center. They rolled it behind Milo. The tears in one of the paramedic's eyes glistened in the police cruiser's headlights. Short of the waiting ambulance, a puff of wind caught the sheet and it floated off the body. The corner caught under one wheel and the sheet pulled away like a game show curtain revealing a prize.

Natalie Olsen lay on the gurney. Her gray, still eyes were nothing like the sparkling green ones Scott knew so well. Her wan skin looked waxy in the strange lighting. One button kept her Brownie uniform blouse closed across her bony chest. Her skirt was gone, leaving her exposed from the waist down, where blood coated the area between her legs. Two bloody handprints on her knees testified to where her legs had been forced apart.

Scott gasped. Allie let out a stifled scream. Scott whirled to block her view of the dead girl. All the color had drained from Allie's face. She stared through Scott to where the girl had been, as if the afterimage still burned in her mind.

"Allie," he whispered. "You don't need to see this."

Scott reached behind her and opened the passenger door. He guided her back into the truck and softly shut the door, as if a sudden slam might shatter her. He turned back to Milo. The frazzled paramedics had re-draped the now-muddy sheet over Natalie's corpse. They lifted it into the ambulance.

"Jesus, Milo," Scott said. "Was that Natalie Olsen? What the hell is going on here?"

"The chief said that he'd answer all the questions," Milo said. "The investigation into the deaths is ongoing."

"Deaths?"

The paramedics trudged back up the road to a second covered gurney and began to trundle it back to the ambulance, this time with far less care than they'd shown with Natalie. Scott checked the second gurney as it passed.

"Who else is dead?"

Milo held his hands up, palms facing Scott. "Chief's gonna answer all the questions."

Scott was about to remind Milo that the town selectmen oversaw all police activities. A flash of white across the road caught his eye.

In the wood line across Canale Road, at the edge of the illumination of his truck's headlights, stood a tall thin man with a crew cut of gray hair and

THE PORTAL • 65

a wispy, trimmed gray beard. He seemed to blend into the darkness, dressed all in black, except for the small flash of white at his collar.

"Reverend Snow," Scott whispered to himself. "What's he doing here?"

The reverend made no indication he was going to get involved or even move closer. He just stood motionless in the tree line, like one more maple.

The paramedics closed up the ambulance and then entered through the front doors. The ambulance made a U-turn on the road and headed back to the clinic. The red lights went dark, and the big van rolled on well within the speed limit.

No rush now, Scott thought.

Scaravelli walked down the dirt road in the glare of Milo's cruiser's headlights. Milo gestured Scott out of the way. The officer ceremoniously untied the crime scene tape from a tree and walked it back across the road. Scaravelli passed and Milo retied the yellow tape.

"What are you doing here, Tackett?" Scaravelli said.

He looked at Allie in the truck with a vague sense of recognition. Scott didn't want the questioning to veer in her direction.

"I think the question is," Scott said, "what are both of you doing here? Who's in that ambulance?"

"This is police business, part of an ongoing investigation."

"Which selectmen have full access to. You do remember you work for the town through us, right?"

Blood flushed Scaravelli's cheeks. If there hadn't been an audience, Scott knew Scaravelli would have let loose with both barrels about worthless civilian oversight. He'd heard the speech before.

"About 5 p.m., Carl Krieger, who works at Captain Nate's Boatyard, kidnapped Natalie Olsen from West Street. It appears that he drove her up here, then raped and killed her sometime tonight."

Scott's stomach sank. How could this be real? Natalie and her parents were wonderful people. He knew of Krieger, in a peripheral kind of way. He was low-rent, but a rapist and murderer....

"I received a call from Colleen Olsen," the chief continued, "and tracked Krieger to this location. When confronted, he drew a weapon and fired at me twice. I returned fire and killed him. Then I found Natalie's body in the back of his van."

"How did you know to look for Krieger?" Scott asked.

"Look, that's more than you need to know already," Scaravelli said. "Go home and let us do our job."

Scaravelli turned and started back to the other cruiser parked down the dirt road.

"Officer Mimms," he called over his shoulder.

Milo straightened up to an approximate version of a soldier at attention. "Chief?"

"I want this area kept clear all night. All the woods from the road to the hilltop. Starting now. Starting with getting rid of those two."

"You heard the chief," he told Scott. "Move it along."

"Now wait a minute—" Scott started.

"Scottie," cut in Allie. The truck's closed window muffled her voice, but it sounded a thousand miles farther away than that. "C-can we just go?"

Tears had washed tracks of eyeliner down her cheeks. Fear filled her reddened eyes. Scott kicked himself for stopping here with her in the truck in the first place.

"Sure, Allie."

Officer Mimms stood grim and dutiful at the yellow tape. As Scott walked around the front of the truck, he noticed that Reverend Snow was gone and the maples again stood alone.

He and Allie sat in silence as they drove to Allie's house. Allie looked shattered. Tucked up into her corner of the car, she stared out the window at the darkness. They pulled down the long driveway to her house and Scott rolled the truck to a stop.

"Allie, I'm so sorry. Are you all right?"

"Sure," she said without conviction. "That whole horrible scene back there…. I just need some sleep. It's been a full day. I'm not usually out this much."

They both got out of the car and stood on opposite sides. Allie backed away before he could start for her side of the truck.

"I'll check on you in the morning," Scott said across the truck's hood.

"Yeah, okay," Allie said.

Her weak smile made him long to comfort her in his arms. She walked to her porch as if dazed. She never looked back. He watched until she closed the front door behind her.

Scott slammed his hand on the fender. The best night he'd had in years had just become one of the worst.

On the drive back home, on a route that didn't include Canale Road, questions about the murder began to bubble up through his devastation at Natalie's death. How did Scaravelli find Krieger in the woods, or even know to look for him? On an island this small, how could Krieger think he'd get away with child rape and murder? Why such a large crime scene area if the incident was as cut and dry as Scaravelli claimed? What was Reverend Snow doing watching from the woods?

He decided Harbor Hardware might have to open late tomorrow. This whole thing didn't sit right at all. But first thing tomorrow, he needed to console Colleen and Stan Olsen.

★   ★   ★

As soon as the door closed behind her, Allie let her trickle of tears turn to a flood. She slid to the cold wood floor and sobbed in the darkness.

A murky shadow had spread across her idyllic island escape. Thirty minutes ago, everything was bright and beautiful. Now a girl was raped and murdered. This wasn't a sweet Stone Harbor thing. This was a seedy LA thing. She felt like some evil had tracked her across the country and finally caught up, injecting itself into her world of clarinet music and home-style pizza.

Memories of the Dark Thing broke through the ground she had shoveled over its grave, and began to track muddy footprints through her mind. The strength she'd felt earlier in the day crumbled. The supposedly solid foundation she thought she'd built turned out to be more like a hollow shell, one that cracked at the first sharp blow.

She needed an escape. The sweet burn of alcohol, the mellowing warmth of pot, the euphoric rush of cocaine. All the old vices volunteered, with smirking promises both she and they knew would never be kept. The easy path beckoned, the downhill stroll that always ended as a plummet off a cliff. Were she still in LA, she'd have herself hooked up in minutes.

And that was why she was at Stone Harbor. Three thousand miles of land and thirty miles of sea between her and the twisted temptations she'd indulged. All that to insulate her from the rest of the world, and the screwed-up crap that filled it. But somehow, the crap had found its way here.

She glanced at a wall clock, counted the hours before sunrise, and despaired at the number.

CHAPTER SEVENTEEN

Waves beat the car ferry's hull as it cut through the eastern reaches of Long Island Sound. All summer, the lumbering ship left a miles-long, frothy wake as it plied the waters between Stone Harbor and the mainland. But this morning, the rough fall seas scrubbed all records of its passage, like an accomplice covering the tracks of a criminal.

Though down to two trips a week, the lightly loaded ferry still rode high in the water. The nearly empty car deck spread out open to the sun's feeble rays. A glossy black pickup towered between two squat Subarus near the exit ramp. Off-road suspension raised its fender wells above the smaller cars' hoods. A windowless cab covered the rear bed. Three stubby antennae sprouted from its center like shark fins.

Almost all the passengers had abandoned their cold vehicles for the warmth of the enclosed cabin above the car deck's center. Five exceptions remained out on the open lower deck, men spread out at irregular intervals along the railing, backs to the sea, watching nothing happen with far too much intensity.

All had walked aboard, arrivals staggered. None exchanged a word with another, but it was clear they were all together.

They all looked older than their actual mid-forties ages. Deep-lined faces and crooked noses told stories of misspent years. Scars enjoyed a liberal distribution, faded unprofessional tattoos came in a close second. All wore dark pants and white, short-sleeve button-down shirts so new that the collars had chafed a few necks red. A small overnight bag lay at each one's feet.

At the halfway point across the Sound, Rene Kyler stepped out of the driver's seat of the pickup. A blast of spray crossed the deck and coated his face. He didn't flinch. Over his arm, he carried five black nylon jackets too light for the weather. His dark eyes scanned the perimeter of the deck and paused at each of the nervous, white-shirted men.

Kyler approached the first man, one with a shaved head and a Fu Manchu biker moustache that stretched past the edge of his mouth in two long black streaks. A small hoop earring hung from his left ear and an unlit cigarette dangled from his mouth. The big guy pushed two hundred and twenty-five pounds, easy. Fu Manchu's eyes never met Kyler's as he approached, but tension ratcheted up in his arm muscles the closer Kyler got. Kyler stopped three feet away.

"Ramirez," Kyler said.

Ramirez rolled the cigarette to the other side of his mouth. It quivered between his lips. "Is Oates on board?"

"Already on the island."

The tension melted from Ramirez's shoulders. "I don't like the setup. Ain't no way off that rock."

"We're making our own exit. Of course, if you'd rather pay your debt in full now, I'll arrange it."

"No, no, it's all good. I'm cool with it as is."

Kyler handed him a jacket. "Head to the truck."

The sky turned to gray overcast as Stone Harbor Island appeared on the horizon. Kyler moved on to the next passenger, whose pockmarked face sported a ropy scar that ran from the corner of his mouth across his cheek to his ear, like half of a demented clown's smile.

He addressed the man as Ricco and had a similar exchange. Three more, Washington, Santiago, and Culpepper, got the same instructions and all five met at the truck's tailgate.

The ferry whistle blew at the Stone Harbor channel marker, the crew's signal to docking stations. Deckhands emerged from the warm cabin and climbed down to positions at the bow and along the starboard side. The engine slowed to half speed as the ship passed the harbor's breakwater.

Kyler and the five at the truck donned the dark jackets, *FBI* stenciled in white on the back of each one. Kyler dropped the tailgate. Two green wooden footlockers lay in line down the center. The five climbed inside the truck's bed.

The ferry pulled up to the mass of pilings that made up its berth. Kyler glanced over the ship's side and across the empty marina dock. The low, sleek mass of the *Killin' Time* floated on the pier's far side. The ferry's wake washed against it, but it did not move. Kyler straightened his jacket.

The boss is on the job, he thought. *Time to get to work.*

The ferry's engines went into full reverse. The ship shuddered and its forward momentum slowed. The pilings strained in their footings as the ship nosed into them. The ferry slipped a few feet right, and lined up with the exit ramp. The pilings and the ship relaxed. Crewmen tossed heavy ropes to waiting dockhands.

Kyler reached in and flipped a footlocker open to reveal six M4 assault rifles. The five's faces had been filled with apprehension from the minute Kyler first spoke to each. Now they all smiled.

"Pistols and ammo in the other box," he said. "Load up. We're about to get busy."

CHAPTER EIGHTEEN

Something in Stone Harbor was going very wrong, very fast.

Scott had barely slept all night. He hadn't had nightmares, per se, but every time he nodded off, memories of the previous day's chilling events brought him back wide-awake.

For Scott, the slow and steady heartbeat of life in Stone Harbor had skipped a beat, twice in fact, in one day. First, Joey Oates had arrived at his hardware store with some wild story about Scott's father, and then Natalie Olsen was dead at the hand of Carl Krieger. He could even add in the emotional peak and valley of his half-day reunion with Allie. He got out of bed before dawn, resolved to take action on all three. Considering the hour, getting to the bottom of Oates' story was first on the list.

Oates had walked into Scott's store Thursday, and autumn ferry service was down to a Friday and a Saturday run. Oates sure as hell hadn't been here all week. Old handyman Len, master of the gossip grapevine, would have given Scott an earful about it by now. By the look of Oates, he was no Olympic swimmer. That meant he had to come in by boat, that boat had to come into the harbor, and Charlie Cauble would know all about it.

Scott pulled into the harbor parking lot. The sun had yet to fully crest the eastern hills and long shadows painted the empty streets in shades of gray. The bed-and-breakfasts and souvenir shops had closed for the season. A few owners who still courted trade swept the sidewalks in front of their shops, the signs in the windows flipped to *Closed* until the clock struck nine.

Scott rolled down his window. A sharp, stiff breeze washed him in the rejuvenating scent of dried algae and salt. The deep bellow of the ferry's horn rolled in from a few miles outside the harbor entrance.

"Hey there, Scott," he heard from behind him.

He hung his left elbow out the window and looked back. Charlie Cauble sauntered up to the driver's door.

"Awful news about the Olsen girl," Charlie said. "So sorry. I know you're friends with Stan and Colleen."

"It's hard to believe it happened here," Scott said.

"Well, I always knew Krieger was scum," Charlie said. "Just not *that* scummy. Glad he saw some justice."

Scott hadn't bought Scaravelli's version of Natalie's murder, and was a little surprised that Charlie had taken it in whole.

"Any new boats in the harbor?" Scott said. "Maybe came in yesterday?"

Charlie's eyes narrowed and he made a quick, disgusted gesture toward the town dock.

"Just one here. Black speedboat came in yesterday morning. Don't like the guy on board one whit. No sir. Bad mojo with that one for sure."

Scott followed Charlie's pointing to the town dock, but the tide was on its way out, and the speedboat rode low in the water on the pier's far side. Only the two lines tying it off were visible.

"Short, bald guy with a goatee?" Scott said.

"Dressed black as midnight with a personality to match."

"Did he say what he's in town for?"

Charlie shot a contemptuous glance at the ship's berth. "Don't know. Don't care to know. Hoped he was leaving today with the tide, but there he sits."

A second, louder blast of the ferry's horn signaled its entrance into the harbor. The shore crew exited the tiny ticket stand where they'd sheltered themselves from the wind and headed for the ferry ramp.

"A speedboat, huh?" Scott said. An odd choice of craft. Sailboats filled Long Island Sound, rigged any way from simple sloops to gaff-headed schooners. There was also a plethora of powerboats, the younger crowd favoring runabouts, the older set preferring staid cabin cruisers. Saltwater racers were rare, being loud, thirsty, and impractical for anything but being the fastest way from point A to point B.

The ferry neared the dock. With a final blast of the horn, the ship's engines roared in reverse. The ship nosed into the pilings. Shipboard crewmen tossed lines over the side. The lines uncoiled through the air like striking snakes and were caught by the crew ashore.

The metal car ramp slowly lowered onto the ferry deck. When the plates clanged into contact, the ship's crew rolled back the gates to let the cars depart. Scott recognized every car but one as returning islanders.

One by one, the crew waved the cars forward and they disembarked. Their tight formation split and they scattered in all directions like pool balls at the break.

An unfamiliar big black Dodge Ram pickup started with a throaty rumble. It chirped the tires as it left the ferry, and barely missed the edge of the ship as it disembarked. It executed a rolling stop at the parking lot's exit, and then roared up Main Street.

"Judas Priest!" Charlie said. "Mainlanders drive like fools. Where's a cop when you need one?"

Scott knew right where they were. They were on the other side of the island, with weightier problems than traffic violations.

CHAPTER NINETEEN

Scaravelli's gun belt pinched him in the kidney. He shifted in the seat of his cruiser and gave the belt a twist. He checked the clock again.

"Two-and-a-half damn hours," he muttered. Following Oates' orders, he'd relieved Milo at 7 a.m. To do what? He had no idea. "Keep the crime scene secure," was all Oates said. With the population of sheep in this town, crime tape worked even better than an electric fence. There wasn't even any police work to do. Milo had happily spent the night taking pictures, bagging the .38 revolver and boxes of other useless evidence. Willett's Auto had even towed the van back to the impound lot behind the station. So Scaravelli sat executing a complete waste of his time.

His performance last night for the grieving Olsen family had been just the opposite. He played the concerned cop to the hilt, slathering on layers of false empathy and taking full credit for slaying a killer the courts would have somehow set free. The grieving Colleen even cried on his shoulder. Even that jackass Tackett would have to give him a little respect after that recital.

So Oates had been right and right again. Krieger had been where Oates said when Oates predicted. And Scaravelli had wasted him with zero repercussions and, judging by the early reaction of the townies he'd met so far, earned the exact popularity boost Oates had forecast. This hand was coming up all face cards. So if Oates wanted him to hang out in the woods a while, what the hell. The guy had a plan.

A gust of wind sent a jet of cold air through the bullet hole in the windshield. Scaravelli bent over and turned the heater blower up a notch. When he looked back up, a big black pickup had its chrome grill pressed against the police tape at the end of the dirt road.

Scaravelli rubbed his chin. He knew every truck on the island, and this four-by-four brute sure wasn't one of them. It must have crossed on the morning ferry. Word couldn't have spread quickly enough that mainlanders were here to ogle the crime scene. That would be more shit than he was ready to deal with.

Something about this truck made him think of Oates, but he'd lay ten-to-one Oates managed to get around the island without transportation. The day the Devil needed a pickup truck….

The front doors opened and the tailgate dropped. Six men with assault rifles wearing FBI jackets got out and clustered around the truck's nose.

Scaravelli's mood took a nosedive. One look at them told him that these thugs weren't FBI. He was more likely to see these goons through a set of bars than in front of them. The adulation of the townspeople for their hero chief of police would evaporate as soon as they got wind of a gang armed with assault rifles wandering about the woods. He gave his bushy moustache a nervous pull and levered himself out of his cruiser.

The pickup's driver broke from the group and went straight for Scaravelli. His muscular physique and short black hair announced him as some kind of military veteran. He looked the least thuggish of them, but that wasn't saying much.

Scaravelli squared his shoulders. He could handle these types. Once they knew he was in charge, everything would be fine. A pack always followed the alpha male. Stone Harbor was Scaravelli's territory, and these fake agents weren't going to be marking it with their piss. The truck's driver stopped in front of Scaravelli.

"Where do you want to start, sir?" the man said.

Scaravelli internally smiled at the deferential tone. An excellent start.

"Start the search at the edge of the road," Oates said from behind Scaravelli.

Scaravelli spun around. Oates stood just feet behind him.

"Go from there to the hilltop, Mr. Kyler," Oates said. "Find the stone. I expect my property by nightfall."

"Understood," Kyler answered. He turned to the five men standing by the truck and waved them forward and onto the dirt road. Each of them passed under the yellow crime scene tape and around Scaravelli, as if neither made much difference. All but Kyler avoided eye contact with Oates.

"What the hell's going on?" Scaravelli asked Oates. "Who are these felons in cop costumes?"

"These *associates* of mine are here to retrieve me a lost item," Oates replied, "and you've secured the area so we can search without raising no suspicions."

"These guys aren't cops," Scaravelli said. "These breathing mug shots have no authority here. I don't want them on the island."

Oates looked deep into Scaravelli's eyes. An icy chill formed in the center of Scaravelli's chest. His lungs locked in place.

"These gentlemen, they're here at my pleasure," Oates said. "Same as you. You forget that?"

Scaravelli's eyes bulged. His face flushed bright red. Oates looked away. Scaravelli's diaphragm dropped, and his lungs sucked in gallons of air. He sagged forward and rested his hands on his knees. Fear that they'd destroy his carefully laid trail of evidence pointing to Krieger's guilt hit him. He looked up with bleary eyes at the real alpha male of Stone Harbor.

"But the crime scene," he gasped, "the evidence…."

"You have all the evidence you need to cover your ass. No one's gonna ask no questions when all the facts are out." Oates smiled in a way that was anything but reassuring.

"Well, these guys, they weren't part of the deal," Scaravelli wheezed. It came out more like a whine than the bold statement Scaravelli had intended.

Oates squatted down in front of Scaravelli. He grabbed Scaravelli's chin with a hand cold as a corpse. His eyes flashed ruby red. His lips parted to reveal two rows of shark-like teeth.

"Watch your tongue before I rip it out," Oates said, "I always keep my deals. Always. I told you I'd take care of things after you killed Krieger, and I am. You'd best stay on my good side or I'm gonna realize that you ain't useful no more, and call in your debt."

Scaravelli quivered. He slid his tongue into the painful, empty socket in his lower jaw.

"No need for that," he pleaded.

Oates released him and stood up. His eyes and teeth went back to normal.

"Now," Oates said, "your presence ain't required here. First, go to Krieger's apartment. Find the necklace he kept from the Dickey girl and tag it as evidence. You'll also find a hoard of child porn you're gonna use as character witnesses. Take that back to the office. I need you answering questions from the curious public."

"What do I tell them?"

"Whatever you want, just keep 'em away from here. *Capisce*?"

"*Capisce*," Scaravelli replied.

Scaravelli returned to his cruiser and collapsed into the front seat.

Through the shattered windshield, he saw the six men from the black pickup formed in a long line in the woods. They trudged uphill, kicking through leaves and prodding the ground with sticks. Oates was suddenly gone.

Scaravelli closed his eyes and rested his head against the steering wheel. In minutes, he'd lost control of the situation, and had no leverage to get it back. He lay at the mercy of someone he could not trust, and it scared the hell out of him.

In a rare moment of insight, he realized this specific emotion had filled Carl Krieger's face in the last seconds of his life.

CHAPTER TWENTY

Scott looked out his windshield at Stan and Colleen Olsen's house. Bright blue shutters offset the gray cedar shingles, and a red box kite sat on a porch chair. A wind chime plinked out a random, mournful tune in the morning breeze.

He'd known Stan and Colleen since they were kids. He'd been here a half dozen times for dinner and each time the house absolutely radiated energy, between Colleen's infectious smile and Natalie's unquenchable enthusiasm. To pass through their door was to enter a land of bright colors, loud music, and rolling laughter.

But on this overcast morning, the house had all the energy of a snuffed candle. The bright box kite Natalie flew down at the beach sat crooked on the porch. Its red seemed to have faded to rust overnight. The cedar shingles wept great gray trails he'd never noticed before. The low, diffused sun leached the shutters' and trim's usual brilliance into a muted approximation of faded denim. The aura, the essence, the life force of the house was gone.

When Scott knocked on the door, Stan answered, though he seemed more like the ghost of Stan, with sagging, sallow skin and empty eyes.

"Scott?" Loss had drained the life from Stan's voice as well, and left it little more than a whisper.

Stan reached out to shake Scott's hand. Scott pulled him in for a quick, rugged hug instead.

"Stan, I'm so sorry. How are you holding up?"

"I'm managing. But Colleen…."

"She's upstairs?"

Stan nodded and stepped aside. Scott entered and climbed the stairs. At the top, the door to Natalie's bedroom stood open. He paused in the threshold.

Colleen sat on Natalie's bed. The vivacious, vibrant woman, the perky blonde who bought that box kite at his store, who dropped Christmas cookies off around town each year, sat shattered almost beyond recognition.

She clutched a framed eight-by-ten-inch against her chest, picture facing out. The shot was of Natalie in a yellow dress, flashing her usual dazzling smile. Colleen rocked back and forth, a human metronome marking hollow seconds that had to feel like days. She stared off into space. Long black streaks down her cheeks confessed that she'd wept away this morning's attempt at normalcy. She repeated the same phrase to herself in a low, faraway voice as she swayed on the bed.

"We didn't need rolls. No, we didn't need rolls."

She didn't acknowledge Scott.

He wanted to hug her, console her, try to absorb some of that loss that consumed her. But he was afraid to even speak, as if his words might break the eggshell that guilt had left of her sanity. He backed out into the hallway and halfway down the stairs.

A knot of friends and family stood in silent mourning in the living room, cups of coffee clenched in their hands, their tethers to a world where little girls weren't raped and murdered. The incomprehensible horror seemed to leave them all at a loss, only able to offer their presence as consolation, to Stan and Colleen, and each other.

Stan held a phone to his ear and looked a thousand miles in the distance as he couldn't say when the medical examiner would release the body for burial. Scott tapped him on the shoulder as he passed and whispered that he'd be back later. Stan nodded, though Scott wasn't sure it was in response. Scott passed through the front door, depressed by the injustice of the Olsens outliving their daughter, and disappointed at how little he could do to help.

He got into his truck as another car of mourners pulled up behind him. He opted to channel his frustration into action. He was certain there was more to this than Scaravelli had told him. Scaravelli's story was too neat, his role too heroic. The other two selectmen were off-island, which was a plus since they tended to back Scaravelli on everything, so it would be up to him to get some real answers for the Olsens.

*　　*　　*

Scott marched into the police station. Scaravelli looked up from his desk in disgust.

"What do you want, Tackett?"

"An update and some answers for a start."

"I don't owe you shit."

"You report to the Board of Selectmen, jackass."

"Yeah, well, then call a meeting, we'll have a chat. Oh wait, two-thirds of the board are off-island. Gotta wait for a quorum. Call me when you get one."

"Christ, Scaravelli, a girl's dead and so's her alleged killer. The town needs to know how this could have happened."

"I already told you what happened. Krieger killed her, and I killed him in self-defense. And I'll add a few other items I've uncovered."

The idea of Scaravelli conducting a professional investigation was absurd.

"Krieger was a bigger scumbag than we thought," Scaravelli started. He pulled a plastic bag from his drawer and tossed it on his desk. Inside was a cheap necklace with a scallop shell on it. "I found this in Krieger's apartment, belonged to the drowned Dickey girl from the summer. Also found a pretty disgusting collection of kiddie porn. I'd always suspected that he had something to do with the Dickey girl's death."

"You did?"

"Yeah, Tackett, I was a cop while you were still in diapers, you know."

"You thought that Krieger killed the Dickey girl all along?"

"Well," Scaravelli said, "I got a sense of these things. I've seen a lot of child molesters in my line of work, and he fit the mold. After the Dickey girl went missing, I talked to Krieger to see if he'd seen anything suspicious around Captain Nate's Boatyard that day. He seemed real nervous, like he was hiding something. Had him in my sights ever since."

"So when Natalie disappeared…?" Scott asked.

"I went straight to Krieger's. His van was gone. By the time I found it, it was too late."

This whole scenario was preposterous. Scaravelli hadn't processed crimes greater than a parking ticket since he'd arrived here.

"I see the van's out back. Mind if I check it out?"

"Sure. Soon as you become a cop. It's evidence."

Scott wanted to punch the haughty jerk. "I'll just head back up to Canale Road myself."

Scaravelli's face paled. The smugness left his voice.

"That crime scene is still off-limits and secured," he said.

"Milo is up there working by himself?" Scott said.

"No," Scaravelli said. He hesitated slightly. "I've got some help from the

Feds covering that." He gave a forced little chuckle and an artificial smile. "We were a bit undermanned on this one. They cover kidnappings."

Scott assembled a quick mental timeline. It was impossible for Scaravelli to have asked for help in time for the FBI to make the morning ferry the next day. A vision of the jet-black pickup-on-steroids flashed in his head, like an errant puzzle piece that finally fit somewhere.

Scott's anger at this double talk was about at a boil. Scaravelli was just going to keep feeding him lies, when what he and the Olsens needed was the truth. He took a deep breath to gain control. "I'll be back later to check on any developments."

"Don't strain yourself," Scaravelli said. "I'll call *you*."

Scott spun around and went straight for the front door. He'd always disliked Scaravelli, but this turn of events made him despise the man. Incompetence was one thing. But it seemed like Scaravelli had crossed that line into covering up something that felt plain evil.

He was tempted to go out and check on Allie, then shook his head at her self-imposed tech isolation. Colleen Olsen had Stan's support. He wanted to offer Allie his. She'd been deeply upset after he exposed her, firsthand, to Krieger's nightmare come true. Would she even want to see him after that?

But first things first. He needed to head out to Canale Road and get a look at everything in the daytime, see if he could get something that made sense from the FBI agents on the scene. There sure as hell was something Scaravelli was covering up.

CHAPTER TWENTY-ONE

Allie didn't wake up that Friday morning alone. Despair shared her bed, that dark, life-sucking companion she'd hoped to leave in the plastic world of LA. Last night's tragedy called it back and now it lay heavy beside her, its black magnetism holding her beneath the stifling comforter, its curtain of hopelessness blocking the sun's rays.

The tragedy of Natalie Olsen's death blew through the thin wall of normalcy she'd built since returning to Stone Harbor. She'd thought she'd conquered her demons and re-centered herself, but all that concrete accomplishment now seemed only sand. In LA, one call would have brought her a solution to all this, a ziplock bag of white powder, doorstep delivered in a red Carrera, in less time than a Domino's pizza.

Newly sober actors always decried the evils of cocaine in interviews, lamenting how awful it was to be hooked. They were all full of it. Being high on coke was the greatest feeling in the world. Anxiety, exhaustion, fear, all banished when the drug hit the bloodstream. The white powder always assured Allie she could handle any problem, overcome any obstacle. There was nothing miserable about being on cocaine.

There was, however, something miserable about *not* being on cocaine. The rush of reality's return and the punctured sense of invincibility were hellish, like returning to mortality after being a god.

And 'recovering' addicts were blowing smoke when they said that the cravings got weaker over time. There was no bigger lie. Did someone crave ice water less the longer she stayed in the desert? Drugs were a tempting shortcut to happiness. Who would choose the long route up the mountainside when the valley route beckoned?

If she had still been in California, she could have seen her program mentor for support. But even if she went into town and found a phone, a disembodied voice through a tinny speaker would not cut it at all. Human contact made such a difference, contact with someone she could trust.

Scottie was the first person who came to mind. The connection they'd had years ago had somehow survived the storm she'd unleashed upon it. But she dared not lay bare her vulnerability. She was sorely disappointed by the person her LA years had created. The more of that she shielded from Scottie, the better. There was no point both of them being ashamed of the person she had become.

The hearty Puritan fishermen who founded Stone Harbor left a legacy of self-reliant DNA and a proud reticence when it came to airing emotional problems. LA sprouted shrinks on every street corner, but Stone Harbor boasted a count of zero. There'd be no help available from a pro.

Then she remembered seeing Reverend Snow out on Canale Road last night, across the road in the shadows. He had been the rector at All Souls Church since before her mother had been born, absolving sins and nurturing the needy. Allie had sung in the choir during middle school. He'd at least remember her as someone other than starlet Allison Layton, a good enough start. She wasn't going to shock him. National news had already overshared the part of her life she was willing to discuss.

She threw back the comforter and rolled out of bed. With a sweep of her arm, she pulled back the drapes. Sunlight streamed across the empty, rumpled bedsheets. The bright light lit a flame of hope.

*   *   *

An hour later, she passed out of town and pulled into the tree-shaded parking lot of All Souls Church.

The church's slender spire had watched over Stone Harbor since 1790. Flush with the promise of religious freedom, the congregation had built the church, which still stood today. A high-peaked roof of black shingles covered the simple white wooden structure. The tall, narrow windows along the side were done in precious stained-glass, made back in the days when true artisans created it for the glory of God.

The bell tower, long silent for fear the vibrations of the bell's peals would weaken it, stood a story higher than the main roof. It was said that on a clear day it afforded simultaneous views of Massachusetts and Long Island. Allie remembered how the reverend hung a star of white lights on the tower each Christmas, a tradition that stretched back to a candle-powered version during the church's first year. A set of steps led to two large black doors at the steeple's base. Two enormous fir trees flanked the entrance.

New nagging doubts surfaced as she ascended the church steps. Her last visit was at Easter when she was 16, a distracted final pantomime of worship after years of increasingly intermittent attendance. Would Reverend Snow remember her? Would he really want to help her out, given the mess she'd made of her life? Natalie Olsen had been brutally murdered last night. What weight could he give to her problems compared to that?

She pulled open the heavy door and entered the church. It closed behind her and her eyes adjusted to the dim interior as she stood under the small choir loft at the rear. The air was redolent with the familiar scent from those old holiday services, a combination of old wood, melting wax, and incense's sweet aroma. Multicolored beams of soft light cascaded down on the rows of stark wooden pews that faced a simple altar.

A life-size wooden replica of the crucified Christ hung on a massive cross, suspended by two ropes that passed through ceiling mounts and down to cleats in the wall. Jesus' head hung down, his eyes closed. Allie had wondered as a child whether Jesus was dead or just resting in the statue, and always decided on the latter.

The warm familiarity experienced on Scottie's porch washed over Allie again. This house of God, witness to countless baptismal inductions, seemed to reach out and welcome her back, as if it remembered her christening amongst the thousands. Allie smiled as she walked down the aisle, and just a bit back in time.

In the center of the main aisle, a tombstone lay flush with the floor. The polished marble inscription read:

ZEBEDEE SNOW
FIRST RECTOR OF ALL SOULS CHURCH
APRIL 14, 1680 – OCTOBER 22, 1770
"With God, all things are possible."

When she was a child, the reinterment of the first rector's body underneath the church had always struck her as just a little creepy.

"Can I help you?" she heard from the altar.

She looked up to see Reverend Snow. Even in daylight instead of the darkness on Canale Road, he hadn't seemed to age a bit.

She stopped several pews short of the altar and braced for a stiff welcome. "Reverend Snow? You may not remember me…."

"Allison Layton," the reverend said with a smile. "Of course I remember you. You sang in the youth choir. First girl to ever play Gabriel in the church Christmas pageant. Ever since then it's always been played by a girl. How nice to have you back."

Allie sighed. No judgment, no condemnation, none of the appraising looks people gave as they compared Allie past to Allie present and came up disappointed.

"What brings you back to All Souls, Allison?"

Well, this is it, she thought. *Either I give him a BS answer about randomly visiting familiar sites, or he gets the truth.*

Sympathy and strength shone in his eyes.

"Can I talk with you a moment?" she asked.

Reverend Snow stepped down and sat in the first row of pews. He turned to face Allie and gestured to the pew behind him with a sweep of his hand. "My time is yours. Have a seat."

She sat down and already felt less burdened.

"Reverend, I've made some mistakes the last few years."

"So I've heard."

She blushed and looked at the floor.

"I run a parish, Allison," he said, "not a monastery. I have plenty of contact with the world outside of Stone Harbor." He patted her shoulder. "I'm not here to judge you."

"I was in a dark place before I returned to Stone Harbor," she said.

She paused, then chose her words carefully, unsure of whether the reverend would admit his clandestine observance on Canale Road last night. "You've heard about Natalie?"

"Horrible," he said. "Just horrible. I visited with Colleen and Stan this morning. They are having a tough time of it."

That non-admission didn't help her much. She decided not to confirm she was there either.

"Last night, when I found out about little Natalie, I started to slip back to that dark place. I mean, such an awful, disgusting thing…here in Stone Harbor…I came home to escape things like that, you know?"

"I'm sure everyone on the island feels the same way," he said. "If you didn't feel sorrow for the girl, then you would really have a problem."

"It's my reaction to it that scares me, Reverend. I had a serious drug problem in California. It almost killed me. I beat it back in rehab, but my first instinct last night was to use again. If I had access, I know I would have."

"Now think before you answer, Allison," Reverend Snow said. "Do you really *know* that you would have used?"

She imagined the line of powder across a glass tabletop, the demon in white, promising her escape. She remembered the hell she went through to get clean, the worse hell of doing it all again. She imagined the look on Scottie's face if he saw her as the addicted mess she had been a year ago, all her worst weaknesses front and center.

"No," she said. "I really don't know that I would have used. The temptation though...."

Reverend Snow nodded in confirmation. He reached out and held her hand. His rough skin was warm, his grip firm.

"That's the part that really upset you," he said. "The temptation. Since you had surrendered to it before, you assumed it inevitable that you would do so again. Now you realize that was not the case. Temptations never vanish. The nature of our struggle with evil is that it always returns to tempt us. Even Jesus was tempted by Satan himself, who offered Christ the world for his allegiance. God will not provide temptations you cannot decline. He will not test you past your limit. Don't look at temptation as an exploitation of weakness, but an opportunity to reaffirm your strength."

Some of the emotional weight she'd carried in on her shoulders eased off.

"You really think so?" she said.

"I know so." Reverend Snow leaned back. "So, have you reconnected with old friends since you've been back?"

"I've spent some time with Scottie Tackett."

"I'm sure that seeing Scott again was very nice," Reverend Snow said.

Allie felt like some preteen having to admit she had a crush on a boy in her class.

"Well...yes. I think he's helping me center myself."

Reverend Snow stood up.

"I'm sure that he will, Allison," he said, looking down at her. "I've got a pre-marital counseling appointment I'm due for. Stop by anytime you want to talk."

Allie rose.

"Thank you, Reverend," she said. "I'll do that."

She wanted to hug him, but Reverend Snow had already turned and headed to the sacristy door behind the altar.

She walked back down the aisle between the pews, treading lightly on the stone that marked the resting place of the first Reverend Snow. She opened the door to leave, and the bright sunlight hurt her eyes. The morning overcast had burned away to reveal a resplendent blue sky and a few stray white puffy clouds.

Maybe she could handle all this. The island had given her things stronger than a sandbar to stand on. Reverend Snow could be a source of strength, and Scottie made her feel more like the person she used to be, and wanted to be again. She returned to her car, much less fearful about facing the rest of the day.

*   *   *

Reverend Snow watched from a sacristy window as Allie departed the church.

Did she see me last night? he wondered.

He chided himself for getting old and careless. Ten generations later, the prophecies were coming to pass. Months of premonitions had warned him that Satan's return was imminent. His last one sent him out to Canale Road last night, a premonition he'd hoped in vain he'd misinterpreted. What he'd seen was horrible, but he was certain darker events approached from just beyond the horizon.

In fifty years of spiritual leadership, he thought that he had become a decent judge of character. He now had a clear read on Allison. Something still unspoken troubled her kind heart. But she was strong.

But she'd reconnected with Scott Tackett. That was another story. A good man, but his family history wasn't at all reassuring. Under great stress, which way would he bend? There would be no second chances when the remaining prophecies came true.

He shifted his weight right and leaned against the wall to relieve the pain on his arthritic knees. Awful trials were certain to come in the next few days. He was an old man boxing an immortal opponent. Odds were, he wouldn't go the distance. He'd need someone in his corner, maybe sooner than he thought.

Could she be the one to help? he thought. *Is that why God brought her home now?*

Trusting her with centuries-old family secrets would be a step he couldn't take lightly. He looked at her sitting in her car. He gripped the edge of the window frame. She was about to leave, and he had a feeling that any delay in recruiting her would be catastrophic.

He did what he always did when the decision was difficult. He took a deep breath, and sought divine inspiration.

He realized that if she trusted him with her dark secrets, he could trust her with his.

He rushed out the sacristy door as Allie pulled through the parking lot. He waved her down. She stopped and rolled down her window.

"Yes, Reverend?" she said.

"Allie, I'd love for you to come tonight at six for the adult Bible group," he said. "We discuss the Scripture, not our lives, and tonight there are passages I think you will find meaningful."

She answered, without reservation, that she'd love to.

The reverend watched her pull away. She gave a little wave as she went out.

Reverend Snow crossed himself for his lie. The adult Bible group never met on Fridays.

CHAPTER TWENTY-TWO

Scott rolled up to where the dirt path split off from Canale Road. The obsidian-black pickup truck he'd seen in town sat on the edge of the yellow crime scene tape. The tailgate and cab hung open.

Scott scratched his chin. Farmers brought men to work in pickup trucks; the FBI didn't use them to shuttle agents.

Off up in the woods, five men in FBI windbreakers walked between the trees, too intently focused on the ground to notice his presence. Each had an assault rifle slung across their back. Most were smoking. One glance said none of these men was an employee of the federal government, unless felony convictions had gone from exclusionary to minimum standard in the hiring process. Crude tattoos, broken noses, scars. If law enforcement really looked this scary, there'd be no crime.

Scott didn't know anything about doing an area evidence search, but was sure it wasn't done like this. The men wandered around at random, using sticks and poles to make desultory scrapes through the underbrush. If what they were looking for was smaller than a washing machine, they'd probably miss it. Pigs did a better job rooting for truffles.

One of the men, a heavyset Hispanic with bad skin, swung a long stick back and forth across the ground. At the end of one arc, it slipped from his hand. The stick sailed through the air and hit a guy with a prison-issue Fu Manchu squarely in the back of his bald head. Fu Manchu spun to face the other man with rage in his eyes.

The two burst into a profane shouting match. The rest of the searchers backed away, and waited for the fireworks. The two closed to within a foot of each other. They traded taunts, dared the other to make a move.

Fu Manchu pulled a hunting knife from his belt. The well-honed edge flashed in the sunlight. The Hispanic man scooped a stout branch from the forest floor and raised it like a knight's sword to parry the coming thrust.

A sixth man, also in an FBI windbreaker, streaked in through the trees. He pulled an automatic pistol from a holster at his side and wedged himself between the two men. He shoved them apart like he was separating two angry pit bulls.

"What the hell are you two doing?" The tall, crew-cut man looked furious. "I leave you alone one goddamn minute and this shit happens?" He turned to Fu Manchu.

"You pulled a knife?" He pointed his pistol at the man's head. "I should just shoot you now."

Fu Manchu's steely look didn't waver, like a man who'd faced the dark end of a gun barrel plenty of times before. The leader let the pistol fall away.

"Better yet," the leader said, "how about I tell Mr. Oates you've decided not to play well with others?"

Scott's stomach did a flip at the mention of Oates. Apparently, so did Fu Manchu's. The man's eyes went wide. His jaw sagged. He sheathed his knife.

"Ain't no need for that, Kyler. We're cool. Little misunderstanding is all."

"No, no, dude," pleaded the Hispanic man. "No need to get Oates into it."

Scott backed up to his truck and got in. He closed the door without a sound and prayed he could get away from here without being noticed. As soon as the men began searching the forest floor again, he started the engine and backed away until he could do a discreet U-turn.

Nothing about this added up. Those guys were no more FBI agents than he was. Scaravelli said they were working for him, but from the looks of them, they'd spit on Scaravelli, or any cop, on sight. The guy called Kyler was obviously in charge. And he wasn't reporting to Scaravelli, he was reporting to Oates.

Which reminded Scott of that disk he'd found hidden in the hardware store, the one that seemed to get all buzzy when Oates came to visit. How did that work into this? Even more important, what about that black speedster Oates arrived in? Charlie Cauble sure didn't think there was anything normal about it.

It was late in the morning and Scott hadn't opened the store yet. Len had probably been by to get some hardware for today's minor fix-it. A contractor had a delivery due in the afternoon. The horrific and the strange surrounded him, and still the needs of the family business somehow worked their way to the surface anyway. He thought that maybe practicing a bit of normalcy for a few hours would help him clear his head.

But later today, when that was done, he'd pull that disk out from under the counter for a closer inspection. And then after closing time, after sundown, downtown would turn out the lights and be just about deserted. That would be a good time to check out the boat at the marina without gathering a crowd. The more he could find out about the mysterious Mr. Oates, the better he'd feel.

And then tonight, no matter what, he'd check on Allie, and see if the day had given her time to forgive him for dragging her through last night's horror show.

Pretty stressful schedule for living in a town where nothing ever happens, he thought.

CHAPTER TWENTY-THREE

Officer Milo Mimms hadn't slept much all day. Graveyard-shift sleep was usually rough, but the excitement from the previous night made it impossible.

When Scaravelli relieved him that morning, he really hadn't wanted to go off duty. There was so much real policing to do; documenting the scene, processing Krieger's van, preparing reports for the state. With a big cup of coffee and a candy bar, Milo could have gone on for hours. But Scaravelli had been insistent, to the point of fury, adding instructions to talk to no one, and to report back to the crime scene the next day.

That afternoon, Milo paced a thousand laps in his apartment, and tried diverting himself with the mindless drivel of daytime television. By 5 p.m., he couldn't wait any longer. He put on his uniform and got ready for work. He strapped on his gun belt and checked himself in the mirror.

For the first time in a long time, a law enforcement officer stared back at him. Maybe it was because he was about to do some real law enforcement work. Maybe it was because in a few small ways, Scaravelli had finally *treated him* like a law enforcement officer. Until last night, Scaravelli had never called him *Officer Mimms*. It had always been *Milo*, always couched in an exasperated sigh. Last night, Scaravelli had entrusted Milo with securing the Canale Road scene. That said something right there.

Sure, Scaravelli had some lousy traits. He was a miserable communicator and he had the interpersonal skills of a porcupine. He was overweight and looked permanently rumpled. But he had been a real NYPD cop.

Milo's insecurity had swelled starting on Scaravelli's first day. Scaravelli hung pictures of his NYPD glory days on the wall, shots of him flanked by ripped, smiling cops. Milo became self-conscious about his own ill-fitting uniforms. He stopped wearing his bulletproof vest after Scaravelli told him he looked like a kid in a life jacket. Scaravelli's favorite phrase seemed to be 'Do I have to teach you everything?' Every day during the drive to work, Milo felt smaller than the day before, flapping around in oversized clothes, stretching to reach the controls in the wide police cruiser, everything mocking him as a kid playing in a man's world.

Milo hated to admit it, but Scaravelli's approval meant a lot to him. Former Chief Anderson had hired Milo and praised him, but he'd known Milo since he was a kid. Scaravelli wasn't influenced by any sentimentality. Earning Scaravelli's approval meant Milo was a real cop.

As he drove out to Canale Road in the setting sun's red light, everything was a perfect fit. His shirt's shoulder seam sat square, the American flag patch beneath it straight and proud. He piloted the cruiser through town, left arm cocked out the open window, right hand on the fat steering wheel, fingerless leather glove tight on the rim. On the open stretch of Canale Road, he flicked on the high beams and punched the gas.

He coasted to a stop at the crime scene's dirt trail. He cocked an eyebrow at the scene. A big black Dodge Ram with a cargo bed shell sat parked on the trail, the front bumper stretching the yellow police tape he'd run between the trees. The plates were out of state. The chief's cruiser was nowhere to be seen. Anxiety prickled the hairs on the back of his neck.

He stepped out of his car and walked up to the truck. Three empty, grease-stained boxes from Angelo's Pizzeria lay on the hood. Crushed cans and cups littered the ground. Voices and the sound of rustling leaves drifted in from the forest's growing shadows.

He ducked under the yellow police tape and started up the dirt path. He rested one hand on the butt of his pistol. Ahead, sweaty, tired-looking men in black jackets jabbed at the leaf litter with branches and long sticks. The one closest to the road seemed to be directing the other five. An M4 assault rifle hung from his shoulder. The man saw Milo, shook his head in disgust, and moved in Milo's direction. Everyone's jacket had FBI on it in big white letters. FBI jacket lettering was always bright yellow.

"Can I help you?' The man's offer came across as an accusation.

"I'm Officer Mimms," Milo said. "Night shift in Stone Harbor. Who are you?"

"I'm Special Agent Kyler," the man replied. "My men and I are here for the investigation."

Milo looked past Kyler's shoulder at the search team. Even the gathering gloom couldn't mask hardscrabble faces that belonged to FBI agents about as much as those bogus jackets did.

"How come I don't know about this?" Milo said. "I'm the chief's right-hand man."

Kyler looked Mimm's beanpole physique up and down with a bemused look. Milo felt the shoulder seams on his shirt droop.

"Take it up with Scaravelli, Milo," Kyler said. Milo hadn't told him his first name. "We have the scene secure. Go back to the station."

Milo wasn't about to take condescending directions from a total stranger in a fake FBI jacket.

"Look *Agent* Kyler," he said. "I don't know what's going—"

Kyler stuck his finger against Milo's chest. He pushed hard and Milo rocked back a step.

"I said we're busy here, kid. Take it up with Scaravelli."

One of the other men emerged from the woods, Milo's height, but stocky. The sleeves on his jacket were pulled up to the elbows and his forearms were a blur of faded tattoos. His black hair was brushed straight back from his broad olive face, which bore a pineapple-skin of deep acne pits. A horrific scar stretched from the corner of his mouth across his cheek to his ear, as if a knife had been stuck between his teeth and yanked to the right.

The man glanced over at Milo. Milo tucked his thumbs in his gun belt and puffed his chest. The man stifled a laugh. Milo's chest deflated and his gun belt sagged lower on his hips. He backed away to his cruiser.

"Boss," the scarred man said to Kyler, "the goddamn thing ain't here. We been back and forth, up and down, nine hours straight. Maybe someone already took the piece of shit. All I know is, it ain't here, and I don't want the blame."

Kyler looked pissed.

"You're getting to be a lot of trouble, Ricco. First, I gotta keep you from killing Ramirez, and now this bitching. It's here in the woods, or you wouldn't be here looking for it. We stay until we find it. You'd rather quit? Let me know. I'll pass the word to Mr. Oates that you want out."

Ramirez's toughness faded.

"I ain't quittin'," Ramirez said. "I'm just statin' facts."

None of this made any sense to Milo. These guys were more crook than cop, and whatever they were doing out here had nothing to do with Natalie's murder. He finished his slow, backward shuffle to the cruiser, convinced that staying under these guys' radar would be very healthy.

He got in the cruiser and closed the door. A muffled, sometimes animated conversation continued between Ricco and Kyler, with each intermittently pointing to spots in the woods behind them.

If the chief thought these agents were the real thing, he needed to know the truth now. Milo picked up the radio mike.

"Chief Scaravelli, this is Officer Mimms in Unit 2."

"This is Scaravelli." He sounded frustrated. "Where the hell are you?"

"I'm on my way in, Chief," was all he said.

"Hurry it up," Scaravelli replied.

*　　*　　*

Minutes later, Scaravelli greeted Milo's entrance to the station with an irritated "Where've you been?"

Scaravelli looked awful. Dark circles shadowed his bloodshot eyes. It looked like he'd combed his hair with a rake. His nose and cheeks were flushed.

"Chief, I went straight to Canale Road."

Scaravelli rolled his eyes and sighed. "Did I tell you to go up there?"

"Uh, yes, this morning."

"Everything up there is under control," Scaravelli said.

"I don't know, Chief," Milo said. "Those guys up there look like they're—"

"Doing just what I want them to do," Scaravelli cut in. "They're professionals. I don't want you up there in their way."

"Chief," Milo said, "they seem to be looking for something. I saw the van impounded behind the station. What exactly do you have them looking for?"

"Milo, just leave the crime scene to those men. Understood? Sit your ass here all night. Tell anyone with questions to call back in the morning."

The chief stood up and had to steady himself against the desk. He closed the open desk drawer in front of him. A bottle rolled along the drawer's metal pan and clinked to a stop. He turned the key to lock it.

"You stick right here," Scaravelli emphasized. "Anything at all happens tonight, you call me at home. Understood?"

"Yes, Chief, I understand," was all he could say.

Scaravelli slammed the door behind him as he left.

Milo collapsed into his well-worn chair. Whatever perversion of law enforcement was unfolding in Stone Harbor, Chief Scaravelli looked like he was up to his eyeballs in it. And who was the Mr. Oates whose mention had stopped Ricco in his tracks? Scaravelli was the ultimate authority on the island, but there had to be some other law enforcement avenue Milo could take to find help. State police? The real FBI? Would anyone listen to a nineteen-year-old, even believe he was a cop? Right now, he couldn't even convince himself.

He had an interminable, lonely shift to think about it.

CHAPTER TWENTY-FOUR

Rene Kyler swallowed two caffeine pills dry and prepped himself for a long night.

Darkness's arrival on Canale Road wouldn't stop the search. Oates said the wooden artifact was out here, hidden under a piece of shale, and Kyler had never known Oates to be wrong.

Unlike the other five, Kyler had spent years in Oates' direct employ. He specialized in solo work: assassinations, theft, arson. His first instinct was to balk when Oates told him he'd have five weak links added to his chain, but he nodded and accepted the mission. Oates tended to have pretty violent reactions to the word *no*. However, as Kyler met each addition to his crew on the ferry that morning, his faith in their ability to execute ebbed lower and lower. He figured that if you were Oates, it was hard to find good help. In Kyler's experience, the criminal masterminds on TV only occurred in fiction.

That threat of Oates' retribution was what made Kyler so uneasy as night fell and the object of the search remained undiscovered. Every slab of shale had been flipped, every square inch of the leaf litter probed with no result. He dreaded the conversation he'd have when Oates inevitably arrived to check on progress.

"Think of the Devil, and he shall appear...." Kyler heard.

Joey Oates stood beside him in the same long-sleeved black shirt and black pants he'd assumed for this event. His gold chain gleamed red in the dying sunlight.

"I don't see what I'm looking for," Oates said, eyeing the ground as if the Portal should be lying there.

A few of the men searching in the woods noticed Oates' appearance. Hushed whispers passed between them. A more energetic prodding and scraping of the forest floor commenced.

"Sir, we've been over this area for ten hours," Kyler said. "We've raked every leaf and dug up every rock. I've been out here every minute hounding these bastards myself and keeping them from maiming each other. We haven't missed an inch, and it isn't here."

Oates surveyed the darkening landscape.

"It's here somewhere," he said. "Only the girl knew where she hid it. We're gonna stay 'til we find it." He added the last sentence loud enough to reach the five laboring in the woods.

"It'll be pitch-black soon," Kyler said. He was explaining, not excusing. "I'd better go into town for some lighting."

A yelp from Ricco came from just up the hill. He stood between two tall trees, smacking a stick on something hard between them.

"Kyler! Check this out!"

Kyler, Oates, and the other men converged around the two trees. Ricco dropped to his hands and knees. He swept aside the detritus to uncover a flat piece of gray shale beneath the trees' crisscrossed roots.

Oates bent down and fingered the edge, broken into a jagged Z pattern. He smiled and nodded.

"That's it," Oates said. He turned and started away. Over his shoulder he added, "You have an hour, Mr. Kyler."

The men let out a collective sigh of relief. Their remaining time on Earth had just been extended.

"There are axes in the truck," Kyler commanded. "Let's take down these trees."

CHAPTER TWENTY-FIVE

Allie arrived at All Souls Church for the adult Bible group thirty minutes early. The empty parking lot made her smile. Beating the rest of the group here meant a little extra time alone with Reverend Snow, and perhaps the answers to some questions. She thought that since he'd been so open with her before, he might want to share a few details about his presence out at the Canale Road murder scene.

The stained-glass windows glowed in defiance of the gathering darkness. One front door stood open and sent a shaft of inviting light across the front steps.

Allie stepped inside to see Reverend Snow sweeping the floor around the altar. He faced the huge crucifix on the wall, back to the empty pews. She watched him for a moment. Each slow, deliberate pass of his broom brought a little shudder to the back of his neck. His steps were more like shuffles, short slides as if to lighten the impact on knees and hips. He bent with a slight stoop that Allie had not noticed before. Her first take on the reverend was wrong. He had aged since she'd left Stone Harbor. In the low amber light, he looked every bit of the eighty years old he had to be by now.

Greeting the reverend with a shout across the sanctuary struck her as sacrilegious. She walked down the main aisle, stepped around the first Reverend Snow's marker, and stopped just short of the altar.

"Hi there," she ventured.

Bones creaked as Reverend Snow straightened to his full height. His grip on the broom tightened and he took a deep breath. He turned and shone a broad smile down on Allie.

"Allison, my dear," he said. "I'm so glad you came." He stepped down from the altar and laid his broom against the first pew.

"I'm early."

"Indeed you are," Reverend Snow replied. He lowered himself down onto the altar's base. "Sit beside me for a moment."

A personal conversation with the reverend was going to be easier to start than she'd thought. She took a seat beside him.

"Allison," he said. "As a change of pace, I'll confess something to you. The adult Bible group doesn't meet tonight. I just thought we needed to talk a bit."

Her plan was to get some answers from him. She really didn't want to go back over her sordid personal history at this point. She slid a few inches away.

"Oh, Reverend, I feel much better after our talk today. You don't have to worry about me."

The reverend smiled and patted her knee.

"You misunderstand, Allison. We're going to talk about problems bigger than the sum of both of ours. We're going to talk about Stone Harbor's problems."

This conversation was going to work her way after all. "This is about Natalie's murder?"

"Yes, dear, and much more."

The reverend paused for a moment, like a weightlifter preparing to clean jerk hundreds of pounds off the floor. He looked out across the church, but the glaze in his eyes said he was seeing well past the walls.

"Ten generations ago," he said, pointing to the gravestone in the center of the church floor, "a Reverend Snow started this very congregation. His sons nailed the boards of this church into place. It's by more than just tradition that a Snow has always led this congregation. Each of us has felt more than just the calling to serve God. We inherited the responsibility to protect Stone Harbor, and the world."

"The world?"

"Do you remember learning about the local witchcraft trial in elementary school?" the reverend said.

"Five girls were burned alive for practicing witchcraft before the Revolution," Allie said. "We all know the story. I think the blame fell on moldy wheat that gave the girls an LSD-type experience. It was never as famous as the trials at Salem, and I'm sure glad that we didn't get that kind of reputation. Most people want to pretend it never happened."

"But it certainly did happen," the reverend said. "In school you learned the myth, a watered-down tale that the elders told, for just the reasons you say. No one wanted Salem's notoriety. But any myth is only half the truth, and even tonight, I can't tell you the full tale. But circumstances compel me to tell you some of it."

Reverend Snow's face registered a deeper degree of solemn.

"I'll start by telling you that Satan walks among us," the reverend said, "and not in the non-corporeal state most people believe. He is a physical manifestation, as when he tempted Jesus in the desert, or became a snake in the Garden of Eden. Wherever he walks the Earth, people do evil things that may otherwise only inhabit their fleeting fantasies. He pulls them along in his horrible slipstream, leads them into great sin."

"Like Carl Krieger," Allie said.

"Yes, like Carl," the reverend said. "Natalie's terrible death is what convinced me that Satan walks our island again."

"Again?"

"Without him," the reverend said, "there would have been no witch trial. The girls didn't hallucinate. They practiced true witchcraft, under his guidance. He came to Stone Harbor in the guise of a merchant from the East India Company, looking to use our village as a port. He won over the girls with promises of wealth and excitement. But he was using the girls to his own end, one that held the fate of more than Stone Harbor in the balance.

"Our island is a special place. You know that it's a lateral link halfway between Massachusetts and Long Island. But it's also a vertical link. For some reason, this place on Earth is some potential shortcut between our world and Hell. Whatever fabric separates the two places is threadbare here. If that cloth tears, the demons in that world can pass into ours, and I don't even want to imagine the consequences.

"The story goes back even further. Norsemen knew of this weak place to what they called Valhalla. The search for it fueled their early visits to the New World. The weak points in both worlds align about every three hundred years. Using the sum of the magic they'd encountered around the world, they created a disk, a portal, that was of our island, bonded to this place so strongly it cannot leave, so coated in magic it cannot be destroyed. It could gather and direct the energy of five souls and focus it on that fragile point between the two dimensions.

"Legend is that the Norsemen opened the gateway, discovered it was to an evil afterlife and slammed it shut. No one knows what, if anything, happened at the next three-hundred-year opportunity, but at the second event, six hundred years later, Satan tricked the girls of Stone Harbor into trying to reopen that path between the worlds. With the five gathered around the Portal, chanting the right incantations, they would be able to open the door to the Netherworld."

"That's nothing like the story we learned in school," Allie said.

"In the 1700s, the truth would have panicked the town," the reverend said. "Stone Harbor would have been abandoned. The town elders broke up the circle before the girls could start, arresting four of them. A fifth, Providence Neely, escaped with the Portal into the forest. When the townspeople finally came upon her, she was dead from snakebite, in a month when snakes always hibernate. The Portal was nowhere to be found."

"Everything going on now has to do with the missing Portal?" Allie said.

"It had been prophesized. Later, Zebedee Snow had a visitation by an angel that told him of the weakening of the membrane between the worlds every three hundred years. Until then, the Portal is of no use. Our family knew, when the worlds aligned, Satan would return to use the Portal again. That time has come."

Reverend Snow's forthright, solemn delivery made the unbelievable story entirely credible. Allie became a believer. Two people dead in a matter of hours in Stone Harbor was too bizarre to be a coincidence. "So your family took up the mission of guarding Stone Harbor's future?"

The reverend raised his chin, just a bit.

"For generations," he said with pride, "we have kept the truth alive. Right here inside these walls." He patted the floor of the church. "Each Christmas Eve, one generation retells the story to the next, and the younger Snows repeat it back. Details I have not shared with you are passed on so that each new minister will be ready to defend his flock. We would be prepared for that day when Lucifer would return to find what he had lost."

"Reverend," Allie said, "I'm honored, but why share all this with me?"

"Allison, my girl, I did not fulfill my duty. The mandate was to leave a son so that a fresh generation was always ready to carry on the fight. But in my life, I found no spouse. I could not bring myself to try to marry, committing another to a lifetime on our small island, without a mutual bond of love. That love never blossomed. So now the danger generations of Snows prepared for has arrived, all I can send into battle is one tired old man."

Allie imagined the weight of this responsibility settling on Reverend Snow over the years. It was no wonder that he looked so drained.

"I'm not strong enough for the task ahead," he said. "I will need some help. I think that you are that person."

"Me?" Allie said. "I'm the last one qualified for that job."

"Don't worry, girl," Reverend Snow said. "Trust that I have good reasons. That is enough."

"I'll do whatever I can," Allie said.

"You must be careful. We never trusted our secrets to anyone outside the family. We were warned that Satan's agents would be waiting on the island, generations waiting to open the Portal just as we waited to keep it closed."

The reverend moved to rise. He grimaced. Allie stood and helped him up. He looked away for a moment in embarrassment.

"For now, go home, girl," the reverend said. "Come back at eleven tomorrow. There is more to share with you. We will need a good plan. I sense that bad things are happening all across the island tonight."

CHAPTER TWENTY-SIX

Later that night, Scott pulled his truck into the empty marina parking lot and rolled into a spot near the water. He killed the lights. Only the two lamps at the edge of the dock lit the area. Scott drew some comfort from the cloaking darkness between him and the speedboat tied to the dock.

He didn't doubt Charlie Cauble's warning that the boat was wicked. The thing delivered Oates, the match that lit the fuse of everything suddenly wrong at Stone Harbor. Even this far away, Scott felt some sort of ominous threat from the craft.

If it brought Oates here, it might tell Scott more about the man. With the Canale Road search running hot, heavy, and apparently behind schedule, Oates would no doubt be there. If Scott was going to check out the boat, now was the time.

Scott got out of his truck and closed the door with barely a click. The wind blew a damp, frigid taste of the upcoming winter from across the harbor. He jammed his hands in his coat pockets, hunched his shoulders against the cold, and headed for the dock. His pulse beat faster with each step. The marina was unnaturally still, the only sound the lapping of the waves against the abutments.

The tide was in. At the dock's end floated the long black speedboat, riding high, deck nearly even with the thick wooden slats.

At first, he thought it was an optical illusion, a trick of the pier's shadow and the water's reflection. But as he got closer, his pulse bumped up a notch. The boat didn't move. A shallow-hulled boat should rock with the waves, but this boat just stayed parallel with the dock. The securing lines didn't flex an inch.

Scott inched down the dock, eyes locked on the ship with every step. His feet edged along the thick yellow safety line on the plank's edge farthest from the boat. He pulled his hands from his pockets and the cold air chilled the sweat on his palms. He caught himself holding his breath.

He passed the boat amidships, and then looked down at the stern. Gold letters on the transom read:

Killin' Time

Nothing about that name made him feel any better.

Scott stepped over to the boat and looked over the transom. The spotless cockpit was empty of the usual pleasure-boating debris, no stray lines, no empty beer cans. The fiberglass bench seats had no cushions. The boat looked like it would on a showroom floor. It was hard to believe that someone had driven her across the Sound.

Smoked-glass hatch covers blocked his view inside the cabin. Even in broad daylight, he doubted he would be able to make out anything inside. The rear hatch, though closed, was unlocked. All he had to do was step into the cockpit and slide it open.

Now that he stood beside it, the idea of boarding the boat set every warning alarm in his head off at once. If stopping at Canale Road was stupid, then getting on this boat would be stupid times ten. But answers to his questions lay secreted within that glossy black fiberglass. With no one around, this might be his only chance.

The gap from dock to boat was small. He crouched to leap.

He spied a symbol on the cockpit deck between the seats and froze. His heart skipped a beat. A circle with two odd concave triangles inside it, the same symbol on the disk his father had left hidden in the hardware store.

"What the hell?" he whispered.

"You recognize my mark, little Scottie?" Oates said.

His voice nearly startled Scott off the edge of the dock. He spun around. Oates stood two feet away, between him and the safety of land. The sense of dread he'd felt the last time he saw Oates rolled back in at twice the intensity, this time coupled with the panic of a trapped rat.

"I-I don't know what you mean."

"I taught mankind how to lie, don't insult me by thinking you can do it convincingly. Your father's brand."

This time, Scott really didn't know what Oates was talking about.

"My gift?" Oates said. "The receipt for the special contract?"

Oates waved his hand in a circle. A ghostly, 3-D vision whirled into existence to their left. The setting was the main counter of the hardware store. Scott's father stood in front of the counter.

"Dad?" Scott said.

The hallucination, or whatever it was, had to be almost ten years old, before his father had grown a beard after his mother's funeral, before he'd gotten sick himself. This was the father Scott remembered, robust, strong, commanding. Scott had erased the images of his father in his hollow, final days.

Oates stepped into the frame. He looked the same, but wore a black turtleneck.

"May I call you Gary?" Turtleneck Oates said. "After all, this kind of transaction puts us on a first-name basis."

"Should I call you Lucifer?" Gary said.

"Most do. I'm good with it. But let's stick with Mr. Oates."

The revelation that Scott stood in the presence of Satan was somehow anticlimactic. But his father speaking to Oates was like a nightmare.

"Now, you understand what you're about to do is murder," Turtleneck Oates said to Gary. "Murder has consequences. In prison, you'll lose all this, and your son."

Gary nodded. "I don't see any other options."

"No one ever does. I'll wipe away the consequences. You'll never be caught, never punished."

"For my soul, I assume?"

Oates laughed. "No, once you kill, I've already got your soul. But while I keep you free, you work for me."

"I'm not killing anyone else."

"Nothing so active is necessary. You're just gonna watch. Something valuable of mine is on the island. If it surfaces, you'll tell me. Simple."

Gary gave Oates a wary look. "And no one, especially my son, will ever know I'm a murderer?"

"You'll die with your name untarnished. All you have you'll leave to him."

Real-life Oates spun his hand in a circle. The vision went into fast-forward. "There's some negotiations over details here." His hand stopped and the vision went back to normal speed.

"You have a deal," Gary said.

Turtleneck Oates nodded at Gary. Gary screamed in pain and dropped to his knees. A patch of his shirt above the left breast pocket flashed into flames. When they extinguished, Oates' symbol glowed red on Gary's pectoral. It cooled to white scar tissue. Gary's head sagged to his chest.

Real-life Oates waved his hand and the vision vanished.

"That symbol there? You saying you never saw it?"

Scott never had. Even through his father's illness, Scott had never seen him without his shirt on, which did not seem odd at the time. But now he remembered in his last years how his father had stopped going shirtless, even out on the water, how at the depths of his illness he'd never let Scott help him dress or bathe. Scott had chalked that all up to pride, but maybe this was the real, darker reason. The revelation made his stomach turn.

And he'd seen the symbol on the disk under the hardware store counter. That thing had some connection to Oates. If that was Oates' missing property Scott wasn't about to return it. But if Satan really could spot him lying....

"I never saw that scar on my father's chest," he said.

Oates cocked his head, "Yeah, I guess not. A shame he never showed it off. I only bestow the gift on the specially recruited, those with chosen tasks."

The whole scenario was more than he wanted to absorb. His father, who he idolized, shown as a murderer in league with the Devil. He refused to accept it.

"This is all a lie," Scott said. "The Devil lies."

Anger flashed red in Oates eyes. "Watch it, kid. I never lie. My contracts hold up because I never lie. Never have to. They all come to me, they all sell cheap. Like your father did."

"Never lie? I just saw you promise that his son would never know what he did."

"I promised he'd die with his reputation untarnished. And he did. Untarnished enough for you to sacrifice it all to live your life like he did."

Scott hadn't thought of it that way, true though it was. "My father wasn't a killer."

"Little Scottie, you're so clueless. You're all murderers given the chance. And he took to it. The gleam in his eye, the thrill of ending a life. The whole thing awakened him. Kinda like Krieger. Afterward, I had to stop him from doing it again. He had a job working for *me* then."

Scott thought about all the people on the news who always said the mass-murdering neighbor seemed so nice. Then the cops find a dozen skeletons under the guy's floorboards. But not his father....

"Big things are gonna happen around here," Oates said. "I'd advise you not to try to intervene." He waved a hand like he was erasing a whiteboard. "Strike that. Please do. Because when times get tight, you'll break my way, just like your old man did. Weakness is in your genes, boy. He sold out, you'll sell out."

"You don't know me."

"I'll prove I do." Oates stepped aside and gestured toward the parking lot. "You're free to go. You ain't no threat." Oates vanished and reappeared in the cockpit. "See, no tricks. Take yourself a hike."

Scott backed away down the dock. Oates began to examine his fingernails.

"You go on back to little Allie Cat."

Scott bristled as Allie's nickname touched Oates' poisoned tongue. Fear flamed to life inside him. First, he'd exposed Allie to Natalie's murder, and now she might get dragged into something spun from his father's dealings with Oates. If Oates had Allie in his sights as well….

Scott turned and jogged off the end of the ramp and across the parking lot to his truck. Oates' laughter rolled across the water, infused the darkness surrounding Scott, and sent a chill down his spine.

CHAPTER TWENTY-SEVEN

Scott went straight to the hardware store. The unnerving experience with Oates and the revelation about his father was a double gut punch. He had to disprove the little drama Oates had just shown him. The place to start was with whatever that was hidden under the counter. He parked in back and went in the rear door.

He'd planned on reexamining the disk earlier. But deliveries took forever, and then customers came in all day. Well, more visitors than customers, everyone looking for someone to talk with about poor Natalie, or to offer Scott condolences since he'd been friends with the Olsens so long.

A part of him had been happy for the interruption. If he didn't pull the disk out again, he could continue in the state of half denial about his father's connection to the satanic. But Oates' little display on the dock had sent denial packing, and he had to see what the disk was about.

There was no reason to announce his late-night visit to the store to the world by having all the lights on. He took the emergency flashlight he left plugged in by the door and switched it on instead. The beam lit his way straight to the cash register. He knelt and pulled the cover off the hiding place. With a groan, he slid the granite slab out onto the floor.

He set the flashlight to the side and swiveled its head down so the beam illuminated the circle-and-triangles symbol. In the angled light, the handprints were just a dark shadow, as if their interiors plunged deep into some eternal abyss. No question the symbol around it was the one from Oates' boat, and the same one seared into his father's skin in whatever that hologram was. Upon closer inspection, the edge lettering appeared to be Latin, with some letters like A and E combined into one. But while sometimes Latin words often resembled their English descendants, none of these words looked familiar.

This time the slab dragged out a piece of paper pinched between it and the floor. Scott moved the slab and pulled the paper the rest of the way out. It was actually several sheets of paper, stapled together and crushed where the stone had shoved them back into the recess of the hiding spot. Scott straightened them out on top of the stone.

The pages had been run off a computer printer, the one at the hardware store to be exact. The telltale black streak along the right side was a dead giveaway. The first page was a printout from a website. Scribbled notes along the margins were unmistakably in his father's handwriting. The text contained a description of the relationship between the realms of Heaven and Hell, with Earth being the buffer between the two. Angels came down, demons came up. The Devil himself could not cross over. Scott's dad had crossed out that sentence and written *BULLSHIT* in capital letters in the margin.

Scott flipped to the second page. It contained a drawing of the diagram etched in the stone. It wasn't an exact replica. A pentagram filled the center rather than the stone's twin triangle symbol. Also, the inscription along the edge was made up of random letters. But the handprints were there, dead center.

The description underneath referred to the stone as a Summoner, a direct link to the demonic. This was like having a demon's personal cell phone number. It created a connection strong enough to travel around the world or between the realms of Earth and Hell. The paper described the link it would create and it was exactly like the hologram Oates had conjured up on the dock. A demon gave a Summoner only to the most trusted, because the demon had no call waiting. The link always went through. In the margin, Scott's father had written an equation about power dissipation over distance, then scribbled *Closer = Stronger* and *Can't ignore. Loud.*

The letters around the edge of the drawing were nonsense because no one knew the actual text inscribed in a Summoner. Each inscription, in reversed Latin, was specific to only one demon. Recite it three times, with your hands in the center, and you were connected.

Scott traced his fingers counterclockwise along the stone's inscription and now *nomead* spelled *daemon* and *eratacov* spelled *vocatare* which looked a lot like calling someone. He pulled his finger away, afraid that touching it or sounding out the words in his mind might somehow dial up some demonic wrong number.

Scott's father had never been a wizard on the internet, but it looked like his encounter with Oates (and there was no denying it now for Scott) had prodded him into it. He flipped to the next page.

This page contained a recipe for blessed iron, a concoction of iron, gold, and holy oils forged over a wormwood fire. Supposedly a demon repellent.

Rusting spots of inlaid iron dotted the edge of the Summoner. Apparently Scott's father didn't want Oates to repossess the Summoner.

The last page of the packet was the most detailed. Scrawled across the top in blunt pencil were the words *Demon Trap*. Underneath was a diagram of strange symbols around a circle, and several measurements like the circle's diameter and the distance between symbols. *Must be in red* ran along the paper's edge. Each symbol had smudged notes scribbled beside it, most of which Scott couldn't decipher. At the bottom, Scott's father had written *Temporary prison or permanent??*

Scott sat back against the wall and flicked off the flashlight. He let the quiet darkness cover him like a quilt, and took a deep breath.

His father had really made a deal with Satan to kill someone. Scott couldn't imagine a scenario where his father would plot a murder. It probably hadn't been on the island, because a murder would have been big news, Carl Krieger being Exhibit A on that one. The reality was hard to accept, but even harder to accept was that on top of it he'd made a deal with the Devil. But it looked like his father had second thoughts about the arrangement. He'd researched what he could, and came up with a viable defense, or maybe he thought the demon trap was more like a viable *offense*. Whichever it was, his father had sought a way to put Oates on ice.

Scott had a premonition that that kind of information might come in pretty handy. And soon.

CHAPTER TWENTY-EIGHT

The door of the old police cruiser creaked closed with a comforting thud. The car's thick glass and heavy insulation sealed Scaravelli away from the outside world. He exhaled into the comforting silence as he sat in the car outside the station. A few moments alone were just what he needed now. The seams that joined the fabric of his plan with Oates were starting to unravel, and he needed a place to figure out how to stitch them back up.

All day he'd relished his clean dispatch of Krieger. The arrival of Kyler and his fake agents recast him as a bit player. His primary task completed, Scaravelli feared Oates now had him tagged as expendable.

All day, he'd reacquainted himself with his favorite remedy for worry, a bottle of Russia's great contribution to the world, vodka. The odor-free, on-the-job drinking favorite was clear and mixed with anything. By the time Milo had arrived to relieve him just now, Scaravelli's minor buzz had been all that kept him from firing the clueless dipshit.

Scaravelli now nursed a bout of healthy paranoia. He looked through the bullet hole in his windshield to Krieger's van, parked cockeyed behind the station where the tow truck had dumped it. He replayed his story in his head, reviewed the evidence in his cruiser and in the van. He tested for inconsistencies, anything that would contradict the fiction he'd passed around town. He knew he'd missed something. The guilty always do. But his blood alcohol level muddied his thoughts. He decided to obliterate them altogether.

Minutes later, he pulled his cruiser into the Rusty Nail's pitted gravel parking lot. A history of haphazard additions left the worn-out white building looking like a collection of adjoining mismatched boxes. The bar's moniker graced the façade, with a crude picture of a clipper ship in the background. A single steel door faced the parking lot, and the building was devoid of any windows, permitting the patrons to avoid daylight, darkness, and any other intrusions from the outside world.

Scaravelli's car was no odd sight at the bar. It was common for him to stop for a visit with Mr. Jack Daniel, the sum of his company at the Rusty Nail. He was there for alcohol, not fellowship. He couldn't imagine backslapping with these inbred island yahoos over a Pabst Blue Ribbon. He had his table. He drank alone. No one approached the imperial chief of police, and that suited him. Especially tonight. He got out of the cruiser and went inside.

It seemed as if only the neon ads on the barroom walls challenged the shadows of the Rusty Nail's dim lighting. Scattered tables tried in vain to attract errant chairs. Sagging stools stood sentinel at the bar, and a smoke-hazed mirror covered the wall behind it. The pungent aroma of ancient beer and long-vanished cigarettes scented the stale air. Scaravelli felt right at home.

The locals scattered around the room took no notice of Scaravelli as he entered the bar. With a nod to the bartender, he went to his usual table in the far corner. The bartender poured two shots of whiskey, the usual first delivery. Scaravelli dropped into a seat facing the room.

The bartender brought the drinks to his table without a word. Scaravelli downed the first one with one gulp, in a hurry to get hammered.

"Chief?" he heard from his right.

Scaravelli looked up at Chet Wheeler's round, ruddy face. He owned Wheeler's Wheels, the used-car lot in town.

"Yeah?" Scaravelli replied in a tone he hoped conveyed he was in no mood to hear the usual petty complaints.

Chet extended his right hand like a man trying to pat a lion.

"I just wanted to say thanks. You hunted down that son of a bitch Krieger and delivered a dose of real justice. You're a hell of a police chief."

Scaravelli relaxed and grinned. This was what he envisioned when Oates told him the plan. He reached out and gave Chet's hand one firm, hard pump.

"Just doing my job," Scaravelli said, emulating the modesty he'd seen others display. "Anybody would do the same."

"No they wouldn't," said a voice on his left.

Three other faces hovered at the side of his table, like moths to a streetlight. Several more shots of Jack landed in front of him.

"You iced that bastard good," the admirer continued. Scaravelli did not even recognize him. "Saved the town an expensive trial. Probably woulda gone free on some technicality, anyhow. Best thing you could have done."

Scaravelli beamed and downed his next shot in one swallow, this time in celebration rather than escape. Faces began to fill the opposite side of his table.

"Tell us the story, Chief," someone asked from behind the growing knot of men.

Scaravelli began the tale he'd spun earlier for Tackett. Patrons gravitated to his table and jockeyed for a ringside seat, way more receptive than Tackett had been. Their eyes locked on Scaravelli's. They hung on every word. Scaravelli added a few superlatives he might have overlooked in the first telling. The crowd soaked it up like a sponge.

Questions rolled in from the group.

"How did you catch him?"

"How close was the bullet when he shot at you?"

"What did he do to Natalie?"

Scaravelli rose and added some embellished details, punctuated with a sloshing thrust of his drink for enriched emphasis. Adoring eyes stared riveted, heads nodded as the crowd followed his every word. He enhanced his expertise and diminished Krieger's humanity, as he gave birth to a myth he was certain generations would retell.

"How *did* you get such a clean shot at him from inside your cruiser?" interrupted someone from the crowd.

Even with the Jack coursing through his bloodstream, his fogged perception caught the question as more of an accusation. He squinted and failed to identify the questioner. The crowd quieted awaiting his answer.

"It's training...you just fall back on it...."

The adulation in the eyes of the gathering drifted away, replaced by confusion.

Chet looked down at his hands and crossed his right over his left. "But sitting in your car, you'd have had to shoot left-handed...."

"Kind of odd you'd know Krieger was out in that exact spot in the woods, isn't it?" boomed a question from the other side of the room.

"Well, I had this hunch...." Scaravelli felt the crowd's opinion take a U-turn. The throng of admirers had transformed into a tainted jury. The claustrophobic press of people trapped him in the bar's dark corner. The exit seemed a thousand miles away, and between it and his table floated a sea of eyes, staring at him, staring *through* him, waiting for him to tell the truth.

"Chief, why'd you sell out to Oates?"

Scaravelli's glass slipped from his hand and smashed on the floor. He flattened against the wall. Sweat broke out along his bushy moustache.

"Who said that?" he yelled. "Who knows about Oates?"

"Who said what?" Chet asked. "Who's Oates?"

"Get out of my way!" Scaravelli ordered.

He pushed his way through the crowd. Whispers passed between them, more questions he did not want to answer. He practically ran the last few feet to the door.

He threw it open and burst outside into the night. The cool, clean air washed over him.

"Now that I think about it," Chet Wheeler said as the door swung shut, "the whole thing's kind of odd."

Scaravelli took a deep breath and decided he needed to get home, do less thinking, and way more drinking.

*   *   *

The crowd in the bar broke into groups of two or three. Concurrent animated discussions about Scaravelli's story blended into a low, anxious rumble. In the back of the room, a stout, bald man dressed in black stepped back into the corner's shadows, all his questions for the night asked. No one had noticed his arrival, and no one noticed when he disappeared.

CHAPTER TWENTY-NINE

Scott couldn't put it off any longer. Even if she'd had access to all the normal, less personal, but more immediate, twenty-first century methods of communication, Scott had to see Allie face-to-face. He'd immersed her into something horrible last night, and now he was certain that his dealings with Oates were about to enmesh her in something even worse. Even if all that happened was she told him to go away, he'd settle for that right now.

He pulled up into her driveway. Her car was there, but the dark house was silent, no radio, no TV. A light burned somewhere within. Dread built as he approached her front door. He knocked. No answer. He knocked again.

His first, blackest thought was that Oates had beaten him here, done something terrible to her. His heart sank. He grabbed at the doorknob. Locked. Panic started to take hold.

From behind the house, he heard something soft and beautiful, light as a whisper, musical. He ran to the side of the house. When he turned the corner to the backyard, it became crystal-clear and he stopped in his tracks.

A clarinet.

A small fire pit on the rear patio lit the area in a warm, buttery glow and fought back the descending evening chill. Allie sat cross-legged on a lounge chair in a pair of baggy sweats and an old flannel shirt. The clarinet was to her lips, and the most beautiful sounds floated from it.

He watched her play with the awe of the musically incompetent. Joy filled her face as her fingers danced over the instrument and called sweet cascading notes out into the air. Allie looked radiant as she created a melody out of thin air and talent.

In high school, Allie's singing and acting had garnered the accolades of her peers. But Scott had loved her music. He would often cut class during sixth period, sneak into the school auditorium, and watch from the darkened back row as Allie practiced with the band, just as he watched her now, filled with awe and adoration.

Allie finished the last note. The clarinet left her lips and she smiled.

"That was beautiful," Scott said.

Allie looked up, startled.

"Scottie!" she said.

She smiled in recognition. Scott exhaled in relief that she was okay, and seemed happy to see him. He took a chair beside her on the patio. The fire warmed his face.

"You still play beautifully," Scott said

"I just started again when I came home. It really sounds awful, but it feels wonderful."

"It looks like it does," Scott said.

"Well, I appreciate a sympathetic, if surreptitious, audience," Allie said.

"It's late, but I had to check on you," he said, "after last night."

Allie's face got serious.

"Oh, last night was awful," she said. "That poor girl. I had to get home. I was about to start crying, the kind of performance that didn't need an audience."

"I understand," Scott said. "I should have never stopped there with you in the car. The important thing is that you feel okay now."

"I do," Allie said. "Believe it or not, I went over and talked to Reverend Snow. He was a big help."

"It's in his genes," Scott said. "His family's been consoling Stone Harbor for generations."

"He's been doing more than that," she said. "He shared something with me. Natalie's murder is just part of what's going on here. Something's been hidden here for three hundred years."

Allie proceeded to tell Scott everything the reverend had shared with her about the Portal, the witches, and his family's role keeping the Portal from being reopened. Scott had to wait for her to catch her breath before he could ask a question.

"Who's come looking for this Portal?" Scott asked.

"It sounds incredible," Allie said, holding her hands up in a sign of embarrassed resignation, "but Satan himself. I know that's hard to swallow."

Scott sighed in relief at someone validating his own terrifying experiences.

"Not really," Scott said. "I'm taking it in smaller bites than you think. I've met him."

Allie's eyes widened. "You're kidding."

Scott filled her in on the boat at the dock and the mysterious Oates, the man who made a frozen wilderness sprout in your chest. He left out his discovery of his father's involvement, and the Summoner in the hardware store.

The flames in the fire pit died down. Allie's face fell half into shadow. She shivered.

"Let's go inside," she said.

Scott followed her in through the sliding glass door. She flipped on the living room light. Two big couches faced an enormous television. Original oil paintings of coastal scenes hung on the walls. Allie locked the door behind them. She returned her clarinet to the case on the counter to the kitchen.

Scott marveled at how completely comfortable he felt walking into a stranger's house rented by a woman who, before yesterday, he hadn't seen in ten years.

Maybe that bond we had back then never really dissolved, he thought. *Maybe over the years it twisted and curled and stretched very thin, but never severed.*

He took a seat on a couch. She sat down beside him.

Scott told her about the dangerous-looking men posing as FBI agents who were scouring the woods north of town. "Since they didn't look like they were searching for clues to the crime, and they were reporting to Oates, I'll bet they were looking for the Portal."

"Reverend Snow admitted he's too old and frail to defend the Portal," Allie said. "He asked for my help and I agreed. I think you should too."

"We were always a good team," he said.

Allie smiled. She slid down and on her side, tucked her legs and laid her head against his thigh. He ran his fingers through her hair. It still felt like silk. He rested his hand on her shoulder and gave her a squeeze. They just stayed like that in silence for minutes. Scott felt the rise and fall of her breathing against his leg. The weight of the tasks ahead of them sank onto Scott's shoulders.

"I'm sorry," she said.

"For?"

"For ten years ago," Allie said. "Fame got ahold of me and I let everyone and everything go. I abandoned you without even a goodbye. I'm sure you think it was just teenager stuff, but I owe you an apology. I'm way late. I missed your part of my Twelve Step Process."

The conversation Scott dreaded yesterday now seemed like a relief compared to the events that had unfolded since. "I appreciate that. I took it hard at the time. It would have worked out different if we'd gone to school together, I guess."

Allie sighed. "I couldn't convince you."

"Huh?"

"There was no talking you out of following in your father's footsteps to RPI. I floated several places we could both pursue our majors, and you never bit on any of them. UCLA offered an aid package, so I took it."

Scott couldn't remember any conversations like that. He racked his memory. Well, maybe something similar. She had brochures from schools once.... Did he listen to her? Really listen? He had been hot on Rensselaer Polytechnic Institute at the time. Was it because of his father? How could he have never put that together before?

And how had he never put any of the responsibility for their lost relationship on his own doorstep? He'd rescued her from a broken-down Mustang plenty of times, but when she needed a rescue from the siren call of Hollywood, where had he been? A little support at the start, from someone who loved her, might have made all the difference in the world.

"I'm sorry, Allie Cat. I wish we'd stayed together then."

"We're together now," she slurred. Her breathing became heavy and regular.

Scott stroked her shoulder, leaned back into the couch, and thought about summer nights on the porch swing at home. He started to plan tomorrow in his head, and got no further than visiting Reverend Snow. His thoughts began to grow fuzzy, and he realized that his eyes were closed. He tried to force them open, but quickly surrendered to the call of sleep. He drifted off to a pleasant place, one without dead children, portals to Hell, and black speedboats.

CHAPTER THIRTY

Out on Canale Road, the massive lights on the black Ram's brush bar banished the night from a patch in the woods. In the spotlights' center, the splintered remnants of two stumps reached up from the earth, as if the forest floor was reaching out in a cry for mercy. Five men, stripped of jackets, some even of shirts, dug and hacked at the trees' stubborn grasp on the piece of jagged-edged shale.

Kyler supervised from a few feet away. He gave the butt of his holstered pistol a nervous massage with the palm of his hand. This pack of thugs was bordering on unmanageable. Since he'd broken up Ricco and Ramirez, the two of them had been itching for a chance to kill each other. He didn't assess the others as much better. Only the fear of Oates kept them in line.

Axes and shovels tore earth and roots from the ground in big clumps, and exposed more of the gray slab of rock. The stump on the right was nearly fully excavated. Kyler stepped up beside the men.

"All right now," Kyler commanded. "Get some leverage underneath that one on the right and rip that son of a bitch out."

All five men wedged shovels and axes under the base of the stump.

"On three," Kyler said. "One...two...*three!*"

With a rumbly groan, the men collectively strained against the maple's last stand. The roots held firm.

"Again," Kyler said. "One...two...*three!*"

The group pulled one more time. One of the maple's roots snapped with a sharp crack, followed milliseconds later by a second one.

"This is it," Kyler said. "Last shot. One...two...*three!*"

The five pulled against the unyielding tree stump. A series of short, sharp pops filled the air. The stump rose and rotated away from the grunting men. With one thunderous crash, the main roots parted, and the stump fell on its side. The men tumbled after it.

The five stood and stepped back from the fresh hole. The earthy smell of decomposition rose up in a cloud of steam as warm dirt touched cold air. The lightning-bolt edge of the shale slab lay exposed.

Kyler knew this was it. Oates had been too demanding, too certain. The powerful artifact that cost the lives of many lay underneath this stone. The initial elation of the men at their success shifted to foreboding. No one moved.

"What have we got, Mr. Kyler?" Oates' voice boomed in the darkness.

After all these years, a sudden appearance no longer startled Kyler. Oates stood behind him, his back to the Dodge Ram. The spotlights backlit him into a dark, ominous outline. The men around the shale took several quick steps back.

"We've just cleared the tree, sir," Kyler said.

Oates stepped forward and knelt beside the slab. He tucked his hands under the edge, his fingers fitting into the saw-toothed edge, shattered three hundred years ago. He lifted it effortlessly and tossed it aside. He bent his head and peered into the depression under the rock's resting place.

The spotlight beams left the hole in shadow. Oates lowered his hands into the darkness beyond the rim. Kyler saw rare emotions in Oates, his eyes aflame in expectation, his mouth curled in a wide, hideous grin. He'd never seen Oates so alive with anticipation.

Then the look on Oates' face changed. The smile transformed to confusion, and then to anger. Oates' hands scrambled from side to side in the hole. He scooped up a handful of something and lifted it into the spotlight beams. The remnants of a burlap sack, ravaged by insects, time, and weather.

Oates' normally pale face turned a deep shade of red. His eyes went ablaze, like windows into Hell. He cast his face up to the night sky and raised a fist clenching the sack's tattered shreds.

"You know they can't hide this from me!" he shouted at the stars. The rags in Oates' hand smoldered, and then burst into flames. He hurled them down into the empty hole. The rags struck the earth and a fountain of yellow fire erupted six feet high. The flickering glow gave Oates' face an orange cast. His facial muscles writhed like a den of snakes. His cheekbones rose, his chin extended. A bony ridge swelled from his nose to across his bald head as he turned more monster than man.

All but Kyler ducked and cowered.

Oates clenched his fists and closed his eyes. He took a deep breath and seemed to gather control of himself. The flames at his feet died. His ruddy face returned to normal. The anger left his voice and it returned to its usual emotionless monotone.

"Mr. Kyler," Oates said, "this town's got my artifact. Compel them to return it." He looked with derision at the five cowering thugs. "The weak here need rest. Five hours, then follow the plan."

"Yes, sir," Kyler said. He turned to the men in the woods. "You heard the man. Let's go." He jerked his thumb in the direction of the truck.

The five dropped everything, grabbed their shirts and coats, and scrambled for the truck. They climbed into the back with sighs of relief. Kyler turned to Oates.

"The usual operational constraints, sir?" he asked.

Oates nodded. "The usual."

Kyler knew that meant there were none. Oates walked off into the darkness without rustling a leaf.

★   ★   ★

On the way back into town, Kyler plotted how to feed and house these scumbags until they'd outlived their usefulness. His five-hour clock had already started ticking. Oates never revised his timetables.

A place caught his eye as he neared Main Street. He hit the brakes hard and the Dodge's nose dove for the pavement. He threw the truck in reverse and backed up to the front of a rambling blue-and-white Gothic, well-lit by small floodlights. Several interior lights were on. The wooden sign near the porch had *Blue Fin Bed-and-Breakfast* carved into it in black letters. Underneath was a smaller, matching sign that said *Closed for the Season*.

"Here's betting I can convince the owner to open for us," he muttered.

He pulled into the driveway and killed the engine. He got out and banged twice on the truck's bed cap. The five tumbled out the back. Several groaned.

"Follow me," he said.

Kyler led the men up onto the porch. He opened the screen door and hammered his fist against the wooden front door. Two seconds later, he impatiently repeated the staccato call.

"Hold on, I'm coming," a creaky voice said from the other side of the door.

Kyler pulled the automatic from its holster and flipped off the safety. A deadbolt clicked. He took one step back. The knob turned and a splinter of light appeared between the door and the jamb.

Kyler reared back and delivered a powerful kick to the door's center. A thud and a surprised cry sounded from the other side. Kyler burst through the doorway.

On the floor lay a slight man in his fifties, wearing a brown cardigan sweater, blue jeans, and slippers. His short silver hair was parted in the middle, though mussed around the edges. Large gold wire-rimmed glasses sat askew on his face. Bright red blood flowed from his nose and mouth. He looked around, dazed.

Kyler bent down and grabbed the man by the sweater. He pulled him to a half-sitting position. Their faces were inches apart. He put the muzzle of the automatic to the side of the man's head. The little man's eyes widened.

"Who's here with you?" he said to the man.

"N-n-no one," the man managed to spit out. "I live here alone."

"Wonderful," Kyler said. He squeezed the trigger and sent a bullet through the innkeeper's head. Skull and brains exploded against the wall in a design worthy of Rorschach. The man went limp. Kyler dropped him to the floor.

He turned to the men on the porch. Each had varying looks of pleasant surprise and anticipation on their faces. Kyler had legitimized mayhem. They were now five kids in a candy store. Kyler felt magnanimous. This was probably the last night any of the five would spend breathing.

"Make yourselves at home, gentlemen," Kyler said.

The men fanned out through the B&B amidst an echoing series of whoops.

The dull eyes of the dead man on the floor looked larger than life through his glasses. The lenses made him look surprised.

You're just the first, Kyler thought.

CHAPTER THIRTY-ONE

In the pre-dawn hours, Kyler stalked down the second-floor hallway of the Blue Fin Bed-and-Breakfast. R&R was over. They were on Mr. Oates' timetable again.

"Let's go!" He kicked on doors and banged his fist against walls as he moved down the hall. "This is your goddamn wakeup call. Downstairs in fifteen minutes. Let's move."

He knew there was as much chance of these shit bags being ready to roll in fifteen minutes as there was of him becoming pope. Thirty minutes would even be a stretch.

He went downstairs and entered the kitchen. It looked like a pack of wild boar had been through it. Half-eaten everything lay strewn all over the table and countertops. A dozen drained bottles of very expensive wine lay on their sides in the corner. Kyler laughed remembering how one of the men had gone over and kicked the shit out of the innkeeper's corpse, punishment for a beer-free refrigerator. Only the wine cellar's discovery kept the innkeeper from heading into the afterlife as a pile of goo.

Kyler started a pot of coffee. He needed it anytime the day started at oh-dark-thirty in the morning. While the coffee perked, Kyler went into what had originally been the house's living room. It was now some type of community lounge. Two floral print couches flanked a long, low wicker table. The owner had attempted to give the place a nautical ambiance with pictures of tall ships on the wall alongside a clock mounted in a ship's wheel.

One of the miscreants upstairs had propped the innkeeper's lifeless body up on one of the couches. A bent cigarette hung wedged between his blue lips. His glasses were on upside down and the arm on one side hung out into empty space over the gaping exit wound in his skull. His pallid, waxy face still had that look of shock on it.

Kyler sat beside the stiff. He picked up a binder off the table. The homemade cover read: *FUN THINGS TO DO IN STONE HARBOR.* Inside was a collection of ads and brochures for local businesses. He flipped a few pages and found a map of the town. It showed only four roads leading out of town to the rest of the sparsely populated island. That was good. Even better, he saw that the harbor was the only place to land a boat. He could seal this place up tight, even with the losers at his disposal.

He tore out the map and went back to the kitchen. He went to the cupboard and pulled out a mug that said *WORLD'S GREATEST GRANDPA* on it. He studied the map as he filled the mug with coffee.

He checked his watch. The upstairs crew was due another kick in the ass about now. He grabbed his coffee and went over to the base of the stairs. The assault rifles stood propped in a corner by the door.

"Move it up there! You want to keep Oates waiting?"

Heavy footfalls sounded upstairs. One by one, the men staggered down to the ground floor. They looked like shit, bleary eyed and ragged, wrapped in hopelessly wrinkled fake FBI jackets. Each grabbed a weapon as he headed out the front door.

Kyler slammed home the rest of his coffee. He entered the living room and propped the empty cup in the dead innkeeper's lap so that the *WORLD'S BEST GRANDPA* accolade faced forward. He gave the corpse two little pats on its cold cheek and headed out the door.

The men climbed into the back of the truck. Kyler entered the cab alone. He double-checked that the police scanner under the dash was on. He didn't want any double-crossing from Scaravelli or Officer Dopey he met last night. The other band could track the state police if necessary, but in under an hour, no one would be calling them for help.

False dawn edged the eastern hills in a rosy glow. The town itself seemed asleep as Kyler drove the big Dodge down its deserted streets. He turned down Clipper Street and pulled over under the lights of a small used-car lot a block off the Main Street tourist trap. Six cars and a truck flanked a cheap white clapboard box of an office. A sign on it read *Wheeler's Wheels* and advertised on-the-lot financing with easy terms.

Not as easy as the terms Kyler would negotiate.

Kyler left the engine running, got out and banged twice on the cargo bed cap. "Everybody out!"

The hungover men exited the truck with the finesse of beached walruses. The clatter of poorly handled weapons against steel and concrete set Kyler's teeth on edge. The men surrounded him and he flattened his stolen town map against the side of the truck, high enough that they all could see it.

"Oates says we lock this town down," he said. "Here's the plan. Ricco, you take Constitution Avenue." He pointed out a spot on the map to Ricco, who nodded.

"Ramirez, West Street. Washington, Canale Road. Culpepper, Harbor Road." He identified a spot on the map for each of them. "Get to the edge of town, and keep everyone off the streets until I tell you otherwise."

He reached into the cab and pulled a big green duffel bag out of the passenger footwell. He unzipped it and dropped it on the ground. It brimmed with long, curved, thirty-round ammunition magazines, all loaded with sharp-pointed, glimmering bullets.

"Santiago," he said to the last man. "You take the dock at the end of Main Street." He handed him an M16. It had a grenade launcher strapped underneath it. He passed him a sack of grenades.

"It loads like a shotgun," Kyler said. "If any boat so much as starts an engine, blow it out of the water."

A big smile filled Santiago's fat face under his curly mat of greasy hair. A hint of insanity flared in his eyes.

"But if you so much as scratch the black speedboat at the dock," Kyler added, "you might as well eat one grenade yourself." Kyler pointed to the lot's office hut. "Find some keys, get a car, and take up your positions. No one in this town gets on the street. Shoot any car that moves."

"Even the cops?" Ricco asked.

"Except the cops," Kyler said. "They're with us on this one. Everyone else dies. Do not leave your positions until Oates or I tell you to. Understood?"

There was a muttering of assent and the men headed for the sales hut. Kyler heard breaking glass and a victory whoop as he refolded the map. The men in the sales hut argued over the keys and who'd get the 'pussy Beetle' at the lot's far end. Culpepper drew the short straw. The men hustled out of the building. Five vehicles roared to life, and then scattered like dogs released for a hunt.

Kyler gave the situation forty-eight hours at best before it degenerated into a bloodbath. In the Middle East, he'd seen the results of giving weapons to undisciplined maniacs, and these five were maniac material. But by then it wouldn't matter. He and Oates and the whatever-this-artifact-was would be on their way back to civilization aboard the *Killin' Time*, and this town would no longer be important.

He had a few things to do before he went looking for the artifact with Oates. Step one was to get a little information from Officer Dopey.

He left the lot, turned right, and a few blocks down, stopped in front of the police station. The light was on, a police cruiser parked in the lot.

He wondered if Officer Dopey was going to want to do this the hard way.

*   *   *

The pre-dawn hours were always Milo's worst. Nothing was open in town, even the drunks were passed out at home, and his body always made one last push for sleep before the sun declared it another day. The usual antidote was a patrol around the island, sometimes on foot. But tonight the chief's orders, dumb as they were, were to stay in the office and answer the phone that never rang.

Kyler's black Dodge pulled up outside the front door. Milo jolted wide awake.

Kyler and the heavies on Canale Road weren't cops (no matter what the fake jackets said) and whatever it was that they were looking for would probably do the world a lot more good by staying hidden. Kyler was only the tip of the iceberg, since it appeared that someone named Oates was running the show. The guy pulling Kyler's strings was probably the one pulling the chief's as well. Maybe a mob boss or drug kingpin, but what any of them hoped to find in the woods outside Stone Harbor was a mystery.

Kyler pulled open the front door. A holstered pistol hung on his hip. He wore tight black leather gloves and a determined, angry look. Milo shivered. He stood up behind his desk.

"Agent Kyler," he said. "What can I do for you?"

Kyler barely looked Milo in the eye. He unfolded a wrinkled tourist map with *Blue Fin B&B* stamped on the lower right-hand corner. He laid it on the desk and held it in place with one hand.

"I need the main power station and the phone exchange from the mainland. Where are they?" Kyler's eyes never left the map.

Milo thought fast. Once inside there, these men could cut power and communication, even cell and satellite. Stone Harbor would be isolated from the world.

He considered giving Kyler the wrong locations. But this killer would be back in twenty minutes, waving that automatic in Milo's face, or worse. It wasn't like the buildings didn't have big signs on them anyway. Whatever he did, Kyler would find both places eventually.

But knowing what Kyler was up to, Milo thought he might be able to protect some of the townspeople. They were the important thing. If he could play the fool here, he might live to play the hero later.

"The power substation's here, Agent," Milo said, pointing at the map, "and the phone exchange's in the basement of this building here. The door's in a stairwell in the rear."

Kyler marked the two spots on the map with a pen from Milo's desk. He finally looked Milo in the eyes.

"Shit's going to hit the fan in a few hours," he said. "The town is going to be dark and scary. People who stay in their homes don't get hurt. You keep them there. Understood?"

Kyler had dropped all pretense of having a legitimate purpose in Stone Harbor. This authoritative show of strength was supposed to leave Milo cowed. To stay invisible, and fight these men using inside information, Milo figured he needed to act like the threat worked.

"You don't have to hurt anybody," Milo pleaded. "Tell your men. I'll help keep people off the streets."

Milo did his best to look frightened. He was surprised that he wasn't.

Kyler eyed Milo as if checking Milo's bullshit against some internal bullshit database, looking for a match, and a solid reason to shoot Milo as a liability. Milo's heart pounded so hard he was sure Kyler could hear it.

"Anyone we kill," Kyler said, "is on you."

A smug look of satisfaction crossed Kyler's face as he turned for the door. Milo held his breath. The door closed behind Kyler. Milo stood until the Ram pulled away. Then he collapsed back into his chair.

His heart rate slowed back to normal. He needed to call Scaravelli and tell him what happened. Scaravelli wouldn't do anything about it, but calling would be what Scaravelli expected him to do. He had to stay in character. Once Scaravelli relieved him, he could start doing something to save the town.

An image of John Wayne raising a posse in some old Western popped into his head. Wayne always wore his star prominently when he played a sheriff. Milo looked down at the badge on his chest.

To Protect and Serve was inscribed on the rounded bottom.

Milo stood back up behind his desk. He adjusted his gun belt. This was going to be a long day.

★   ★   ★

Kyler chirped the Ram's tires as he pulled away from the station. He smiled with self-satisfaction at how quickly the little boy playing cop had caved. Just the threat of force had him quivering. He'd have lasted five minutes at Quantico.

Kyler pulled in behind the phone exchange building, under the town's only cell tower. An underground stairwell led to the exchange door. Kyler got out and folded the seat forward to access the behind-the-seat storage. He pulled out some hand grenades from ammo pouches and clipped them to his belt, along with several spare magazines. Before this was all over, he'd probably have to send some of the five he'd brought here to Oates' final reward ahead of schedule. He needed to be armed for it.

"Time to get this party started," he said.

He jogged down the steps to the thick metal phone exchange door. A cheap silver padlock hung on a crooked clasp. Rust bubbled up through a faded white outline of a telephone and an outdated warning that read:

PROPERTY OF NEW ENGLAND BELL
NO UNAUTHORIZED ACCESS

"May I present my authorization?" he said. He pulled his pistol, aimed it at the lock, and fired. The gun's blast echoed in the stairwell. The lock exploded into pieces and fell to the ground.

He kicked open the door and flicked on the light. Thousands of wires of all different colors ran in and out of junctions on the walls. Tiny lights flickered red and green. The wires' labels were coded with tags filled with short strings of numbers and letters. Kyler started trying to trace the lines to find the main junction. It quickly grew frustrating.

"Screw this shit," he said. He stepped outside and pulled a grenade from an ammo pouch. He turned and yanked the pin. The handle flipped off and hit the concrete with a ping. He tossed the grenade into the exchange, and then slammed the door. He leaned against it and covered his ears.

A muffled boom sounded on the other side of the door and it expanded from the doorframe for a split second and then relaxed. Acrid white smoke drifted out from the door's edges.

Kyler cracked open the door. The beautiful smell of spent explosives wafted out. He breathed in deeply, to savor the sensation. Inside, the room lay in shadow, the fluorescent overheads shattered by the detonation. Smoke rose from the junction boxes. All were dark, their green and red telltales snuffed out.

He closed the door and walked back to the Dodge Ram.

Fifteen minutes later, another dull thud at the power station severed electricity to every house on the island. As the residents slept, every water heater went cold, every refrigerator began to warm, every digital clock faded to black. Being late for work wouldn't be a problem though. Oates and Company had declared a holiday.

CHAPTER THIRTY-TWO

As Kyler drove away from the power substation, Oates materialized in the passenger seat of the truck.

"Are we on track, Mr. Kyler?"

"The men have the town surrounded, sir," Kyler answered without looking over. "Power and communication are down." He paused and decided that he needed to add the rest, even if it meant consequences. "They won't be enough to hold the town. It's too much area. They're too undisciplined."

"I'll arrange support," Oates said.

Kyler did not know what that meant, but he knew enough not to ask. "Next step, sir?"

"Somebody here's got my property," Oates said. "We're gonna find out who. It's gotta be one of the older families. They would have found it back then and hidden it. I want the descendants questioned."

Interrogation was one of Kyler's favorite parts of the job. It was brutal and sadistic, and unlike the other brutal and sadistic things he did, interrogation actually had a purpose. Over the years, he had learned how to inflict intense physical suffering while prolonging life. He considered it a gift.

"First stop, sir?"

"Top of the list," Oates said. "All Souls Church. Let's start with Reverend Snow."

Kyler spun the Dodge Ram around in a tire-smoking maneuver the bulky truck was never designed to execute. He drove back through the blacked-out town and pulled into All Souls parking lot. Though the power was out, dim light glowed behind the church's colored glass windows. Kyler pulled up in front of the big wooden doors.

The two got out of the truck and mounted the steps. At the top, Kyler opened the church door. Oates preceded him in.

In the darkness, a pool of soft light illuminated the altar. Reverend Snow knelt on the bare floor, facing the huge suspended crucifix. A row of candles lined the altar's edge, and two more flickering collections flanked him on either side. The dancing flames reflected in the aisle between the pews like tiny fireflies. The reverend's head was bowed, his eyes closed. He murmured a prayer to himself.

Oates stood behind the last pew and motioned Kyler forward. Kyler advanced down the aisle, the measured thud of his boot heels like a countdown clock. One boot landed on Zebedee Snow's grave marker and left behind a clod of earth. Kyler stepped up to the altar to the reverend's left.

The reverend did not react, perhaps lost in prayer, perhaps afraid to see his own future. Either reason pissed Kyler off. He spun around in a roundhouse kick. The rush of air extinguished the candles on the left.

Kyler's boot struck the reverend's chest. Reverend Snow flew backward away from the altar and crashed on his back in the aisle. The blow knocked the wind out of him and he gasped for breath.

Kyler stepped down and spun the supine cleric around to face Oates. He yanked the reverend into a sitting position, and then pinned both his arms behind his back at the wrists. Kyler slowly lifted the reverend's arms. Ligaments cracked as the man's arms rotated in the wrong direction. Reverend Snow groaned and rose to his knees to relieve the stress on his shoulders. Kyler pointed the reverend's head straight down the main aisle, straight at Oates.

Oates advanced down the aisle with slow, measured paces. He paused atop the white marble marker of the first Reverend Snow and looked down in disgust.

"First in a line of weaklings," he said.

He continued forward until he was a few feet from the reverend. Kyler grabbed the reverend's forehead and yanked the old man's head back. The reverend's eyes met Oates'.

"Reverend," Oates said. "Pleasure to meet you. My name is—"

"I know who you are," the reverend said, his voice strained. "We've waited for you to slink back to the island."

"Do I look like I'm slinking?" Oates said.

Oates began a slow pace before the altar, a few feet down, a few feet back. He gave his goatee a thoughtful stroke. He spoke without looking at Reverend Snow.

"My Portal, it's missing, Rev. I know where Providence hid it, and it's gone. Got a strange feeling you can help me with that."

"Maybe it rotted away," Reverend Snow said. "It's been three hundred years."

Without looking over, Oates raised the pinky finger on his left hand. Kyler reached down and grabbed one of the reverend's pinkies. He quickly bent it backward until the nail touched the wrist. Brittle bones snapped like dried bamboo. Reverend Snow let loose a high-pitched shriek. Tears ran down his cheeks. Kyler dropped the pinky. It drooped limp and crooked.

"Lies from a man of the cloth," Oates said. His pacing did not pause. "Truth's gonna hurt lots less, Rev. In fact don't you always say that the truth will set you free? Now did one of your foolish relations –" he gave the slab on the floor a dismissive wave, "– steal my property? Ain't there some commandment against that?"

"That was three hundred years ago," the reverend gasped. Pain flushed his face a dark red. "How would I know?"

Oates raised his ring finger. Kyler snapped the reverend's ring finger with a twist. The reverend screamed at the second wave of pain. The cry petered out to a whimper and he slumped forward. Kyler jerked him back upright.

"You'd know because your misbegotten family of do-good shitheads would have been proud of it," Oates said.

Kyler blinked as profanity passed Oates' lips. Oates had broken Kyler of the habit when in his presence. But then, last night he also saw Oates angry for the first time.

Oates stopped dead center of the altar. Kyler yanked the reverend's head back again for a proper view. Pain painted the old man's face. Kyler smiled.

"Look who you been working for," Oates said to the reverend. He pointed at the crucifix. "You sacrificed having a real life for him? You got no wife, no kids, nothing. Do you even own a car? Everyone your age worth anything took a ferry out of here. But old Zachariah stayed trapped here in Stone Harbor, tending a flock of idiots."

Oates renewed his pacing, now maintaining eye contact with Snow at each step.

"And you don't get no appreciation," he said. "Do they shower you with rewards for your sacrifice? Do they even give your church the support it needs? No. Just a little lip service to your Sunday sermon, and then off to do as they please the rest of the week. They blow thousands on new cars, and then tip you a buck in the collection plate. You've helped them in their time of need, but where are they now for you? You're taken for granted."

Oates spread his arms and pointed at the walls.

"You ain't a man to them. You're just a fixture, a piece of furniture in this house of misguided worship."

Reverend Snow's shoulders sagged. Kyler had seen Oates turn many a man at this point. The boss knew the right buttons to push. Every time.

"All this for him?" Oates asked, pointing at the crucifix above the altar. "You see him saving you now?"

Oates pointed one finger at each cleat that secured the crucifix's suspending ropes. With a twist of his wrists, the two ropes spun off the cleats. The crucifix seemed to hang in the air unassisted for a second, then fell to the floor with a crash. Christ's head broke off the carving. It rolled across and off the altar, then bounced off each step with a hollow thud. It stopped face-up against the first pew.

"He don't care about none of you," Oates said. "If he did, why would he allow war? Why allow famine? Why create serial killers? Most of all, why would he let me exist?"

Oates paused. The reverend sighed.

"Trust me," Oates said. "I know the guy. To him, you're toys, an amusement."

Oates sat down before the reverend. A subtle change crossed Oates' face. His features relaxed, his eyes calmed. In the candlelight, there was something almost angelic in that face, some of the Lucifer before he was cast out. This was Eden's snake.

"Now, Reverend," Oates said, like an old pal who had just dropped by. His Brooklyn accent retreated, and his normal monotone grew melodic. "The difference is, I do love you. I love all mankind. I encourage all to find their own happiness, unrestricted by some artificial morality."

Oates put his hand on the reverend's shoulder. He cocked his head, his eyes dark brown and soft as seal fur.

"It's not too late to right this injustice. I am magnanimous enough to reward you for your service, even if it was to the wrong cause, because I respect your sacrifice. In an instant, I'll give you more than God has given you in a lifetime. By my side, you will have power, comfort, and respect. I'll restore your youth and you can live life the right way, enjoying it. Kyler will tell you I'm a man of my word. I deliver what I promise. All I need is the Portal, and you will join me as I rule this reality. You will do so little, and I will give so much. What do you say, Zachariah?"

The reverend said nothing. He reared his head back as far as he could in Kyler's grip and spit in Oates' face. The reverend managed a small smile, and then closed his eyes.

"Our Father," he said, "who art in Heaven, hallowed be thy name."

Oates' salesman face vanished in a flash. Cold Brooklyn Oates was back. He slapped the spittle from his face and stood up.

"He's yours," Oates said flatly over the reverend's continued prayer. "Find out what I need. I've other things to set in motion." Oates turned and stormed down the aisle toward the main doors.

Kyler released Reverend Snow's head and yanked the old man's arms straight up with his left hand. The reverend yelped in pain and his prayer was silenced.

Oates stopped beside the last few pews. He pointed up at the sanctuary's back wall. A beam of fire shot from his fingertip. He traced a huge smoking design on the white wall, two inverted concave triangles within a circle. Then he burned a message beneath the diagram, and disappeared into the darkness out the main doors.

Kyler pulled out an old-fashioned straight razor from his pocket. He flicked it open inches from the reverend's eyes. The sharpened edge sparkled in the remaining candlelight.

"Rev," he said, "I once used this to peel an onion skin, one layer at a time. It took forever. Human skin has damn near as many layers."

He gave the reverend's wrist a twist, just to hear him scream again.

CHAPTER THIRTY-THREE

Lucky's ears perked to attention and the chunky black Labrador retriever popped up wide awake, despite the pre-dawn hour. His paws skittered on the hardwood kitchen floor as he scrambled to his feet. He sniffed the air in the dark. Carrot peelings in the trash. Ground coffee beans in the coffee maker for the morning. Lemon oil in the floor cleaner. Moldering kibble behind the refrigerator.

No, none of that awakened him. Someone had called his name. But everyone in the house was asleep. He cocked his head.

He heard it again, somehow not from anywhere without, but from somewhere within. It wasn't a call, so much as a directive, a demand for his presence so urgent that his body practically responded on its own. He bolted through the pet door and into the night.

In the backyard, the command grew stronger. Without hearing it, he shouldn't have been able to determine its location. But somehow, he knew it came from the east, from under the rising moon. The summons promised to fulfill his every desire: the need to belong, the need to be loved, the need to serve. Lucky's heart pounded against his ribs. He danced right and left in anticipation.

A five-foot barrier of chain-link fence blocked his way to the powerful master who called from beyond. He ran along the fence line in vain, doing a blind search for a hole he knew wasn't there. There was only one way out, and that was over. He ran to the far end of the yard, and charged the silver barrier.

Rolls of fat jostled up and down as he sprinted toward the obstacle with the amazing energy level he'd had as a puppy. He closed on the silvery mesh and leapt for the top.

His front legs crested the fence, but his belly grazed the top. A sharp, broken tip along the mesh snagged his rear leg. The metal point ripped a gash along his inner thigh but Lucky hit the grass on the far side and kept running. The tsunami of the master's summons washed away the pain from his leg.

Lucky bounded in a beeline across yards and through woods until he broke out in the parking lot of All Souls Church. A wide, foot-tall circle of crimson flames illuminated the center of the near-empty lot. On the conflagration's other side stood a stout, bald man in black. His eyes flared as red as the flames before him.

He didn't open his mouth, yet Lucky heard his command, louder than ever. It wrapped around his brain, coursed through his muscles, surrounded his heart.

"Come boy," he said. "Into the flames!"

Reason sent a warning about the fire, about pain and blisters and the sickening smell of burned fur. But the magnetic pull called from a place beyond Lucky's rudimentary rational thought. The man's eyes, his alpha-male aura, his unspoken promise of satisfaction drove Lucky straight for the blaze.

He leapt across the low wall of fire and landed in its center. The man raised a hand and spoke an incantation in a language Lucky had never heard, but the translation followed like an echo. *The blood sacrifice of one feeds power to the many.*

Lucky's chest split open like it had been unzipped. Blood gushed onto the pavement and made a glistening red pool in the firelight. He got dizzy and collapsed onto the asphalt with a *splat*.

The puddle around him shifted and swirled until it contracted to form two inverted concave triangles within the circle. The new design erupted into flame and Lucky vanished in a cloud of red smoke.

*   *   *

Across the island, hundreds of dogs' ears snapped straight up as Oates sent them all a new command and awakened their most ancient desires.

CHAPTER THIRTY-FOUR

Deborah Deering's old grandfather clock clicked over to 6:45 a.m. Only the tick of the clock and Deborah's light snore disturbed the silence. Deborah slept under two layers of floral comforters. Her miniature poodle, Precious, curled up sound asleep at the foot of the bed.

Suddenly, Precious's ears perked up and rotated forward, as if some noise only she could hear had just occurred. But there was nothing, just the ticking of the tall hallway clock.

Precious's eyes snapped open, her head popped up, and she was wide-awake. In one motion, she sprang from the bed and ran to the front door, paws ticking all the way down the old linoleum hallway. She stood on her hind legs and scratched at the doorknob, barking in sharp little yips.

The commotion stirred Deborah from her sleep. She swept a tangle of gray hair from her face and frowned. Precious was never up first. Deborah usually had to force the dog off the bed in order to straighten the sheets and comforters.

"What is it, Precious?" she said, her eyes barely open. "What's my Precious darling want?"

Precious fired off a few more insistent barks. Deborah clicked on the lamp beside her bed. Nothing happened. She looked over at the dark, dead face of her digital clock. She sighed. The power must be out.

She swung upright on the bed to get a view down the hall. The dog stood on her hind legs, front paws reaching for the door handle. She looked back at Deborah in expectation. At this early hour, Deborah remained unmoved.

"You'll need to wait, Precious. It's too early for Mommy."

Precious's eyes narrowed, and a low growl escaped her lips. She dropped to all fours and charged back to the bedroom. She crouched at Deborah's feet and growled again.

This got Deborah's attention. In all these years, she had never heard Precious growl. If anything, she seemed more terrified of the world than able to terrorize it. Deborah gave her companion a quizzical look.

"Precious?" she said.

The dog growled again, lower and deeper than before, a guttural threat drawn from deep out of the canine collective subconscious. She bared her teeth and crouched back on her rear legs.

Deborah's heart pounded. Malice gleamed in Precious's eyes. For the first time ever, Deborah feared her dog.

Precious launched herself at Deborah's leg. She sank her teeth into the flare at the hem of Deborah's pajamas, just missing flesh and bone. The dog jerked her head and shredded the flannel into strips.

With a shriek, Deborah recoiled and scrambled backward to her headboard. She tucked her legs to her chin and wrapped her shaking arms around her knees.

"Precious, what's come over you?"

The dog gazed up at her with a look that Deborah swore was victorious. Precious trotted back to the front door, a ragged scrap of pajamas in her mouth like a hunter's kill. She sat on her haunches and put one paw up on the door. She looked over her shoulder at Deborah. A low snarl filtered through the soft cloth clamped between her teeth.

Deborah inched to the edge of the bed, then lowered her bare feet to the cold floor. She shivered, though whether from the chill to her toes or from the look on her dog's face, she couldn't be sure. She shuffled to the front hallway. Her eyes stayed glued to her dog's, Precious following every step she took. Deborah picked up the leash on the hall table.

"Okay, Precious," she said in the soft, artificial tone orderlies used when talking to the insane. "Does Precious want to go for a little walk? Mommy will take you." She hoped at this hour none of the neighbors would see her out barefoot in her shredded pajamas.

She sidled past her dog to the front door. Precious's eyes tracked her with the intensity of a hunting jackal. The rag dropped from the dog's mouth. Deborah managed an unconvincing smile. Her back creaked as she bent over to attach the leash to Precious's jeweled collar.

The dog struck like a coiled spring. She exploded up from the floor, and sank her teeth into Deborah's left hand. Bones crunched and blood oozed out between the dog's lips.

Deborah screamed and dropped the leash. Her whole arm felt like it had caught fire. She yanked her hand away, but Precious just clamped down tighter. Deborah flapped her left arm, as if the dog was an errant piece of lint that she could shake off. But Precious only bit down harder and growled with fury as she sailed back and forth through the air. Blood ran down the dog's cheeks, bright crimson streaks on her shiny white coat. With each sweep of Deborah's arm, droplets of red sprayed the foyer's eggshell walls.

In her panic, all she could process was to get the crazed dog out of her house. She pulled open the front door with her free hand.

As soon as the door opened, Precious released her grip. She dropped to the floor and darted out the small gap between the door and the frame.

Searing pain pulsed through Deborah's left hand. She looked at it in uncomprehending horror. The area between her thumb and forefinger looked like ground meat. A steady stream of blood ran down her wrist and dripped into a growing puddle on the tan throw rug. Deborah tucked her mangled hand under her right armpit and squeezed. Tears of pain and heartbreak ran down her cheeks. She looked through the gap in the doorway and into her yard.

Precious trotted down the front walk. In the low dawn light the small dog cast an outsized, long shadow. She looked back at Deborah. Blood painted the dog's jaws red like some twisted interpretation of canine clown makeup. She bared her teeth one more time in Deborah's direction. Deborah swore she was gloating.

Five other dogs sat at the edge of her property, a perfect row of spectators, watching Precious come their way. One was a Lab, one a German shepherd, but the rest defied a single classification. The Lab was the Gleasons' over on Clipper Street. Its collar had about two feet of broken chain attached to it, and the shepherd carried his own red badge of rebellion with blood smeared on its cheek. All five sat motionless until Precious joined them, then in unison, they all turned right, and the pack loped up the street.

Deborah slammed the door shut and locked it. She ran to the kitchen and picked up the phone with her good hand. She looked out the back window and saw three other dogs trot through her yard, arrayed in a perfect V, headed for downtown.

"Good Lord, they're everywhere," she whispered to herself in disbelief.

She pressed the talk button.

No dial tone rose in response.

CHAPTER THIRTY-FIVE

At the island's other end, Allie slept. She dreamed she was on the patio, playing the clarinet on a warm afternoon, a melodious counterpoint to the sharp crash of the sea on the shore beyond.

A breeze ruffled the edges of her sheet music, then lifted the three pages off the table, and sent them flying in orbit around her head. The clarinet fell silent and she dropped it from her lips. She reached for the sheets but they flitted just out of reach.

The pages spun around her. The edges grew indistinct and the contours morphed. Feathers came into focus, and each sheet became a beautiful white dove. The three doves circled her head, and then paused and hovered in place all around her. She sighed at their angelic beauty.

Small black clouds bloomed from nowhere all across the sky. The clouds spread like cancer until their edges touched and drove out the daylight. Jagged arcs of blue lightning flashed across the sky. Allie shivered. A blast of wind sent trash and dead leaves across her yard in a swirling dance.

The soft dark eyes of the dove in front of her flickered bright red, like a torch bursting to life. She caught her breath and recoiled.

Each bird swelled, wings spreading wider, color changing. A flow of black that spread like an oil slick from the point of their beaks until it consumed the tips of their feathers. Their eyes widened and swept upward. The corners of the beaks twisted up in an unholy smile and the birds became three enormous ravens.

The one hovering in front of Allie opened its beak and cawed so loudly that her ears rang. Its fetid breath stank of something dead and rotting. She choked and fought back the urge to vomit.

The birds attacked. The ravens' chilling screeches and the pounding of jet-black feathers filled the air. They dove at her from all angles, fiery eyes ablaze. Allie ducked and shielded her head with her arms. Beaks and talons gashed her forearms. She scattered the birds with a panicked flail of her arms. They flew off and aligned for another attack.

Allie screamed and ran for the side of the house. The three ravens banked and followed in hot pursuit. One bird dove in and grabbed a chunk of her hair in its talons, then yanked it hard. Pain cut through Allie's head like a knife. A bloody clump of hair came out by the roots. She ran for her car.

A second raven dived in on her shoulder, sinking both feet into her flesh. She reached back, grabbed the bird by the neck, and threw it against the car's hood. It let out a surprised squawk, and then lay still, upside-down on the hood, wings spread and head bent at a right angle.

Allie sealed herself inside the car. The remaining duo circled like sharks. Allie struggled with blood-slickened hands to grasp the keys in her pocket. One bird dived and crashed feet-first into the driver's side window. The ice pick tips of its talons punched through. Cracks spread from the impact area like ripples in a pond. The bird looked into the car, and into her, with its blazing crimson eyes.

Allie finally gripped the keys and jammed one into the ignition. The bird on the hood stirred. It flapped its wings and righted itself. Its head hung at an obscene angle, rocking back and forth on its splintered neck. The eyes still glowed as it walked up the hood, its talons making a spine-tingling scratch as they gouged the paint. At the hood's edge, it reached over with its upside-down beak and tore the windshield wiper in two.

The other bird's wings beat outside the window beside her head. Its talons gripped the punctured glass tighter. The window creaked and flexed outward.

Allie spun the key. The car fired up and the tires squealed as she punched it in reverse down the driveway. The bird in front of her rolled backward off the hood and landed with a thud on the concrete.

At the road, Allie threw the car into drive and floored it. She reared back her left arm and rammed her elbow against the driver's side window. The window popped free, the raven's talons still embedded in it. Both hit the ground in an explosion of shattered glass and thrashing black feathers. Allie pushed the car past sixty and headed into town for the only safe place she could think of, Scottie's house.

"There's no running, dear Allison," said a rough Brooklyn voice from the back seat.

Allie shot a panicked glance to the rearview mirror. A man's round pale face with a dark goatee filled it. His black clothing blended into the back-seat shadows, and his bald head almost appeared to be floating.

She screamed and whirled to face the back seat. It was empty. She turned back to the road. Two ravens flew just ahead of the car, pacing it, one off each fender, like an escort from the Underworld.

The head reappeared in her rearview mirror. "It's all gonna come back, Allison. Some things ain't never forgotten."

Allie pushed the accelerator harder, hoping against reason to put some distance between the front seat and the back.

"We got a deal," he said. "Remember?"

In the mirror, the man's eyes burned red as the ravens'. Her back turned cold, like the seat back had iced over.

The view flash-changed. Stone Harbor vanished, replaced by the winding roads over Topanga Canyon, north of LA. It was night, and the unlit road twisted and turned as it hugged the canyon wall. On the other side, the road's wispy shoulder waxed and waned at the edge of a steep drop off. She knew this road well. Too well.

No, not here, she thought. *I'm not going back here.*

"You know what's around this curve, don't you, dear Allison?" the man said.

I know too goddamn well, she thought. *The Dark Thing.*

She hit the brakes, but the car kept going. She twisted the wheel, but the car tracked along the road on its own, Satan as autopilot, taking her to her personal hell.

"It's right past here, ain't it?" the voice said. A hand reached out from the back seat and pointed ahead past her shoulder. Red skin stretched out along long bony fingers. A black claw ticked against the windshield. The same reek from the ravens' breath engulfed her.

"Here it comes. Our little secret." The *s* sounded like a cobra's hiss.

Allie shrieked.

CHAPTER THIRTY-SIX

Scott's sleep was no calmer. In his dream, a guillotine stood on a platform beside the Stone Harbor dock. Torches burned on both sides of the platform and cast an amber flicker dancing along the suspended blade's razor-sharp edge. A tan wicker basket sat under the stocks at the base, ready to receive the guillotine's gift. Tall ships tied off at the town dock behind the platform. Scott stood front-row in the crowd facing the execution site. Though he wore a T-shirt and jeans, they all wore Colonial period dress. The thick scent of burned wood filled the air. This was the 1720 Stone Harbor from Scott's history books.

Scott's father appeared before him. Not the Gary Tackett who Scott had laid to rest, not the withered, weak old shell of a man disease had left his father. This was his father in his prime, mid-thirties and strong as an ox, face afire with enthusiasm. He wore rough, homespun clothes.

"Dad?" The surreal situation screamed that it was a dream, but the warmth and comfort of seeing his father, of feeling his father there beside him, was too good to chase away with the admission of reality.

His father put a hand on his shoulder, real, heavy, substantial. "How's it been going, Scott?"

"Rough at first, but getting better."

"A little sacrifice pays back big. All I ask is a little sacrifice."

His father grinned. Not his usual smile, but an upward twist of the lips that telegraphed an unnatural, blood-chilling menace. He disappeared and reappeared beside the guillotine. He now wore an ankle-length, hooded black robe. The hood covered his head and his face had an ethereal glow from within the cowl's recess. His appearance on the platform brought a muffled roar of approval from the crowd.

Scott realized that no one around him had a face. Each was just a blank stretch of flesh with a bump for a nose and shallow pits for eyes. Their muted, distorted cheers came from within them, deep in mouthless throats.

"When asked, we must give," his father said. The cowl seemed to amplify his voice, and add a rich, powerful reverb. "Always give to receive."

Aaron Siegel appeared in the guillotine. The gray-haired old man in thick glasses ran Scott's former engineering firm. He'd picked Scott out of the class of a hundred graduates, given him some high-profile first assignments, really taken him under his wing.

"First, the career. There is no calling greater than home, none greater than the store. Who was this man to pull you away from Stone Harbor?"

Aaron peered out from the guillotine's stocks at Scott and mouthed, "Why?"

Scott's whole body went cold. What was this? Who was this person in his father's body? His father wouldn't do this. He was no murderer.

"But he is," Oates' voice rumbled out of nowhere and everywhere at once.

Scott's father pulled a rope. The blade dropped with a scraping *whoosh*. Aaron's head popped off like a champagne bottle stopper and dropped into the basket. Blood exploded across the platform. The crowd uttered a distorted cheer.

In a flash, the blade was back at the guillotine's top. Blood dripped from the sharp, canted edge. Aaron's body was gone, another in its place in the stocks. Petite, with short curly red hair and a cute, slightly upswept nose. Scott gasped. *Anita!*

"Next, this marriage, this woman who returned here with you, not out of love, but out of obligation, and that obligation discharged, ran as fast as she could for the mainland. Faithless! You don't need her."

"Scott!" Anita screamed. "Stop him! Stop this!"

Scott moved toward the platform. Villagers' hands clamped around his arms and shoulders and locked him in place.

Scott's father's pupils flared red. He pulled the release with malicious gusto. The blade sailed down and severed Anita's head mid-scream. This time, blood poured from her severed neck in thick, gushing pulses and splashed villagers at the crowd's edge.

Scott closed his eyes against the horror. The villagers shook him until he opened them again.

Now they held him right before the platform, face a foot from the open maw of the stocks at the guillotine's base. The warm, coppery smell of blood roiled his stomach. His father towered over him. His skin had turned sunset-red. His teeth were now white sharpened spikes. The woodsmoke air suddenly reeked of sulfur.

"The best sacrifices are those made twice," his father said. "Ah, to have loved and lost twice...."

Allie appeared in the stocks. She looked confused. Scott's heart stumbled.

"Scottie? Where am I? What are you doing to me?"

"Allie, it's not me!" He tried to reach for her, but the villagers gripped him like steel bindings.

His father laughed, a deep rumbling laugh. His face elongated. Oates' voice replaced his father's.

"He's me, I'm him," Oates said. "And soon we'll be you." His face swirled again and then Scott was staring at himself. His alter ego flashed a set of those wicked, pointed teeth. "One big, happy, murderous family. It's your destiny."

Oates laughed so high it registered as a shriek. He pulled the release rope like starting an outboard.

"Scottie!" Allie begged.

The blade whistled down. With a crunch and *thunk*, it chopped through Allie's neck. Searing-hot blood exploded from the stump and drenched Scott's face.

The world turned red, then black.

CHAPTER THIRTY-SEVEN

Scott popped wide awake. His heart slammed in his chest, his pulse raced full speed. Even through closed drapes, the morning sun seemed to sizzle his eyes. He sighed with relief as he recognized Allie's living room had replaced the guillotine.

Something stirred in his lap. He realized he'd slept sitting up, and then remembered falling asleep on the couch. Allie still slept beside him. She thrashed in the grip of her own nightmare. Scott reached down, slid an arm around her waist, and tucked her close.

"Allie," he whispered. "Everything's okay. Wake up, Allie Cat. It's just a dream."

Allie's eyes shot open. She jerked upright, every muscle tight as guitar strings. She looked at him in stark terror.

"Scottie!" she said. She squinted, blinked, and relaxed. "Oh, my God. I had such a nightmare. There was a man. So evil. And the birds. The horrible birds."

"Talk it out of your system," Scott said.

"Well, I was home…." Allie started, then looked scared, as if the full memory of the nightmare came rushing back. She shook her head. "Nothing. Nonsense images. A jumble."

"Well, from the way you were squirming," Scott said, "that one was best forgotten."

Allie raised a hand against the sunlight streaming in around the drapes.

"I guess we fell asleep," she said. "What time is it?"

Scott looked over at the DVR on top of the TV. The omnipresent clock display was dark. He looked at the stereo. It should have still been on, along with the lights in the room. He checked his watch.

"It's 8 a.m.," he said. "Does the power go out a lot way out here?"

"No one mentioned that," Allie said. She got up and went into the kitchen. "I'll call the power company."

"With what?" Scott asked.

"Damn," he heard whispered from the other room.

"It's about time your lack of a phone frustrated someone other than me," he said. "Do you have a battery-powered radio? We could tune in WSHR and see if they report a widespread power outage." WSHR was Stone Harbor's local low-watt radio station.

He walked into the kitchen as Allie was flicking on the portable radio on the kitchen counter. He could hear Boston and Hartford stations as she spun the tuning dial, but there was only silence on the Stone Harbor frequency.

"No WSHR," she said. "It must be a major outage."

Scott didn't like the coincidental power outage. In his memory, the island had never had a blackout. Now at least a portion of the island was dark, on the same day that Satan showed up with six ex-cons to collect a portal to Hell. There was no way these things were unrelated.

"Allie," he said, "I don't think—"

"That it's a coincidence," she finished his sentence. "Something big is going on."

"We need to figure out what," Scott said. He retrieved what little plan he had made last night. "Let's go down to All Souls and see Reverend Snow. We need some more details about the Portal and how he plans to keep it out of Satan's hands."

"You're driving," she said. "Something about that nightmare spooks me about driving Stewie."

Scott wasn't about to admit that the whole situation had him spooked.

CHAPTER THIRTY-EIGHT

Cisco Ramirez was starving.

Until the last few minutes, he really hadn't been hungry, but all of a sudden, he was famished. He wasn't just ready for something to eat, he was hyenas-tearing-at-a-antelope ready to eat. His first choice was chorizo, but he knew that he was at least a thousand miles from a decent batch of that. Between drinking a bottle of whatever that crap was from the old man's basement last night, and Kyler waking him after what seemed like minutes of sleep, his brain felt one size too big for his skull.

Hunger only stoked his simmering anger. He'd spent yesterday rooting around in the woods. Today, he got stuck driving an old, creaky, gutless Taurus while the pickup went to that prick Ricco, a bastard rapidly getting on his nerves and about one inch away from a major ass-kicking. Then Kyler sent him to this lame little outpost on West Street. This whole event was one big shit sandwich.

He sat on the hood of the Taurus in the center of the street and cradled the assault rifle in his lap. Residential homes with sickeningly well-manicured lawns surrounded him. The trees were bare and there wasn't a stray leaf in any yard. A number of the houses even had stupid scale model windmills or cheesy fountains in the front yards. The shit some people thought was important....

And just his luck, he came here with shoot to kill orders, and no one showed up to be shot. Sure, a few sheeplike residents had cracked a door and peered out of their darkened homes, but they quickly ducked back in. One look at Ramirez lounging on the hood of a car with an assault rifle was all the warning they needed. He was their worst nightmare, a well-armed illegal.

There *had* been a little entertainment earlier in the morning. The neighborhood dogs had staged some bizarre simultaneous rebellion. Loud barking started at one end of the block and worked down in a chain reaction. Then came the Spectacle of the Superdogs. From many houses, family pets of all sizes leapt out of their yards, clearing impossibly high fences. Many dragged sections of rope or chain with frayed or shattered ends. Then front doors swung open and more dogs exploded from houses and bolted into the street. Bewildered, sometimes-bloodied owners peered out after them. A few started to cross the threshold and follow their pets, but the sight of Ramirez and an automatic weapon seemed to deter them.

Ramirez had a few bad dog experiences during afterhours visits to impound yards during his car theft years. This parade of psycho dogs made him nervous. But despite their violent turns on their owners, they ignored him. He watched with amazement as the dogs met in the street, and then broke down into smaller groups. In pairs or triples, the dogs went off on well-defined courses, with seemingly specific destinations, like they were setting up patrols.

Indeed, a collie and a retriever made rounds of his neighborhood, passing the nose of his car every twenty minutes or so. A few times, rapid-fire barking sounded in the distance, usually followed by human screams and the sound of a slamming door. Sounded like the dogs were covering his back.

He knew the dog thing was Oates' doing. When the wine kicked in last night, the men had started trading Oates stories. One guy, Culpepper, told him that he'd seen Oates command animals, actually directing two hawks to land at his feet. The man in black definitely had some powers. Was the guy the Devil himself, like some of the men thought? Ramirez wasn't sure. Devil, demon, warlock, whatever he was, Ramirez knew to stay on the dude's good side.

His stomach rumbled again. His position on West Street, unfortunately, wasn't opposite a Dunkin' Donuts or a Denny's. Not that they would be open on the First Annual Oates Day Holiday anyway.

He looked over to the house on his right. A bespectacled old guy peeped out the window and quickly ducked back behind the drapes. He reminded Ramirez of a kid he used to wallop the shit out of in high school, the type that offered no resistance, the kind that turned bitch in prison. Ramirez smiled. That puss would not only hand over breakfast, Ramirez would make him cook it.

He thought about Kyler's instructions. Don't leave this spot until Kyler or Oates told him to.

Yeah, screw that, he thought. *What Kyler doesn't know won't hurt him. What if I had to take a shit? Does he expect me to drop a load in the middle of the street?*

Besides, the dogs have me covered. The mutts are everywhere, keeping these cattle in their pens. I can be gone a few minutes. Not a damn thing has happened here all morning anyhow.

Ramirez slid off the hood of the car. He held his assault rifle casually at his side by the pistol grip, muzzle down. He made a beeline for the house with the wimp. His boots trampled a bed of fall flowers, crushing the blossoms into the earth.

The little man in the house made another furtive glance out the front window. The man's jaw dropped in panic at Ramirez's approach. His face disappeared. The drapes closed and quivered, as if the house itself feared Ramirez's arrival.

Oh, yeah, I'm getting breakfast, Ramirez thought. His finger caressed the rifle's trigger.

Ramirez entered 281 West Street for breakfast. By chance or some other intercession, that left the intersection on West Street unguarded just as Scott Tackett's pickup came into view.

CHAPTER THIRTY-NINE

"This doesn't look good," Scott said.

He feathered the pickup's brake pedal. A rusty dark green Taurus with no license plates blocked West Street. He recognized it from Wheeler's car lot. It sat empty. He nudged his truck's left two wheels over the curb and crept past it.

"Where is everybody?" Allie said. "Even with the power out, or maybe especially with it out, people should be outside. It's Saturday morning."

"Someone," Scott said, "or something, must be keeping them in, scaring them from coming out. Whatever it is, we don't need to meet up with it."

The truck cleared the Taurus and dropped down off the curb. Scott hit the accelerator. "I hope Reverend Snow is all right."

"Amen to that," Allie exhaled.

The next few miles to the church looked like the set of some eerie end-of-the-world movie. The power was out everywhere. Traffic signals hung lifeless at every intersection. Scott and Allie pulled into the empty church parking lot. Scott parked in front of the church's double doors, Allie's door facing the steps.

Loud, deep, furious barking broke the silence. A large German shepherd burst from the tree line at the lot's edge and sprinted for the truck at an unreal speed.

"Oh my God," Allie gasped.

The dog disappeared under the truck's nose. The truck shook, then echoed with the sound of cracking plastic.

The shepherd leapt onto the truck's hood. The lightweight steel crunched and the dog's claws ripped valleys into the paint. Its powerful jaws clamped a jagged chunk of the heavy plastic air dam between them. The dog's eyes burned a chilling red. It spit the shredded plastic aside. Saliva glistened on its bared, sharp teeth. Its head snapped left then right, alternately barraging Scott, then Allie, with an unearthly barking so deep it resonated in the cab. Strings of saliva splattered the windshield with each snap of its jaws.

Allie slid closer to Scott and grabbed his hand.

Scott was more frightened than he wanted Allie to know. He was more frightened than *he* wanted to know. "That's the Campbells' dog. From the other side of town."

"What are we going to do?" Allie said.

The dog's head swung and revealed the remnants of a chain at its collar. A patch of dried blood stained the fur on its neck. The dog wasn't just dangerous. It was deadly.

Scott gauged the distance to the doors of the church. A dozen yards away and up one flight of steps. It would be a quick dash for them, but the dog had come out of the woods like it was launched with a rocket. They'd never make it.

The dog leapt from the hood. As if reading Scott's mind, it ran up the front steps. It crouched back on its hind legs and snarled. Then the shepherd came hurtling at the truck.

Allie slid away from the passenger door. Scott wrapped his arms around her. She spun and braced her feet against the door.

The dog launched itself from the last step. It dropped its head and angled one massive shoulder toward the truck, like an offensive lineman at a tackle dummy. The dog vanished below their sightlines.

The dog hit. The passenger door crushed inward, and Allie locked her knees to push against it. The impact rocked the truck on its springs. Scott thought the dog had to have broken its neck.

It hadn't.

Two front paws slammed against the base of the passenger window. Then the German shepherd's head rose to fill the window frame. A deep, bloody gash sliced its shoulder deep enough to show bone. Its panting fogged the glass, but its blazing red eyes burned through the mist. The dog barked and gave its head a quick jerk back, beckoning to them, daring them to come out of the truck and play rough. It growled.

It loped back up to the top of the steps, strong despite the obvious wear from its kamikaze assault. It began another run at the vehicle. This time it ran faster, leapt later, and hit even harder.

The truck lurched hard. Allie squished Scott against the door. The interior passenger door panel popped off against Allie's feet. A crack formed at the base of the window. The dog retreated for another run.

"Allie, is that church door open?" Scott asked.

"It always has been," she said. "We'll never get to it."

"I'm going to distract the dog," he said, "then you need to run for it."

Allie sat up and looked at him in horror.

"What does that mean?" she said. "I'm not leaving you out here."

"I'll be right behind you. Leave the door open. Just get ready to go."

Allie shook her head.

"Trust me, Allie Cat."

Allie bit her lip, then slid back across the seat. She put her hand on the door handle. She looked at Scott, her eyes wide with fear.

"Don't do something stupid," she said.

Scott rolled down his window and popped the door open an inch.

The dog crouched for its next assault on the crippled truck.

Scott pulled himself out of the window and sat up on its edge. He banged both hands on the roof like a bongo drum. "Right here, Fido!"

The dog's snarl rose to a roar. It leapt from the top step, hit the ground, then sprang straight ahead and jumped to crest the truck's roof.

"Go, Allie! Now!" Scott commanded.

Allie threw herself at the passenger door. Metal moaned and the door popped open just as the shepherd sailed overhead. She tumbled out of the truck.

Scott ducked back in through the window inches ahead of the dog's bared teeth. He dropped back-first onto the bench seat, and pushed the driver's door wide open behind him.

The dog hadn't counted on the open door. It crested the side of the truck, head tucked and snapping in Scott's wake. It flew forward and its belly scraped the top of the doorframe. The pointed corner pierced it just below the breastbone and ripped a canyon into the dog's gut as momentum kept it going. The dog howled in pain and fury.

Allie had scrambled to the top step. Scott slid out of the passenger door feet-first and followed her.

The dog hit the ground on its side. Intestines bulged from the rent in its belly. It sprang to its feet, unfazed, eyes bright as roaring suns. Scott glanced back. The dog crouched and leapt back over the truck cab.

Allie pushed open the church door. Scott hit the church's first step and then soared over the next two in one leap.

The dog cleared the truck with a wet slap of entrails against the roof. It landed at the church's bottom step with a throaty growl.

Scott leapt across the top step and flew in through the open church door like he was sliding face-first for home. Allie swung the door shut behind him.

The latch clicked a split second before the shepherd hit it so hard the hinges wept dust. Frustrated, furious barking bellowed from the front steps, followed by another heavy blow to the door.

Scott rolled on his back. Allie had her back against the church door. She whirled, flipped the two deadbolts, and knelt by his side.

"Are you all right?"

Scott looked himself up and down. "I think so."

Allie punched him in the chest. "Then don't ever do something that stupid again!"

She sat back and looked across the church. Her eyes went wide then filled with tears. Her jaw trembled and she buried her face in her hands.

Scott spun around and looked up at the altar. He had to force himself not to look away.

At the base of the altar, the crucifix's Christ figure lay in a pile, arms, legs, and torso severed and stacked like a rack of kindling. At the top of the heap, Christ's head lay on its side.

In the Savior's place, a nude Reverend Snow hung on the cross over the altar. Yellow nylon rope bound his arms and feet in place. His head hung low, face-down, eyes wide-open because the eyelids were gone. What had been done to him was almost beyond comprehension.

The reverend had been flayed alive. Long thin strips of skin hung down from his feet, nearly touching the altar. Each two-inch-wide strip started at the reverend's shoulder, and the band of skin had been methodically trimmed from the underlying muscle. From his neck down, the body was red exposed tissue, like an anatomy book picture.

Below him, the reverend's blood splattered the white altar cloth. Around the altar, snuffed sacred candles stuck from pools of hardened wax, drooping in silent guilt for illuminating the night's torturous process.

Scott went to Allie. He knelt before her to block her view of the crime, and pulled her close. She collapsed in his arms, buried her head in his shoulder, and wept.

Scott looked up above the main doors of the church. Two concave triangles inside a circle were burned in the back wall. Underneath was scrawled:

Return my Portal.

"Goddamn Oates," Scott whispered.

If this could happen in a church, to the reverend, nowhere was safe.

CHAPTER FORTY

Chief Scaravelli's long night promised to turn into a long morning.

After his escape from the Rusty Nail, Scaravelli had spent the evening at home in the company of a Mr. J. Daniel, who hailed from an oaken barrel in Tennessee. He drank to forget, but all he could do was remember. His present and future were in the hands of Oates, and he dreaded both. The more he drank, the freer his imagination became, and the more terrifying the possibilities. By midnight, he was stumbling around the house with an empty bottle in his hand, praying he would pass out. He finally did.

Hours later, with sand-blasted eyes and a pounding head, he reentered the conscious world. The clock was black, electricity out. He rolled over to pick up the phone. Dead. His stomach slid south into a pit of anxiety. Anything out of the ordinary the last few days was Oates' work. What had ended last night as something going wrong for Scaravelli had developed into something going wrong for all of Stone Harbor. His venal sin had turned mortal.

Scaravelli vaguely remembered a call from Milo in the wee hours of the morning, or he might have dreamed it. He squinted at the painful daylight leaking through the curtains.

Little Milo's going to be relieved late this morning, Scaravelli thought. *A few more hours playing dress-up cop will get him excited.*

He swung his feet out of bed. His head swam in a sea of vertigo and he gripped the edge of the mattress.

He had to get to work. Without power and communications, the locals would be looking for him to save the day, something to rekindle the hero stuff he heard last night. With enough shoveling, maybe he could keep his little sandcastle in one piece against the waves. Oates would leave soon, the tide would go out, and he would be Chief for Life.

An hour later, driving down Clipper Street, Scaravelli got the first big clue that his sandcastle had long since washed away. A beat-up blue hatchback faced him in the middle of the street. He recognized the car, a summer-long fixture at Wheeler's used-car lot. The hatch gaped open. Someone sat in the back, feet dangling over the bumper. Rough work boots and black slacks.

Scaravelli crept by. The man sitting inside was one of the reprobates from up on Canale Road. He still wore a black FBI jacket. Scaravelli wondered how many other intersections Oates' thugs had commandeered. The story got worse when he saw that the man absentmindedly cradled an assault rifle in his lap. The pistol at Scaravelli's side would be useless against a weapon like that. Scaravelli's anxiety meter maxed out. Scaravelli was too tired and hungover, and in no mood for a fight, especially one he couldn't win.

The man gave a casual wave as the cruiser rolled by.

The town might have turned against him, but Oates' crew still thought he was on their side. When the thugs pulled out, he'd get credit for that. It was the last bit of hope he could foster about his life in Stone Harbor.

Scaravelli looked ahead just in time to jam on the brakes. He nearly collided with old Mel Feingold's silver Cadillac El Dorado, stopped dead in the middle of the street. It was a bullet-ridden mess.

Both front tires sagged flat. Rounds that missed the tires had punched a pattern of holes in the fenders. Thick green liquid puddled under the car's nose where the Caddy had bled out its antifreeze before expiring. The driver's side door hung wide open.

Mel's corpse lay under the open door, face-down, arms and legs spread to his sides. One leg of his gray slacks had ridden up to expose a thin black sock and a band of pale calf. Two tight entrance wounds punctured the back of his yellow button-down shirt. A spray of drying blood dappled the asphalt around him.

Scaravelli could see what happened here. Mel had left his home, for whatever ill-advised reason. The thug in the hatchback shot the Caddy to a standstill, yanked Mel out, tossed him to the ground, and wasted him. Then as a warning to the neighborhood, he left his handiwork on display for all. His casual wave to Scaravelli said he was sure the chief of police would approve.

Scaravelli swiftly abandoned any illusions that this shit was going to work out all right. A corpse lay on a residential street. Who knew how many bodies Oates and his armed sociopaths had dropped around the island? Lifetime tenure as chief of police? Christ, he'd be lucky to avoid prison time.

Scaravelli reached the station hung over *and* depressed. He wanted to see little go-getter Mimms as much as he wanted to change a two-day diaper. The last thing he needed now was his insipid officer jumping around like a Chihuahua begging to do his next trick.

When Scaravelli walked in the door, Milo's jaw dropped. Scaravelli looked down and realized he looked like a shit sundae. His wrinkled uniform looked like he'd stored it on the floor overnight (which he had) and his face told the tale of his night of drinking. He really didn't give a crap.

"Chief?" Milo said.

"Milo."

Milo came around from his side of the desk.

"The power and phones are still out across the island," Milo said. "I've been here like you said, in case anyone came in, but the streets are deserted. Everyone's staying inside, which is probably safer."

"Yeah, safer," Scaravelli said.

He brushed by Milo and plopped down in the chair. He had his own problems and his own agenda. He remembered the bottle of vodka in the top drawer of his desk, just what he needed to take the edge off this hangover. Milo needed to get the hell out of here so he could take care of business.

"Kyler has men placed all around," Milo said. "I checked out the town at sunrise. They have the main roads and dock blocked off."

Scaravelli barely heard him. His head pounded in thunderous harmony with every beat of his heart.

"Chief, there's something strange about all the dogs too."

The vodka in his desk sang to Scaravelli, and it was a sweeter tune than Milo could carry.

"Christ," he said. "Go the hell home, Milo. It's been a long night. Anyone you see, tell them to get back in their houses. Tell them this will all be over soon."

"Chief, do you want me to "

"Just go home!" Scaravelli yelled. Shouting just made his head hurt more. "Go," he whispered.

Milo turned and took a few steps toward the door. He stopped and looked back.

"Chief," Milo said, "who's Oates?"

Scaravelli felt the blood drain from his face. "Where did you hear about him?"

"I overheard Kyler mention him," Milo said. "It sounded like Kyler took orders from him."

Scaravelli took a long bleary look at Milo. For a moment, Scaravelli's alcoholic haze lifted. A sprout of decency emerged from his twisted personality. He looked at Milo and felt sorry for him.

"Stay clear of Oates," Scaravelli said. "As far and as wide as you can if you want to get out of this alive. Am I clear?"

"Sure, Chief," Milo said, a little taken aback. "I'm going right home. See you tonight."

Scaravelli made a grunting noise and looked down at his desk. Milo went out the front door.

As soon as the door closed, Scaravelli unlocked and pulled open his desk drawer. The vodka bottle rolled toward him, stopping right next to his gut like a special delivery.

He pulled it out, unscrewed the cap, and took a swig. The vodka burned all the way down, and it felt good. Just the kind of help Scaravelli needed to get through the day.

He put the bottle down and looked in the drawer. He knit his brow. The Dickey girl's necklace he'd taken from Krieger's apartment was in the drawer, but out of the evidence bag. He picked it up and searched the drawer. The bag was gone. His heart stopped when he realized so was something else.

The gun he'd planted on Krieger was missing.

"Goddamn Milo," he said, all sympathy for his officer evaporating. "Son of a bitch moved it somewhere."

The fuzzy, distant cop part of his brain raised a few objections. Milo didn't know the pistol was in his desk. Milo didn't have a key or a motive to move the gun.

But Milo was the only suspect Scaravelli dared put on his list. Because the person who would know the pistol was in the desk, who wouldn't need a key, and would have some twisted motive, was Oates. Scaravelli was in no condition to deal with that reality.

He wiped some dirt from his coffee mug, and filled it full of vodka.

*   *   *

Outside, Milo pulled away in his cruiser, smirking with pride. Scaravelli didn't suspect him. Kyler didn't suspect him. That gave him the freedom to travel at will. He had a pistol at his side, so he also had some firepower, though strictly defensive compared to what he saw Kyler and his men were packing. All he needed was a little help, and he'd find a way to keep as many people safe as possible.

Milo did find out one important thing from Scaravelli. He'd asked about Oates and Scaravelli went white. The thug Ramirez also turned terrified when Kyler mentioned Oates. Whoever Oates was, he was running the show, including Scaravelli. That put Scaravelli a mile outside Milo's circle of trust.

He'd thought all night about who to put in that circle. He came up with one name. Someone who could be trusted to do what was right, even though it was hard, and someone who loved the town, loved it enough to give up a great job to come back and stay.

He needed to find Scott Tackett.

CHAPTER FORTY-ONE

The Lord won't give you more than you can handle.

Allie approached the edge of a mental cliff over an abyss, and replayed Reverend Snow's words. If they were true yesterday, they still had to hold true today, no matter how awful today had become.

Yeah, well, the Lord gave the reverend a bit more than he could handle, hadn't he? she thought. Tortured to death in his own church. Looked like God was on break when that happened. She couldn't get the vision of his kind face, the echo of the reverend's supportive words out of her mind. Why did this have to happen to him?

Scottie had lowered the cross that bore Reverend Snow, wrapped him in some altar cloths, and laid him in the sacristy behind the altar. She owed Scottie for taking care of Reverend Snow alone. She sat in the church's last pew. Scott walked back down the main aisle. He sat next to her.

"I'm sure he didn't tell them," she said.

"What do you mean?" Scott said.

"He wouldn't give up the Portal," she answered. "They'd come here because they couldn't find it, hunting for people who might know about it from their family history. Reverend Snow would have been first on the list. He'd never tell."

Allie shuddered at the vision of the dead Reverend Snow. She took a deep breath because…

The Lord won't give you more than you can handle.

…she could handle this. Rage at the reverend's torture replaced sorrow. The reverend had asked her for her help and she promised it to him. Time to deliver. She'd grieve for him later, when the town was safe. Allie stood.

"We need to know what he knew," she said. "The Portal's history is in the church somewhere. He as much as told me so. He said that each year on Christmas Eve, the generations would gather here and retell the story, to pass on the responsibility of protecting the Portal."

"Why does that mean there's some physical history here?" Scott said. "They could have just told the story to each other."

"No, no," Allie said, shaking her head. "It's too important to trust to an oral history alone. That could get changed over time. Look around here." She pointed at the church walls. "The stained-glass windows adorned with saints and the Stations of the Cross are all pictures. The reverend always said artwork filled great cathedrals to keep the stories of the church alive and accurate for people who were quite probably illiterate. A family of ministers would know that passing down a responsibility took more than word of mouth. That history is in here somewhere. Why else would they meet here every Christmas Eve, instead of somewhere more comfortable?"

"Christmas Eve in the 1700s had to be cold and dark in this drafty church," Scott said. He started to look convinced. "Okay, let's start looking."

Scott started on the left and Allie on the right. They looked on, under and around every item in the church. They took pictures from walls, checked for hidden panels, and scoured the stained-glass windows for hidden messages.

After several hours, the search appeared fruitless. There were no clues in any of the art in the church. Decades of old paint coated the walls in unbroken uniformity, dimming hope of any hidden doors or panels. The altar area yielded no surprises. The pews were bolted to the solid wood floor, further sealed by layers of wax and varnish. Allie's hope for finding information on the Portal began to wane.

She stood at the rear of the church, running her fingers over the seams of the walls for the tenth time. She was about to have every child's dirty fingerprint there memorized.

"Where would they hold this Christmas Eve meeting?" Scott called from the altar. "As the reverend, where would I go that special night each year to tell my son the most important story of his life, that it was his destiny to save Stone Harbor, and the world, from the reign of Satan?"

Her first inclination was the altar area, but that holiest of places, where the host was consecrated, would be the wrong place to discuss such monstrous evil. Besides, she and Scottie had been all through there.

Allie remembered her Christmas Eves here. The bright light of the evening service made the stained-glass windows reverse their role and send a kaleidoscope of pastel rays out to illuminate the chilly winter darkness. Organ music wafted out into the night, and the lights of the star on the steeple drew the congregation as the Star of Bethlehem drew the Wise Men. A full-scale carved manger scene always stood beside the church entrance, a hundred-year-old tradition, almost as old a tradition as the steeple star.

The steeple star!

"The lit Christmas star in the steeple," she said. "If the Snows met in the actual church, townspeople would have wondered why the stained-glass glowed late into the night. But if they met in the steeple, the extra light there would be normal, expected on Christmas Eve. It would also be isolated, so that no one could overhear what the family passed on. It would be perfect."

Scott walked back from the front of the church. He looked leery.

"Allie, that steeple is so rickety that the bell hasn't been rung since the end of the Civil War. What's to keep you, me, and the bell from crashing straight to the ground? We didn't dodge that dog outside to kill ourselves in here."

"I know it's up there, Scottie," she said. "We have to look. The door is in the choir loft behind the organ."

Allie grabbed Scott's hand and pulled him up the stairs into the choir loft. The dark oak organ sat in a small nave at the rear, centered under the steeple. An array of dull brass pipes rose up from behind it and covered the wall like a metallic fan. The paneling on the nave's left and right looked identical, but on close examination, the right side was actually a door with recessed hinges and a small knob.

Allie pulled Scott to the door. She turned the handle. It was locked.

"That would be expected," Scott said. "How about a key?"

"No idea," Allie said.

Scott quickly surveyed the choir loft, then released Allie's hand.

"Stand back," he said. Allie stepped away and Scott slid the organ's heavy oak bench over to the steeple door. He flipped it up on the short end, and lifted it up over the knob.

He released the bench. The bench dropped and severed the brittle metal knob. The bench hit the floor with a crash. The knob dropped and rolled behind the organ.

Scott slid the bench back out of the way and went down on one knee before the door. He put his finger in the empty socket and pushed. The knob on the other side hit the wooden floor. Scott hooked his finger in the open hole and pulled.

The door creaked open. A cloud of dust rose along the edges.

In contrast to the richly finished choir loft, the timbers in the steeple access were a dull, unfinished gray. Hundreds of years of summers had dried every drop of moisture from the wood. The little room was just a few feet square, with a rough-hewn ladder running up the back wall all the way to the bell tower proper. The light coming in through the door was all that illuminated the access way.

Allie stepped on the dry wooden ladder. The rung emitted a complaining groan as she rested her weight on it.

"Allie, seriously," Scott said. "We're lucky the bell doesn't come crashing down on us."

She bounced up and down a little to test its strength. The rung protested again, but did not give way.

"Reverend Snow comes up here every year to mount the star," she said. She realized she should have used the past tense and shook off the realization. She began to climb.

Each footstep on a rung sent the sharp creak of weakened wood echoing up the tower. Twenty feet up, slivers of light through louvers lit the top. At the top yawned the open mouth of the bell, without a clapper, forever silenced. Dust coated everything like a covering of gray snow.

At the top, she went to the far end of the bell platform. Zebra stripes of light from cracked and missing louvers painted the old bell. The bell's clapper lay on the floor, a long iron shaft, flattened at one end, with a bulbous round tip at the other. She had a quick vision of a severed tongue, and put it out of her mind.

Scott got to the top of the ladder and stood on the platform. He peered out one of the missing louvers that faced the front of the church.

"Hell's watchdog is still waiting for us out there," he said.

Allie peeked out. The German shepherd had planted itself between the truck and the church, and was intently watching the big black doors for the slightest movement. A small puddle of blood lay under its belly. "How can that thing still be alive?"

She began to search the steeple's inner wall of the steeple. Something was written on the north side. She bent down and looked at the marks more closely, ran her fingertips along the letters. A list of names, carved into the wood. The lettering style changed from name to name, with earlier names containing archaic underscoring at the base of the W and M letters. The names read:

Jacob Snow
Joseph Snow
Timothy Snow
John Snow
James Snow
Aaron Snow
Abraham Snow
Benjamin Snow
Zachariah Snow

Beside each one was a dark rectangular smudge, about an inch tall and half-an-inch wide.

"Scottie, look at this."

Scott abandoned his canine surveillance and bent down next to Allie.

"I was right," she said. "These are the names of the nine generations of Snows that tended this church. I'll bet that each boy carved his name here when he reached the age when he would join his father here on Christmas Eve. What do you think these smudges are?"

Scott gave the wall a closer inspection. "Thumbprints. In some I can just make out the swirls of the patterns. Based on the color, I'm guessing that the boys didn't make them with ink. Looks more like blood."

"Can't you imagine a very solemn ritual at that first reading, where it culminates in the boy carving his name in the wall with his knife, then sealing his promise with blood drawn by that same blade? The story of the Portal has to be here."

She reached up into the shadow under the sill over the names. She touched something soft and supple, a tube of some type. Two thin leather straps tied it in place. She worked the knots loose, and the object fell into her hands. She pulled it out into the light of the tower.

A foot-wide roll of dark brown leather lay in her hands. A strap fastened it in the center using a small handmade buckle. Allie unbuckled the strap and unrolled the tube in a patch of light on the floor. It crinkled as it unfurled to about two feet long. Thread attached a yellowed parchment to the inside. A precise flowery cursive, reminiscent of the Declaration of Independence, covered the scroll. If this was what she thought it was, the last time it had seen the light of day was some seventy years ago when her Reverend Snow had his father lay the family secrets out for him. She was probably also the first non-Snow ever to see it.

A date in the upper left-hand corner read 1720.

"Allie Cat," Scott said with a mixture of reverence and amazement, "you were right."

Tires ground against gravel outside in front of the church. Scott stepped back over to the hole in the louvers and looked out.

A police cruiser rolled across the parking lot. As it approached the front of the church, the German shepherd looked at the car, let loose a sharp yip, and loped back off into the woods, as if relieved of duty. A trail of blood drops speckled the ground in its wake. The cruiser parked between Scott's truck and the church. From the spire viewpoint, the car's roof blocked any view of the interior.

"That's got to be Scaravelli," Scott said, "and for once, the police arriving in a dire situation is not good." Scott pointed at the scroll in Allie's hands. "He can't get a hold of that thing."

"He won't," Allie said.

She rolled it back up. Scott started back down the ladder.

"I'll stall him at the door. Stay here. I'll close the access way door. He won't even know where to look."

Allie fastened the leather scroll back under the sill, frustrated she'd have to wait to read it. Scott vanished down the ladder. Someone banged on the front door of the church. She peered out the louvers. The roof blocked any view of the front stoop.

Armed police on the wrong side of the law. What did Scottie think he was going to do to stop Scaravelli? Talk him out of killing the two of them?

From downstairs came a loud wooden snap, then more, louder banging on the door.

She gave the scroll a glance to make sure that it was tied up and out of sight.

It stayed hidden that way for three hundred years, she thought. *That better be good enough.*

Whatever was about to go down in the church, Scottie wouldn't face it alone. Allie grabbed the ladder's top rung and headed down.

If the Lord wasn't giving her more than she could handle, he was sure nudging the upper limit with it.

*   *   *

A pair of red eyes burned from beneath the shadowy cover of the lowest branches of the spruce. The German shepherd crept forward a few inches for a clearer view of All Souls Church. The end of its severed chain jangled across the ground with each step.

The pain from the gash in its belly was somehow distant, muffled. The dog knew its life was draining away, though something external seemed to keep it going.

A police cruiser idled in front of the church. An officer banged on the door.

The dog hunkered down to the ground. It would wait, as Oates commanded, keeping an eye on what the master called 'his sure thing'.

CHAPTER FORTY-TWO

Blood splattered the walls in Franklin Clark's South Avenue house. Kyler had held an impromptu quiz show called *Show Me the Portal*. Franklin Clark didn't seem to know any of the answers.

Clark was the third direct descendant of the original islanders who got to play. The other two had fared no better than Clark. Neither knew about the Portal.

Most civilians broke once a family member died before their eyes. Kyler rarely had to go past the first slit throat before he found out what he wanted to know. But old Clark endured the beheadings of his wife and two children, crying and screaming that he had no idea what Kyler was looking for. This took a level of courage Kyler knew the man didn't have. Kyler believed Clark, so he'd been generous. He'd have let a liar live with the vision of his slaughtered family, a memory guaranteed to eat away at the man's sanity. Instead, Clark got the favor of a 9mm through his temple. Kyler had to admit a bit of frustration as he left Clark's house and reentered his pickup.

"He was telling the truth, sir," Kyler said over his shoulder to Oates in the back seat. "He would have cracked if he'd known."

Oates stared out the window, oddly undisturbed by their lack of progress.

"I didn't expect nothing from any of 'em," Oates said. "We're just playing the long shots, waiting for the sure thing."

Kyler looked at Oates in the rearview mirror and waited for some elaboration. Oates looked out the window.

"For now," Oates said, "take me down this street here." He pointed right. "Fifth house on the left."

Up the next side street, an old, low stone fence ran the length of the road. Early settlers used the most abundant, useless natural resource, rocks, to fence their property. Well behind it stood the original farmhouse where Harry Rogers had lived in 1720. The Rogers barn hadn't fared as well, and newer homes now covered its location and the grazing area that used to surround it.

The Dodge Ram pulled into the driveway of one of the homes, a nice, white, two-story Cape Cod. Two rocking chairs sat on a welcoming covered porch. The attached garage was closed. A small sign at the end of the polished stone walkway read: *The Greenes Welcome You!*

It didn't look like anyone was home, but that was hard to judge today.

"Burn it to the ground," said Oates. "I need this space clear."

"Yes, sir," Kyler said. A smile broke out across his face. "The occupants?"

"Save 'em the trouble of relocating," Oates said.

Kyler stepped out of the truck and slung his assault rifle over his shoulder. He shut the door and strode to the Cape Cod's porch. He tried the front door. Locked. He swung the submachine gun off his shoulder. A short burst from the barrel disintegrated the doorframe in a shower of splinters. He kicked open the door and entered.

Even from the outside, the soundtrack was enough to know what was happening within. Screams. Several bursts of gunfire. Bangs and clatters from within the garage.

Minutes later, Kyler backed out the front door, laying a trail of gasoline from a two-gallon can. He threw the can back inside the house. Stepping off the porch and into the front yard, he grabbed a grenade from his web belt and pulled the pin.

In the cathedral quiet of the day, the handle made a ringing ping as it released from the grenade and cartwheeled to the ground. Kyler lobbed it, underhand and easy, like he was tossing a ball to a child. The grenade almost floated through the air and through the front door. A sharp thump said it hit the far wall inside.

Kyler turned away and bent down. He covered his ears, cracked open his mouth, and closed his eyes.

An explosion rocked the house hard enough to make the ground tremble. Balls of orange flame blew out the glass in every window. Bits of burning curtain and window frame landed in the yard and set miniature bonfires. Kyler stood and appraised the house.

Both stories were ablaze, and burning nicely. Smoke alarms screamed warbling warnings that soon stopped as they too succumbed to the flames. He gave it an hour or so before it was nothing but a concrete pad covered in charcoal dust. He gave his handiwork an approving nod and then took his seat in the pickup.

"Do we need to check out that 'sure thing' you mentioned to get the Portal, sir?"

"No," Oates said, completely dispassionate. "I got my eye on that. We're heading to the marina."

CHAPTER FORTY-THREE

Charlie Cauble shivered in the marina dock house. The propane heater was on, but it took a while to get the chill out of everything inside the little shack, and the weak morning sun wasn't helping out at all. He'd opened on time, despite the power outage that looked like it turned most of the town dark. He was prepared to brag about his old-fashioned wind-up alarm clock to the first person blaming a late start on the lack of electricity.

The vacant dock out the window made him smile. The black speedboat must have slipped out during the night. Charlie thought good riddance to that and the creepy owner, Oates.

While he certainly had no problem keeping his own company, it struck him as strange that he hadn't seen anyone else so far that morning. No one fished the harbor, no one drove down Main Street.

He tapped on his cell phone. No signal at all, and harborside usually had the strongest reception, right near the downtown cell tower. He picked up the dock house landline. No dial tone. He slipped the phone back into the cradle.

The light, happy feeling that bubbled up when he first saw the black boat missing drained away, replaced by the sensation that something had gone very wrong on the island.

The roar of twin motors sounded in the distance. Charlie raised a set of binoculars to his eyes. A boat traversed the harbor breakwater, enveloped in a blast of white spray from the slap of the ocean's chop. Then a black bow cut through the white and the low-slung shape of the black boat he dreaded emerged. It entered the calmer harbor waters and its engines cut back to half throttle. Charlie dropped the binoculars back on the table.

Charlie felt a lot less excited about making it to work on time.

The boat slowed as it approached the dock. Five young, rail-thin women sat in the cockpit. The breeze blew back their long, straight black hair, exposing a tattooed ring of thorns around the base of each one's pale neck. Three of the women were white, one Hispanic and one Asian. Heavy, kohl-colored eyeliner rimmed their eyes and extended to an upswept tip over cheekbones powdered bright white.

The boat glided up to the dock and stopped without reversing engines. It didn't roll, didn't pitch, didn't move one inch from horizontal. The women stood. All wore different cuts of black leather coats, the Hispanic woman's as long as a Western duster. Underneath, two wore long, flowing, high-slit skirts, two wore black pants, and the Asian woman had a black leather mini and fishnet hose. All wore thigh-high boots with five-inch heels.

Back when his wild oats still needed sowing, Charlie'd had his fair share of the opposite sex. At his age now, he'd gone from a quick succession of female purchases to merely window-shopping. But something about these women made his blood race hot, made his heart throb in his chest, something more than their obvious physical allure. They had an aura, a sensation about them.

The Asian woman led the group as they disembarked. She paused on the twin-triangle design carved in the cockpit floor, and turned left. She stepped up onto the gunwale.

The boat still repelled Charlie. Its unnatural arrival made his skin crawl. The women's thorn tattoos were so ultra-realistic that they made him wince and their pale skin reminded him of corpses. Yet he felt hypnotized, even magnetized to approach them, to help them. He walked to the edge of the dock, reached across to the motionless boat, and offered the Asian woman his hand. She laid her palm in his.

Her touch sent a shudder up his arm, like touching a block of ice on a hot summer day. His palm burned, his fingertips went numb. She stepped up and onto the dock. He looked into her eyes and felt the promise of fulfillment of every physical desire he'd ever had, or ever would have. His member went to full, pulsing attention. He sighed and nearly forgot to inhale again.

She released his hand and he felt adrift on a vast ocean. He reached down and took the next woman's hand. The sensation repeated as he helped the next three women from the boat, three more encounters with bliss, three more crashes at its departure.

The Hispanic woman was the last to leave. She carried a twisted wooden staff topped with a golden goat's head. The goat's ruby eyes sparkled as if the thing were alive.

Perfect eyebrows arched over her deep brown eyes, eyes that promised all manners of paradise. The plunging neckline of her jacket revealed her voluptuous breasts. She lowered her chin, and one sweep of her thick black lashes made Charlie's knees weak. His hand shook as he extended it to her.

She took his hand and alighted onto the dock. Charlie stared at her perfect profile and his heart raced.

Something dark and dangerous flashed in the woman's eyes. She bent forward and kissed Charlie's lips. Her mouth was ice-cold but his body caught fire. She squeezed his cheeks with her hand and forced his mouth open. Her tongue darted in, caressed his, and swept him to the edge of ecstasy.

Her warm tongue turned cold and scaly. It thinned and coiled itself around Charlie's like a snake. Every ounce of passion, every drop of desire, fled Charlie. The cold in his hand swept through the rest of his body. Pictures flashed by: blood sacrifice, people tortured, flames, the symbol in the boat cockpit, Oates' face. He jerked his head away, mouth opened wide in terror.

The woman opened hers in a smile and showed a damp, bright red palate, blazing white teeth, and a long forked reptilian tongue. She flicked it out and swept it around her lips. She released Charlie's hand, winked and walked away.

One Thanksgiving, Charlie's mom had prepared a beautiful, golden-brown, glistening turkey. But when his father carved it, a rank stench filled the air. Beneath the golden skin hid a rotting carcass, black as coal. The turkey had spoiled. Decayed flesh oozed as the knife ran across it.

His reaction to that fetid bird filled Charlie's mind as he understood the empty, evil interior of the woman's soul. Anything good in there was long-dead, or more accurately, sacrificed.

The five walked up the dock, symbols of seduction as their butts swayed with each synchronized step of their stiletto heels. The women moved with authority, like five dark queens entering their kingdom at last. They formed a tight, perfect *V*, led by the Hispanic woman with the goat's head cane.

Witch, he corrected himself. The kiss had given him that much insight. *They are witches.*

The Ram pickup pulled up to the end of the dock, the same pickup he'd seen leave the ferry the day before. The five climbed into the cab in the rear and closed the tailgate. The truck drove off up Main Street, turned a corner, and was out of sight.

Charlie fought back the urge to vomit at the realization of what had been in his mouth, and his dazed acquiescence to take it. He grabbed a piling for support. Then he remembered the boat beside him. Oates was still onboard, and whatever evil force those witches commanded, he could certainly best them.

Then he remembered. At the captivating sight of the women, he didn't realize Oates wasn't at the wheel when the boat arrived. No one was.

He spun to face *Killin' Time*. Half-inch lines secured the motionless vessel fore and aft to cleats on the dock. Seconds ago, they hadn't been there. Charlie retreated a few steps back across the pier, then bolted for land.

CHAPTER FORTY-FOUR

Scott stood inside the locked doors of All Soul's Church. The wooden door shook with each pounding knock.

Scaravelli stood on the other side of the door, and waist-deep in this nightmare unfolding around town. The folks working for the Devil were playing for high stakes, and Scaravelli had anted up at the same table. Scott needed a weapon.

He looked around the church. He needed something he could swing. Everything with any weight to it was bolted to the wall or floor. The large wooden cross still lay across the sanctuary floor.

He raced to the altar and propped the cross against its side. He lifted his foot and brought it down hard at the junction. The horizontal cross member broke with a loud crack into a piece five-feet-long, with a jagged, splintered end. Scott picked it up and liked its heft.

Loud banging came from the church door again. Scott ran to the back of the church and stood beside the door. He raised the wooden piece to his shoulder.

"Scott," he heard from the other side of the door. "It's Milo."

Milo? Scott thought. *What the hell is he doing out here?*

"Scott," Milo called. "Things are really bad in town. I need your help. Please let me in."

Scott hesitated. The insanity that had spread through town had fueled a bit of paranoia in him. He remembered how Milo had spoken to him out at Canale Road, ordering him out of the area. That Milo had sounded like he was part of the problem, not part of the solution.

But Canale Road Milo hadn't sounded like himself. This Milo did, and he sounded like he needed help badly. Scott didn't think the deputy had the acting chops to pull that lie off.

Scott reached over and threw the lock to open. His faith came with reservations. If Milo entered with his gun drawn, Scott was going to break his wrist. Scott stepped to the side, five feet of shattered wood at the ready.

"C'mon in, Milo."

The door crept open. Milo entered slowly, his weapon holstered. Scott lowered the broken cross.

"Hey, Milo," Scott said.

Milo looked a bit taken aback by the makeshift club in Scott's hand. "Scott?"

"Hey, sorry, Milo. The town has gone nuts. I have trust issues."

"No," Milo said. "I deserve that. I'm sorry for how I treated you out at the crime scene Thursday night."

"Don't worry about it."

"The town is falling apart. I've been looking all over Stone Harbor for you. I went to your house, the store, and everywhere else. I recognized your truck in the parking lot. Looks like it barely made it here."

"Believe it or not," Scott said, "we got attacked by a dog."

"Oh, I believe it," Milo said. "Dogs have gone wild all over town. I'd swear they're patrolling the town, trying to keep everyone inside their homes."

"So that German shepherd wasn't just after me? That's a relief, sort of."

"That's about all you can feel good about," Milo said. "Did you see those fake FBI agents at the crime scene?"

"Oh, yeah," Scott said.

"Well, Scaravelli is in deep with them," Milo said. "I don't know what to believe about the Krieger killing, or anything else that happened in the last few days. I do know the some guy named Oates is pulling all the strings."

"Milo," Scott said, "he's not just some guy."

Allie came down from the choir loft.

"Hi, Ms. Layton," Milo said.

Scott thought Milo was absurdly formal, and then realized Milo was talking to the big TV star of *Malibu Beach*, whom he'd never met.

"It's 'Allie' back home," she said to Milo. "Nice to meet you. I was afraid you were Scaravelli."

"Looks like Milo is with us," Scott said. "Let's see if we can fill in each other's gaps."

The three stood in the back of the church and exchanged stories. Milo brought Scott and Allie up to date on Scaravelli's state of uselessness back at the station, and the deployment of the five felons around town. He introduced them to Oates' right-hand man, Kyler. Scott filled in Milo on

Oates' true identity. It took a little convincing to get Milo to believe that Satan walked the Earth. Milo bought in when he saw the twin-triangle design burned into the church and remembered how Scaravelli had warned him to give Oates a wide berth. Allie told Milo about the Portal the men were searching for, and how protecting it cost the reverend his life.

"Did the reverend know where it is, this Portal?" Milo asked.

Allie started to answer, but Scott cut her off.

"We're not sure," he said. "We're here trying to figure that part out."

"Wait here a sec," Milo said.

He headed out to his cruiser. He stopped short and looked out toward town. A pillar of black smoke rose from the horizon. He muttered a curse and shook his head. He jogged to the car and popped the trunk. He rooted around inside for a moment, then pulled out a spare police walkie-talkie. He ran to the church, switched on the power, and handed it to Allie.

"Now there's a fire somewhere in town. I need to check it. I'm not sure the fire volunteers will respond and I don't blame them. If you find the Portal, call me on the radio. Just key the mike twice and I'll key it back three times. Don't say anything. I'm sure the chief, Oates, and Kyler are monitoring the radio. You click, and I'll meet you back here. I know where we can hide the Portal."

"Where?" Scott said.

"Down in the vault at the Fisherman's Bank," Milo said. "It's got five inches of steel on all sides. I don't think that there's anything on the island that can blow it open. At a minimum, it'll slow them down. Soon, people on the mainland will realize we're without power and communication, and they'll send help."

"You can get into the vault?" Allie said.

"Sure thing," Milo said. "Local police privileges give me a key to the door. And since my father was the manager for years, the current manager trusted me with the combination to the safe in the event of an emergency. This sure qualifies as one."

Scott looked at Milo, and realized for the first time that Milo really was a police officer. Since they had shared their stories in the church, any anxiety Milo had displayed had vanished. He spoke with authority and self-assurance. His shirt seemed to fit properly for once, not hanging on him in its usual oversized way. Scott thought about Milo sneaking around under the noses of six heavily armed men, risking his life to help keep the townspeople safe. Satan's arrival had let loose some horrible events, but it had also allowed the real Milo to emerge.

"We'll call you as soon as we know anything," Scott said. "Go check on that fire."

Milo nodded and went out to his cruiser. He pulled away and Scott closed and locked the church front door. With Milo gone, he was certain the German shepherd would be back for them, like the crocodile waiting for Captain Hook.

"Why didn't you let me tell him about the scroll?" Allie asked.

"Oates and his men have no limits on getting information," Scott said. "If Milo gets caught, best he knows as little as possible in case that scroll can help us find the Portal."

Allie's face fell a bit at the mention of Milo being tortured. "I guess you're right." She turned and approached the choir loft stairs. "I'll be right back with the scroll. We have a deposit to make at the Fisherman's Bank."

CHAPTER FORTY-FIVE

Allie returned to the first floor with the leather scroll. Scott sat on the floor, his back against the two locked doors. Allie sat next to him. She wrapped her right arm inside his, as she did a hundred times when they used to sit on the porch of his house a few lifetimes ago.

"Scottie," she said, "with Milo's help, we have a good chance, right?"

He grabbed her hand in his.

"You bet, Allie Cat," he said. He kissed her cheek. His lips felt warm, reassuring. "We'll find the Portal first, and lock it up tight."

Allie released Scott's hand and spread the scroll out in front of the two of them. The warm smell of aged leather wafted up. The faded writing was much easier to read in the brighter light of the church than it had been in the bell tower. It read:

Fathers tell ye sons of difficult times
When Satan's footsteps pounded our streets,
When earnest men's courage was put to the trial
The future demands ye copy these feats.

"It's a poem," Allie said.

"And no offense to the Snows, not too good a poem."

"Why a poem?"

"It would be easier to remember," Scott said. "The *Ring Around the Rosie* nursery rhyme was written in the Middle Ages to warn people about the symptoms of the Black Plague. People remember rhymes. The Snows must have known that."

The next section read:

Commit to memory these facts that you read
Which we cull from righteous men's true testament,

And the angelic vision of Brother Snow
Which arrived on the morrow, 'twas Heaven sent.

Five lasses turned witches, virgin and flowing
Did gather at Rogers' humble home manger,
To open the doorway twixt Earth and below
Led by a visiting unholy stranger.

"'Flowing' virgins wouldn't mean what I think, would it?" Scott said, his face betraying his discomfort. "What difference could that make?"

"There are a whole host of higher hormone levels active," Allie said. "The women may be better able to connect with the Portal. What is it with men and periods anyway?" Allie shook her head and kept reading:

Satan did guide the young girls in their studies
Of chanting and summoning spirits condemned,
He sent the Portal that could open the gate
And allow the return of ones who'd descend.

Wooden and gold, the span one fifth of a rod
With carvings that speak of vile creatures and sin,
It can't be destroyed, it can't be reduced
Till its awful purpose completed has been.

"That must describe the Portal," Allie said. "What is a 'span one fifth of a rod'?"

"It's an archaic unit of measurement," Scott said. "I don't remember how long that it, but it must be small enough to carry."

"Indestructible," Allie said. "Just the kind of description I *wasn't* hoping for."

She continued:

Be warned of the powers that Satan commands
Base Lucifer travels through ether at will,
Only water confounds him, binds him to land
So watch sharp, his return wilt be by ship still.

> *Brave men wrested the Portal from Satan's grasp*
> *Sparing the island from the foul witches' worst,*
> *It lies now secreted and safely hidden*
> *Guarded with great care from the very first.*

"That's it?" Scott said. "What kind of explanation is that for where they hid the thing? It has always been guarded, but *where*? Is there more on that?"

Allie scanned ahead.

"Nope," she said, and kept reading:

> *The future wilt come and two worlds wilt align*
> *Again in these places of which we now speak,*
> *Be enlightened, return to combat the evil*
> *With new strength that is born from flesh once so weak.*

"Instructions for each son to go off to divinity school?" Allie said.

"Sounds like it."

> *Trust not the beasts or ones who've made compacts*
> *Through deeds completed with the angel cast down,*
> *The wicked one doth bend weak constitutions*
> *And force a betrayal of God, men, and town.*

> *The Portal's opening can only be blocked*
> *Sealed closed by the blood of descendants of Snow,*
> *Shirk not the commission your birthright demands*
> *When tokens appear, response dare not be slow.*

"That's not good," Allie said. "If only the descendants of the Snow family can stop this thing, we're out of luck."

"Maybe that's not literal," Scott offered. "Perhaps it meant that the knowledge descended from the Snow family."

"Or maybe it's exactly what the angel told Brother Snow in his vision," Allie countered. She wrung her hands. "And now the last Snow is gone."

"But Reverend Snow chose to tell you about the Portal," Scott said. "He had to know you could close it."

"He said he needed help," Allie said. "Not a replacement."

She continued:

> *Commit to your mem'ry this tale of the day*
> *When forefathers halted the end of our times,*
> *For by no mean effort you must do the same*
> *Or pass to your sons this instruction in rhyme.*

"That confirms everything we thought about the reverend's family involvement," Scott said, "and tells us what the Portal looks like."

"And almost where it is," Allie said.

"Almost," Scott said.

The two sat and stared at the stanza that was supposed to direct them to the Portal, hoping that some hidden word had escaped their understanding when they read it the first time.

Allie looked up at the altar, desecrated and damaged. Her eyes passed down the aisle, back to the parchment in front of her. She looked back up the aisle at the marble slab on the floor with the inscription she had memorized as a child:

ZEBEDEE SNOW
FIRST RECTOR OF ALL SOULS CHURCH
APRIL 14, 1680 – OCTOBER 22, 1770
"With God, all things are possible."

The word *first* jumped up off the floor at her.

"Scottie," she said as the realization hit her. "Maybe the scroll doesn't mean that the Portal was guarded 'with great care' from the beginning. It means it is protected 'with great care from the first', or the first Reverend Snow."

She stood up and walked over to the marble slab. She pointed down.

"I'll bet you it is buried right here in Zebedee Snow's grave. The reverend patted the floor when he told me how the Snows had kept the town safe. He wasn't talking about the church, as I assumed. He was talking about what was *under* the church."

Scott stood and walked over to the marker. He knelt and ran his fingers along the edges. The right side's center had a small recess cut into the edge. He blew some dirt out of it.

"Assuming you're right," he said, "and I think you are, we are going to need to get this stone up."

Allie looked out the window.

"And we have at least one rabid dog that will keep us from getting any tools to make that happen," she said.

Scott thought a minute, and then his face lit up.

"I've got it," he said. "Wait here."

He ran back to the rear of the church and up the steps to the choir loft. Allie heard a door slam and seconds later, slam again. Scott returned lugging the tower bell's heavy clapper.

He tapped the clapper's round end against the marble. The result sounded hollow. He flipped it, held the ball end in his hand, and wedged the tongue into the recess between the old oak floor and the marble slab. It was a perfect fit.

"Yeah, that can't be a coincidence," Allie said.

"It explains why the clapper was left on the floor beside the scroll's hiding place," Scott said. He knelt beside it, gave the clapper a wiggle to fully seat it, then wrapped both hands around the bulbous end. "Tell me I'm the first man you've ever desecrated a grave with."

"Sure. If that makes you feel better."

A brief smile flickered across Scott's face, then his jaw set in determination. "Here we go."

He pressed down on the clapper. Stone ground against wood. The marker rose.

CHAPTER FORTY-SIX

Scott leaned all his weight against the clapper. The marker lifted off the floor a few inches. A whoosh of air escaped from the seam, heavy with the smell of mold and damp earth. Scott coughed and turned away.

Allie reached down and wedged her fingers into the fissure. The sharp edge cut into the back of her knuckles. Her biceps burned. She sucked in a deep breath. "Got it, Scottie."

Scott slid the clapper back across the floor. He grabbed the edge beside her. The strain on Allie's shoulders eased.

"Okay," Scott said. "Lift."

They both pulled and the marble marker rose away from them. They heaved until it stood on end, then they gave it a little push and it toppled sideways against the pews. There wasn't just a grave beneath the marker. There was a room.

Scott looked down into the pitch-black hole in the ground. The musty smell intensified, a combination of old earth and rotting wood.

"Allie," he said, "grab some candles from the altar."

Allie went up and removed two white tapers from their gold candleholders. She lit both with the matches nearby, and walked back to Scott, shielding the flames with her hand. She passed one to Scott, and the two knelt together along the opening's edge.

Scott dipped his candle down below the floor. It illuminated a wooden ladder mounted against a packed-earth wall. It was the same design and vintage of the bell tower ladder. The ladder's base disappeared into the darkness.

"Let's see what we've found," Scott said. He swung his feet down into the hole, and descended the ladder. When he stepped off the bottom rung, his head was about four feet below the church floor. He moved away toward the altar. Allie slid over to the ladder, and followed him down.

The light of the two candles was just enough to illuminate the room. It was about twenty feet long and six feet wide, with a floor and walls of hard-packed dark earth. Intermittent thick timbers braced the walls and ran up to attach to the runners of the church subfloor. Several timbers had rotted through at the base and salt rings attested that the subterranean space had harbored standing water several times. The far end of the tomb sat directly under the altar.

The two walked forward. A simple cross hung on the far wall. Below it, at chest height, two stout square beams protruded from the earth and supported a simple black coffin. Insect boreholes peppered the sides. A split board peeled up from the top.

Beneath the coffin, a dark oak chest, three feet square, rested on the floor. Black leather handles hung from each side. The box had no clasp or hinges, and appeared to have been built around what it contained, with no provision for removing the contents. Salt stained the bottom few inches of the buckled wood. Dust-coated cobwebs draped everything like a decaying bridal veil.

Scott reached forward and pulled handfuls of filthy webbing from the casket. In their wake, clouds of dust glittered in the candlelight. The top of the casket had *Z.S.* carved in it.

"It's Zebedee," Allie said. "They really did rebury him under the church when they built it."

"And," Scott said, "they went to all the trouble, and used all the precious manpower, to dig this tomb, so he could stand guard over that." Scott pointed to the box on the floor under the casket.

One of the wall supports behind them creaked.

Scott and Allie shared nervous glances. They went down on their knees. Scott reached out and cleared the cobwebs from the box. Faint lettering read:

Safe from eyes of beast or man
Satan shall not see.
The Portal bur'd 'neath holy ground,
Sealed without a key.

"Holy ground is no protection," Scott said. "Milo's bank vault idea keeps sounding better. Let's get it out of here."

Allie took Scott's candle and placed both of them on the edges of the casket's support beams. Then each reached forward on opposite sides, took a thick leather handle, and lifted. They sidestepped the heavy box from under the casket.

Allie's handle gave way. Her side hit the ground. The box twisted and Scott's handle broke in two. The water-damaged box shattered and crumbled into a pile of rotting wood.

Scott knelt and swept the box's dusty remains away. On the ground lay a three-inch-thick cherry disk, just less than three feet in diameter. Even in the subdued candlelight, the glossy wood shone like it had twenty coats of lacquer. Carved in the center was the twin triangle symbol, inlaid in gold, still brilliant despite its age. Each corner had a strange beast carved into the wood and highlighted in gold. One had the head of a lion grafted to the body of a snake. Another was a hideous half man, half monkey with the wings of a bat. A gryphon. A sea monster. All shared two common traits: they were undeniably malevolent, and each had the furious look of a rabid animal.

In the way fire generates heat, this disk generated the opposite, as if it absorbed the energy and warmth from everything around it. But it wasn't a feeling of cold so much as a feeling of…darkness, an absence of life. An emptiness scarier than anything Scott had ever felt.

Scott's hands trembled and he jerked away from the Portal. The symbols and design reminded him of the stone disk he'd found in the hardware store, the traitorous connection his father had to Oates and ultimately to the evil object at his feet.

"That's got to be…." Scott said.

"Can't you just feel it?" Allie answered.

"I'm glad it's not just me." Scott gritted his teeth and grabbed one edge. The expected cold, hard surface instead felt slimy, like scales on a fish. It almost slithered under his fingertips, as if the Portal was alive. Though he could see his fingers still touching the Portal's face, he sensed that it was drawing him in, enveloping him. His heart galloped in his chest. He dropped the Portal.

"Is it too heavy?" Allie asked, bending over to try to lift it.

"No!" Scott yelled, pushing Allie's hands away from the disk. "Don't touch it. That thing feels…alive."

Allie took a step back from the Portal.

"We need something to carry it in," Scott said.

He climbed out of the crypt. He needed something between his hands and the Portal. He'd settle for two oversized oven mitts.

He saw the white altar cloth, at least six-feet-long and wide enough to wrap the Portal. He approached the altar and grabbed the end of the cloth. Drops of the reverend's dried blood stained its center. A wave of combined loss and anger rolled through him. He flipped one edge over the center to hide the bloodstain, then did the same to the other side, as if burying the reminder of the reverend's suffering in white linen might make it go away. Then he pulled the cloth off the altar and returned to the tomb's edge.

From beneath him, the beams creaked again.

"Scottie?"

The floor sagged a bit at the edge of the opening. The marble slab must have added structural support to the decayed wood. He practically slid down the ladder.

"Let's wrap that thing and get it out of here."

He stepped over and wound the cloth around the Portal, keeping his hands from direct contact, while shielding the bloodstains from Allie. She'd seen more than enough blood today. He wrapped the Portal like a mummy.

"All right," he said. "Let's try this again."

Another moaning creak sounded inside the crypt. The rotted base of one of the timbers snapped. A few pounds of dirt behind it cascaded to the floor in an explosion of dust. One candle snuffed out.

"Scottie?" Allie said, her voice rising.

"Hurry, before we get stuck down here with ol' Zebedee."

They both reached down and lifted an edge of the Portal. The insulation of the altar cloth kept Scott from feeling any of the ill effects of contact. They performed a rapid, awkward sidestep dance to the end of the tomb, the heavy Portal rocking between them. The creak of another beam echoed in the burial vault. A waterfall of dirt flowed over the coffin. The last candle snuffed out. Darkness reclaimed the crypt. The rectangle of light above them from the church offered salvation.

"Hurry, Allie," Scott said. "Up the ladder and I'll pass this to you. Flip it to me."

Allie lifted her end toward Scott. He crouched and bent back. The face of the Portal rested on his chest. His biceps strained. A twinge rippled in his back. No natural wood could be this dense.

"I got it," he gasped. He widened his stance for balance. "Up you go."

Allie scrambled up the ladder into the daylight. Another round of groaning timbers came from the tomb, like some wounded animal trapped in a cave. She lay flat on the floor and looked down at Scott.

"Okay," she said. "Ready!"

Scott flipped the Portal against the ladder and pushed it up, back and forth to clear each rough-hewn rung. Sweat ran into his eyes as the stagnant air began to take its toll on him. His arm muscles started to burn. A sharp crack sounded behind him. Each inch up seemed to take forever.

Clods of earth fell behind him, hard and heavy.

"C'mon, Scottie," Allie said. "I've almost got it."

The edge of the Portal poked above the floor. Allie grabbed the sides and pulled.

Some of the weight lifted off Scott's shoulder. He tucked his right hand under the Portal. He took a deep breath and thrust the Portal skyward like a shot-putter. Allie pulled. The Portal went up, half clearing the floor. For an interminable second, it hung midpoint between the tomb and the church. Then it pivoted and fell to the church floor with a thud.

With two sharp, splintering cracks, the two lower dried-out steps of the ladder gave way. Scott grabbed the ladder rails. The ladder pulled from the wall and he fell backward into the darkness. He slammed the ground hard. Edges of the broken box pierced his back. The shattered ladder pressed down on his chest like prison bars.

"Allie!"

The beam above him exploded with the sound of thunder. A heavy, suffocating rain of earth stormed down on him. The light from the opening winked and disappeared.

Through the falling earth came Allie's muffled scream.

CHAPTER FORTY-SEVEN

The dying flames slow-danced in the charred wreckage of the Greenes' house off South Street. Milo had gotten there way too late. The smell of the arsonist's gasoline still fouled the air. The Greenes' charred corpses were probably somewhere in the steaming wreckage.

As a precaution, he had checked the two homes on either side of the burning house. Both seemed empty. No cars at each house, and no one answered when he knocked. He was glad about that at least. Perhaps they'd already found somewhere safer to hide.

It felt good to meet up with Scott and Allie back at All Souls Church. Saving Stone Harbor, and keeping the Portal out of Oates' hands, wasn't going to be a one-man operation. Scott and Allie weren't law enforcement, but they still moved the odds more in his favor.

He leaned back against the headrest in his cruiser. Waves of exhaustion washed over him. His head seemed to weigh a hundred pounds. He fought to keep his eyes open, but each time he exhaled, his lids drooped lower. He realized that he had been awake for over twenty-four hours. Then, suddenly, he no longer was.

With a jerk, he forced himself awake. Scott and Allie could find the Portal at any time. He slapped his cheeks a few times, hoping the pain would chase away his fatigue. It retreated a bit. But it was just off in the wings, waiting for its cue to return center stage.

From the far end of the street, the black Dodge Ram came his way. He froze at the thought that Oates himself was probably in that truck. Scott had given Milo an excellent description of the stocky, bald man.

The truck approached Milo's cruiser. A bead of sweat rolled down the side of his face. What if they knew he was secretly working against them? Kyler might drive up and pump a dozen rounds from his assault rifle into the cruiser, leaving Milo dead twice over.

He reached down and slid his pistol from its holster. He laid it on his lap, facing the door. He flipped off the safety. No point going down without a fight.

But the pickup never got that far. It pulled into the driveway of the O'Reillys' yellow-trimmed ranch next door. Kyler got out first, rifle at the ready. He went to the front door and knocked with a bold swift kick. The door flew inward and Kyler entered.

Milo slipped his pistol back in his holster.

Seconds later, Kyler reappeared in the doorway. He gave the Ram a thumbs-up. The rear cab door and tailgate popped open. Five young women, all dressed in black seductive clothing, exited the truck. Milo didn't recognize any of them, and he would have because they were all beautiful. They crossed the driveway with purposeful strides. Their high heels clicked against the sidewalk in perfect unison.

Allie had told him about the five witches who tried to activate the Portal three hundred years ago. It was no coincidence that these five monochromatic beauties just happened to arrive in the pickup from Hell. They must be here to cast the spell, mix the potion, or do whatever witches do to activate the gate between the mortal and immortal worlds.

The five women in black might be the last piece Oates needed to be ready to open the Portal, finishing what others interrupted so long ago. If so, it was more important than ever to lock the Portal safely away.

The coven entered the house, then Milo saw him for the first time. Oates got out of the passenger side of the Ram. He was shorter and rounder than Milo expected. He wore all black, an unholy priest without the Roman collar.

Oates crossed the nose of the truck and walked toward the front of the house. He stopped. He turned his head and looked directly at Milo.

Milo was parked one house down from Oates, with old Farmer Rogers' stone fence and a double laminated windshield between them. But it felt as if Oates was right next to him. Milo sensed Oates knew who he was and what he was planning. His skin began to crawl.

Oates smiled, turned, and finished his walk to the front door without another glance back.

Milo exhaled. He shook his head at his sleep-deprived paranoia. There was no way Oates could know what was going on. Milo knew that no one had seen him at the church.

★　　★　　★

Camille led the coven into the O'Reilly house. A white couch, loveseat, and recliner faced a glass coffee table. Framed, homemade needlepoint hung on the wall beside a collection of children's school pictures. Kyler stood at the far end of the living room, in the doorway to the kitchen. He held his rifle high, eyeing the women in black. He flicked the barrel toward the living room furniture.

Camille thought it funny how Kyler had obviously worked so hard to keep some distance between him and her coven since he'd picked them up at the dock, just as he had when they'd met in the apartment. Unlike the old man at the dock, he'd obviously been warned. Took all the fun out of it.

Oates followed them in. Her first sight of him at the dock made her shiver with anticipation. She hadn't seen him since the last witch's recruitment, yet he still stirred that amazing sense of longing for completeness within her, that understanding that being close to him, being part of him, would made her more than she had ever dreamed possible. He'd stayed in the front of the truck all the way back from the dock, hadn't shared a word of greeting with her. It didn't matter. He didn't have to. She knew he felt the same way she did, ecstatic at their reunion, thrilled about their future.

Oates stood in the doorway and cleared his throat.

"Ladies," he started, "your time is here. The moment has come for you to join me forever in my kingdom."

Camille's heart skipped a beat. Smiles broke out on the witches' faces. They all knew why they were here, but it felt good hearing it from Oates.

"Mr. Kyler and I, we're gonna retrieve the Portal. Make yourselves at home. Don't leave."

Oates raised two fingers and motioned Kyler to the door. Kyler tucked his rifle close to his chest and shuffled well around the women to get to Oates. The two passed out of the house. Kyler tried to shut the door behind him, but with the shattered lock, it creaked back open a few inches.

"Well, girls," Camille said to the group. "Years of preparation, all for this."

"The power of two worlds at our fingertips," Ivana, the Asian witch, said dreamily.

"And eternity with the Master," Camille added.

Without discussion, the five sat in a circle on the living room floor, facing each other. They joined hands, closed their eyes, and began to chant in Latin, practicing the phrases that would bring the Portal to life, and transport them to rule in Satan's dominion.

CHAPTER FORTY-EIGHT

Out past the church on West Street, Ramirez sat on the hood of his hated Taurus, a few hours past completely bored. All day, a whole lot of nothing had happened. He'd spent more productive hours in a jail cell. Ramirez had a little fun with the wimp when he went into the man's house for breakfast, but the little guy just couldn't go the distance, and Ramirez had to finish him early. Since then, it had been a dull day watching the sun crawl across the sky.

At the far end of the street, the red Ford F-150 from the used-car lot lumbered toward him. In the front seat sat his favorite chronic asshole, Ricco. Just what he needed. Ricco pulled up next to the Taurus and sprouted a shit-eating grin. Ramirez sat straight up. His finger caressed his rifle's trigger.

"Say, Paco," Ricco said. "Nice wheels."

"What the hell are you doing here? Aren't you supposed to be at the other end of town?"

"I got bored," Ricco said. "Nothing going on, so I went for a drive. What do you care? You my boss now, asswipe?"

"I wouldn't hire a pussy like you," Ramirez fired back.

Ricco's face went deep red. "You know, motherfucker, I've had about enough of your shit. I ought to cap your sorry ass right here."

Ramirez pointed his M4 at the truck cab. "Try it, asshole. I'm begging you to."

They both fired. Muzzle flashes lit up the inside of the truck in concert with a spit of Ramirez's rifle fire. Rounds blew holes both ways through the pickup's door. One caught Ramirez in the leg and spun him off the hood of the car. He hit the pavement hard.

Ricco kicked the truck door open. Smoke wafted from the barrel of the rifle across his lap. He got out of the truck and looked over the car's fender for Ramirez.

Ramirez's thigh screamed in pain but his mind screamed louder for revenge. He raised his rifle up with one hand in the direction of Ricco's triumphant face and fired.

The recoil of the rounds walked the gun up and right like an oscillating sprinkler. A spray of rounds blasted through and then past Ricco to pepper the Ford. Ricco's body jerked like a kid's marionette with each hit. One round tore his jaw from his face. Blood splatter painted the air in a rosy mist. Ricco's rifle flew from his hand, and he fell backward into the truck. His lifeless legs hung askew out the open door.

Ramirez's rifle clicked empty. The gunpowder haze drifted away and exposed a truck that now looked more like a colander. Not one window survived the barrage.

Ramirez felt like he'd just sprayed insecticide on a hornet's nest and exterminated a pest, but his happiness lasted only seconds. His leg throbbed with pain. Blood spurted from his wound like a gusher, keeping perfect time with his fading pulse.

"Son of a bitch," he sighed, and sat up against the Taurus. He knew an arterial wound when he saw one. He clamped a hand over the hole in his leg and squeezed. Pain bolted straight up his spine to his brain. Blood pulsed through his fingers. Without a tourniquet, he'd bleed to death in no time.

He whipped off his belt and strapped it around his leg. He pulled, then screamed as he cinched it tight. He dared look down at the wound. The flow of blood slowed, but didn't stop. A stay of execution, not a pardon.

"Madre de Dios," he whispered. He didn't want to die here on this stinking island in the middle of nowhere. He looked up at the bullet-ridden pickup and at Ricco's still, splayed legs. Blood dripped out of the truck's doorsill.

At least that prick went first, he thought.

*   *   *

Across the rest of the island, similar scenes played out. Without Kyler's enforcement, bloodlust shattered the thugs' thin veneer of discipline. Chaos stepped through.

At the marina, Santiago decided a grenade launcher was a terrible thing to waste. He pumped a few rounds into some pleasure boats, enjoying the thrill of watching gas tanks explode. The toxic fumes from the burning fiberglass drifted over the dock and into the town on the sea breeze.

At the Harbor Road checkpoint, Washington and Culpepper had liberated some hard liquor, and used the street as a shooting gallery. They had made bets on hitting this window or that mailbox, and missed far more than they nailed. The street looked like a war zone.

Isolated and alone, stripped of technology, terrified families huddled together, unclear as to what was happening, and unknowing as to why. People cowered in the back of their homes and prayed that the shooting outside wasn't the precursor to a personal visit. The snarls of patrolling dogs met their glances out back windows.

The chief of police, drunk in the town's only jail cell, looked down and wondered why he hadn't had the good fortune to choke to death on the vomit he'd just sprayed on the floor.

The lock to seal the town's fate clicked closed at the smoking shell of the Greenes' former dream house. Oates pounded an inverted steel cross into the ground. Three hundred years earlier, he had done the same thing when the Rogers barn stood here, the precise location of the weakest spot between the world he could rule below and this one he coveted. Very soon, the planet would begin to re-form in his own glorious image.

CHAPTER FORTY-NINE

Clouds of dust billowed out of the dark opening to the crypt in All Souls Church. Grit filled Allie's eyes as she batted at the brown mist, trying to clear a view into the gloom that had swallowed Scott. She coughed as the dust coated the inside of her throat.

"Scottie!" she yelled. "Answer me!"

A cough rose from inside the crypt. A hand appeared on the lowest visible rung of the ladder.

"I'm here, Allie," Scott said. "Let me get my feet out of this."

Earth scraped and shifted below her, then a second hand reached up and grabbed a higher rung. Two forearms appeared and Scott's face came out of the shadows, covered in dirt and sweat. He'd never looked better.

"Oh, you scared me," she said.

"That time," Scott said, "*I* scared me."

Allie slid back across the floor and Scott pulled himself out of the tomb. He swept the heaviest dust off his clothes and wiped his face partially clean with his shirt. He winced and Allie saw splintered wood sticking out of his back.

"Scottie, don't move," she said. She stepped behind him. Three jagged slivers, each a few inches long, stuck through his shirt. Damp blood stained his shirt around each one.

"Is it as bad back there as it feels?"

"How bad does it feel?"

"Like railroad spikes."

"More like big splinters. I'm going to pull them out."

"Okay, give me some—"

Allie yanked the biggest one out.

"Ow!" Scott winced. "Damn, give me some warning."

"Warning." She pulled out the next two, rapid-fire. Scott flinched with each. None had penetrated very deep. She pressed against the wounds to stop the bleeding.

"Thanks, sort of," Scott said. "The beams collapsed and it was like being trapped in the bottom of an hourglass." He looked down at the Portal, wrapped in white, ready for shipment. "Let's call Milo and put that thing behind steel walls."

Allie pulled her hand from his wounds. Blood blotted her palms. It looked like the blood had clotted. She gave Scott's shoulders a light caress, and then picked up the police walkie-talkie. She keyed the mike twice.

There was no response. She waited another few seconds. Still only silence. She keyed the mike twice again.

"Scottie," she said, "what if—"

Three quick clicks blipped from the walkie-talkie. Milo was on his way.

Scott opened the door an inch and scanned the quiet, empty lot. The passenger door on his battered truck still hung open.

"What's our dog count?" Allie said.

"Looks like zero."

"Do you think it died?"

"Do you think we're having that lucky of a day?"

Minutes later, Milo's cruiser pulled up in front of the church. He bounded out and up the steps.

"You have it?" Milo asked.

"Ready for you to seal in the vault," Scott said.

He ushered Milo up to the Portal. Milo took a wide-eyed look at the ragged, gaping hole in the church floor, then bent down and started to unwrap the altar cloth. Scott reached down and grabbed his hand.

"You don't want to touch it," he said as folded the altar cloth back over the Portal. "The thing feels completely unnerving. I can't describe it, but trust me, it's very unpleasant."

Milo stood up.

"I'll take your word for it," he said. He turned to Allie. "Allie, you said that originally five girls turned to witchcraft and they were the ones who could activate the Portal back in 1720, right?"

"That's the story we have," Allie said.

"Well, I think I've seen their twenty-first-century replacements. Oates and Kyler escorted five women who had the 'witch look' mastered into the O'Reilly house a little while ago. I didn't recognize any of them."

"They're here for Oates' Portal party," Scott said. "If Satan couldn't open the Portal himself back then, he can't do it now. He'll need the strength of their souls to power the doorway open. There's a weak spot between the two realities on the island near the Rogerses' old farmhouse, which is a stone's throw from the O'Reillys'. I'll bet they'll hold the ceremony in the exact same location."

"All the more reason to lock this away now," Allie said, nudging the Portal with her foot. "It looks like Oates may have everything in place that he needs."

"I checked the bank on the way here," Milo said. "The vault is secure ready."

"Let's do it then," Scott said. "We'll follow you in my truck. Allie, get the door. Milo, you and I lift."

Allie went to the front door of the church and opened it a few inches. "It's clear."

Scott and Milo bent down and each took a side of the swaddled Portal. They lifted, and side by side, they shuffled to the rear of the church. Allie opened the door wide and the two of them stepped out into the daylight. They walked down the few steps to the cruiser until they stood behind it, Milo on the driver's side. They rested the Portal on the ground against the rear bumper. Milo popped open the trunk.

Allie stopped halfway down the steps. "Scottie! The scroll! We'd better bring it." She reentered the church.

The edge of the woods exploded with motion. The German shepherd burst from the tree line at an unnatural speed, face twisted in a vicious snarl, broken silver chain whipping behind it. Two other, only slightly smaller dogs followed behind it, teeth bared, eyes blazing red.

Scott and Milo threw the Portal in the trunk and slammed the lid. Scott turned back toward the church.

Deep barking and snarling suddenly surrounded them. Packs of dogs charged from both other sides of the lot. Scott swiveled his head and saw they were about to be swarmed. He identified a Weimaraner, a boxer, and then it was all tails, snouts, and teeth.

The door to the church reopened. Allie stepped out holding the scroll.

Scott's heart stopped. "Allie! No!"

Two mutts split from the pack and rocketed for the front steps. Allie froze and her face went white. In a split second, the dogs hit the front steps. One leapt straight for Allie's neck.

She raised her arms in the nick of time. The dog hit Allie like an avalanche and sank its jaws into her forearm. Teeth ground against bone. Allie screamed.

Allie jumped back through the doorway. She slammed the heavy church door shut on the dog's muzzle with a sickening crunch. The dog yelped and let go. The door closed, and just in time. The second dog hit it head-on and dropped to the steps with a whimper.

Scott's instinct was to run to his wounded Allie. But the rest of the pack was closing fast. Milo jumped into his cruiser's front seat. Scott was closer to his truck. He dove inside and slammed the door behind him.

A roiling sea of fur and fangs engulfed the vehicles. Bodies pounded the sides of the cars. Toenails scratched against steel. Snouts flashed by the window, delivering deafening barks and spitting saliva from bared teeth.

On the church doorstep, the two dogs from the failed assault on Allie had roused themselves to rejoin the attack. Dogs bounded back and forth in the space between the truck and the church door.

Milo started his cruiser. He honked the horn for Scott's attention. He mouthed something unintelligible over the canine din. He shook his head in frustration, pointed to the parking lot exit, then to the trunk of his car, then in the general direction of the bank downtown.

Scott nodded and waved him forward. Milo peeled out. The dogs still moved lightning-quick, and darted out of the way in time to avoid being crushed under the cruiser's wheels.

Scott looked back over the seething pack to the church. Allie's face appeared in a window, scared, but not panicked. Her hand gripped the bleeding wound in her arm. She watched the cruiser scream out of the parking lot, then turned to Scott.

The pack wasn't giving up. With the police car gone, it now filled the space between the church and Scott's truck. The dogs had stopped attempting an outright assault, but they still swirled in the space like a school of circling piranha, filling the air with barking and growling, as if waiting for a chance at the first person out in the open.

Scott's and Allie's eyes met. He knew they shared the same thoughts. Neither was going to get to the other, not now. Time was running out to secure the Portal.

Allie made a circular motion with one finger, and pointed to the parking lot exit. She shouted the silent word, "Go!"

Behind the church's heavy door and thick wall, Allie was safe for now. But still, he couldn't leave her. He couldn't shake the sensation that if he separated from her now, he wouldn't see her again.

Her face turned angry. She pointed again, with twice the emphasis, and mouthed "*Now!*"

He knew she was right. He started the truck. "I'll be back!" he shouted. Since she couldn't hear him, he wondered if he'd said it more to reassure himself.

He punched it and headed for the exit.

Dogs scattered before him, a parting of the Canine Sea. He stopped at the church exit and looked back. The dogs had reformed around the church exits. Whether to keep Allie in or to keep others out he couldn't tell.

He pulled out and headed for the bank.

CHAPTER FIFTY

As he drove to the bank, the fate of the town and more rested squarely on Milo's shoulders. He felt every ounce of the weight. A thousand bad things could happen between the church and the bank vault. Oates' thugs could attack him. He could get a flat tire. The bank vault might not open. Fire from the Greene house could set downtown aflame. Kyler might already be inside the bank. The list seemed endless.

The enormity of the situation threatened to overwhelm him. The Portal. Where did it come from? How did it work? Why was it in Stone Harbor of all places?

There was no denying the otherworldliness of the artifact. Scott had warned Milo how odd it felt to touch it. Milo didn't doubt him. Even locked away in the trunk, its pulsing, unmistakable evil inspired fear and dread. The Portal wasn't some static doorway between the two dimensions, but felt more like a throbbing, living conduit. He couldn't wait to seal it behind a mass of steel and brick.

Milo approached Main Street. He slowed the cruiser to a crawl. The bank was only blocks away. He scanned right and left, looking for Oates or any of his crew, and ready at the first sign of trouble to slam the accelerator through the floorboards. But the streets were empty. He figured Oates and Kyler were still at the O'Reilly place with the wicked witch convention. He only needed them there a few more minutes.

"How ya doin'?" a guttural voice called from the cruiser's back seat.

Milo's heart stopped. Oates' round face filled the rearview mirror.

"Allow me to introduce myself," Oates said. "I'm—"

"Satan," Milo finished for him.

Oates waved his hand dismissively. "You could say. Everyone calls me Joey Oates."

Milo stared at Oates' cold black eyes in the mirror. They both mesmerized and terrified him at the same time.

Kyler's black Dodge Ram roared off Main Street and skidded to a stop across the cruiser's nose. Kyler got out and walked down the cruiser's driver's side. He gave Milo a menacing smile.

Oates disappeared from the back seat and reappeared in the front. Milo startled and slid closer to the door. Kyler opened the rear door and slid into the seat behind Milo.

"Good to see you again, buddy," Kyler said. "I was afraid I'd miss seeing you."

"You got something of mine," Oates said.

"I don't know what you mean," Milo said, lying without conviction. "I'm just out trying to keep everyone in their homes like Kyler asked."

"Please," Oates said. "Lying to me? Like I wouldn't know? I invented it."

Milo glanced back and forth between Kyler in the rearview mirror and Oates beside him. Oates' face displayed no emotion. Kyler looked increasingly excited, like a lion in a cage before feeding time. A metallic click sounded from the back seat. Milo had been a law enforcement officer long enough to recognize a pistol's safety switching off.

"You been working with little Scottie and dear Allison," Oates said. "I know the whole plan. You really think you had a chance? Look around. I control the whole town. No one moves unless I let them."

Oates snapped his fingers and the trunk of Milo's cruiser opened up. "How'd you ever think you'd succeed?"

Milo passed the point of being afraid. He accepted the liberating fact that he wasn't leaving the car alive. No point hitting the exit door listening to this condescending abuse. He turned his head and looked Oates in the eye. Terror welled up within him under Oates' penetrating stare. Milo beat it back down.

"Not making it to the vault isn't failure," Milo said, his tone as sharp as a razor. "My sworn duty was to try. I protect people from evil."

"You suck at it," Kyler said. He reached forward and yanked Milo back in his seat by the neck.

Kyler's 9mm barked twice. Two bullets ripped through the front seat of the cruiser and hit Milo along his spine. The impact tore him out of Kyler's grip. His head struck the steering wheel hard, and his body went still. Blood ran from the corner of his mouth.

Then Oates vanished and reappeared in the front seat of the truck. Kyler stepped out of the cruiser. He lined up an insurance shot at the back of Milo's head. The passenger window of the truck rolled down. Kyler looked up at Oates.

"Get the Portal," Oates commanded. "Then we go straight back to the ladies. Our schedule is getting tight."

Kyler knew not to waste a second when Oates gave an order. He holstered his pistol and went to the cruiser's open trunk. He assumed the Portal was the big round thing wrapped in a sheet.

He flipped it up on its side, slid the linen wrapping down, and exposed the glossy cherry surface with the intricate gold inlays. He grabbed it.

His fingers didn't touch the Portal so much as they entered it, passing just below the surface as they dipped into something soft and immensely discomforting. The Portal swirled around his fingertips like a living thing.

"What the hell?" Kyler thought that after a near lifetime with Oates, he'd run out of fear. He was wrong. The sensation of touching the Portal scared the shit out of him. He dropped it back into the trunk.

He pulled the linen back over the artifact, then grabbed its sides. The insulation helped, but the thing still seemed to radiate an unnerving kind of…void. He lifted it. It was heavy, but he could handle it. He walked it over to the truck and pushed it into the back bed, and slammed the tailgate.

That was the last piece of Oates' Stone Harbor puzzle. Oates' power would soon be unlimited and his dominion over the Earth would be complete.

The suspense was killing Kyler. He couldn't wait.

CHAPTER FIFTY-ONE

Scott turned the corner and slammed on the brakes.

Milo's cruiser was stopped up ahead in the middle of the street, cut off by Kyler's black pickup. Kyler stood next to the driver's door, leaning in the window. It was probably the only reason he hadn't seen Scott arrive.

Scott backed up and out of sight between two other trucks. In the narrow view between them, he watched Kyler get into the police car's back seat. It looked like there was a third person in the car, and that would have to be Oates.

The Portal is still in the trunk, he thought. *If they don't find it—*

On its own, the cruiser's trunk popped open. The linen-wrapped Portal stood out like a full moon against the black trunk interior.

"Son of a bitch," Scott said.

Two gunshots rang out from inside the car. Scott's stomach sank to below his knees.

"No, no, no," he whispered in horror. "Not now." He slammed a hand against the steering wheel.

Milo's head wasn't visible above the cruiser's seat anymore. Kyler got out of the car, smiling. He pointed a pistol at Milo. The truck window rolled down, and Oates barked an order to Kyler. Kyler went to the rear of the cruiser, fumbled with the Portal a bit, then lifted it out and put it in the back of his truck.

Scott curbed his growing panic and dread, and tried to think through his situation. Allie was trapped in the church. Milo was dead. Animals were running wild. Kyler had the Portal, which meant that a coven of witches was about to open a passage to Hell, protected by a gang of psychos. His first thought was to drive up to the O'Reilly place and somehow bring all that to a screeching halt. Of course he'd be doing that alone with information based on his interpretation of a three-hundred-year-old scroll.

He needed a Plan B.

He realized his father had already thought this scenario through. Gary Tackett knew Oates would return someday, and when Oates did, he'd have to keep Oates separated from the Portal. Using the Summoner to lure Oates into the demon's trap was his father's Plan B.

Scott spun the truck around and headed into town down another road. His father had committed murder and become beholden to Satan, but was ready with a double cross, a trap for Satan that no doubt wouldn't hold forever, and would cost his father his life when it finally gave way.

He wished his father had shared something about this with him, given him some insight; more important, given him some warning about the dangerous future Stone Harbor had. Was his father sure about this demon's trap, or was the description in the store just some myth he'd transcribed?

Scott was about to bet on it working. Because once the Summoner delivered Oates, Scott really wanted something between him and the power of Satan.

CHAPTER FIFTY-TWO

Oates sat in the passenger seat as Kyler steered the Dodge Ram into the O'Reillys' driveway.

"Unload the Portal and place it next door by the cross," Oates said. "I'll get the ladies."

Assault rifles crackled off in the distance. Kyler looked in that direction, then down toward the smoke rising from the marina.

"Things are coming unhinged around town, sir," he said. He was sure he was understating what was actually happening. He'd left psychos armed with automatic weapons unsupervised for the better part of a day. He was surprised that the town was still standing. "You want me to take care of the crew?"

"They're immaterial," Oates said. "Let 'em have their last bit of fun. Little Scottie, however, is another story. He could slow things up, and time is of the essence. You'll need to find and kill him now."

Oates got out of the truck and entered the house. Kyler thought Oates' request was a little odd. Not the intent, of course. Oates ordered people killed all the time. He just never asked for it that way. There was always a euphemism, a clever turn of phrase, an obvious innuendo. But here, Oates had been blunt and specific. *Kill him now.*

Kyler went around to the back of the truck and slid out the Portal, making sure the linen cloth still covered it. He carried it to the charred remnants of the Greene house. In the back yard, Kyler found the inverted cross in the ground. It was made of steel tubing and was about four feet tall. He placed the Portal near the base of the cross, sliding it out of the linen wrapping without touching it. He wadded up the sheet and tossed it behind him. A breeze sent it rolling off to the edge of the yard. It looked like it was trying to escape.

He walked back to the truck. As he did, he passed Camille and the other four witches. Camille looked him up and down, smiling. Each of the witches did the same, giving their hips an extra swing as they passed. The last in line gave him a slow wink along with her smile.

Five women, irresistibly attractive, and completely poison. And they all knew it. Oates ordered no touching, but Kyler had a feeling that even without Oates' inevitable retribution, those women always made short work of any man who crossed their paths.

Oates was the last one out of the house, following the coven to the steel cross and the Portal.

"What about the woman with Scott?" Kyler said.

Oates did not reply. He just stared straight ahead, focused on the five, apparently lost in the moment. If Kyler hadn't known better, he'd have sworn he sensed some glee in the perpetually emotionless face of Mr. Joey Oates.

CHAPTER FIFTY-THREE

The thirty minutes since Milo and Scott had left seemed like hours to Allie. It was less than fifteen minutes to the bank and back. Her mangled arm felt like it was stuck in a bonfire.

She lay across the front pew in the church. She clutched her right arm close to her body. Blood ran through her fingers from where the attacking dog had mauled her arm. Tears ran down her cheeks. She shuddered and feared that shock's onset was moments away. She couldn't let that happen.

She stumbled back to the sacristy and found a red stole worn on certain high holy days. The long, thin cloth would have to do.

One at a time, she pulled her fingers away, like a window drape sliding open. She raised her left palm. The dog had done her some serious damage. Some flesh was missing and it looked like Allie's hand was the only thing holding another chunk of it in place.

"Aw, hell."

As best she could with one hand, she wound the stole around her forearm. With one end in her teeth and one in her left hand, she tied the makeshift bandage tight. The pressure sent the pain level from excruciating to unbearable, but it kept the remnants of her shredded flesh in place. And the blood flow seemed to slow to a trickle. She walked down a side aisle and back to the rear pew.

With the problem of bleeding to death at least minimized, she refocused on the missing Scottie and Milo.

There could be a hundred reasons they could be a little late, she thought.

But every one of those reasons was bad news.

Allie picked up the police walkie-talkie. She held a finger over the transmit button.

Radio silence was the plan all along. Not hearing from them didn't mean anything bad happened. Maybe not hearing from them was good news.

Just a quick shout, one 'Milo?' No one would even hear it if they weren't listening at that very second.

But what if someone was? What if that tipped their hand, and they hadn't locked the Portal away yet? Oates and his crew might get to them before they got to the vault.

I'll use the code, Allie thought. *I'll key the mike twice and not say anything. He'll key back three times and then I'll know that he's all right.*

Before she could talk herself out of it, she picked up the radio, and keyed the mike twice. Two loud bursts of static filled the church.

Seconds passed. No response.

Rationalization took over. *Maybe he left the radio in the cruiser when he went into the bank. Maybe he's in the vault right now.* She couldn't convince herself. A bad feeling took up residence in the pit of her stomach.

Allie leaned back into the corner of the pew and closed her eyes. She raised her throbbing arm and propped it along the backrest. The elevation eased the pain. She was kind of glad that the binding around it was red, so she could stay unaware of how much blood might be seeping though. Climbing the steeple stairs for the relatively safer bell tower was out of the question.

"Dear Allison!"

The gravelly voice rolled across the pews from the front of the church. Allie opened her eyes. Oates sat on the altar, looking just as Scott had described him, feet dangling like a little kid. His all-black outfit, so similar to Reverend Snow's clerical garb, added to his abominable disrespect of the sacred location. But any anger Oates kindled in Allie paled in comparison to the sheer terror his presence inspired, some instinctual fear, surfaced from some deep primal level.

"Long time, no see," Oates said.

"We've never met."

"Only in last night's nightmare," Oates said. "But we've done business. You can feel it. That special connection."

She could. The man seethed with malevolence; it came off him in palpable, powerful waves. But that familiarity she felt scared her the most, an association with something repugnant.

"How can you be here," she said. "In this house of God?"

Oates laughed a guttural, mirthless chuckle. "House of God? All houses are houses of man. Man deludes himself into thinking he can sanctify something."

He hopped off the altar and disappeared before he hit the ground. He reappeared in the aisle beside Allie. Startled, she stood and stepped back.

The fire in her arm reignited. Oates' irises flickered red. The stench of sulfur and charred, rotten meat filled the air. She flashed back to the same smell in her nightmare last night. Oates pointed over his shoulder at the broken cross on the floor.

"I had the rev killed, right here, in his own church, strung up on his own replica of his false prophet's destruction. This place ain't nothing special."

Maybe the searing pain in her arm made her apathetic, maybe it was her resignation that she wasn't getting out of the church alive, maybe she thought she needed to buy Scottie and Milo more time. Bravery bubbled up inside her. "Whatever you want, I won't help you."

"You already agreed to," Oates said. He feigned offense. "Have you forgotten our deal?"

He snapped his fingers and a table-sized hologram began to run between them. Allie's bravado evaporated. She recognized the scene.

Her silver Jaguar raced up Topanga Canyon Road north of LA. The headlights sliced the night like a set of knives. The car headed into a curve, well over the posted speed limit and straight for the guard rail. At the last second, the wheels yanked left. Tires squealed and the car jerked back to hug the double yellow centerline.

"I'll set the stage," Oates said. "Rushing home after a long day at the studio. Little too tired, little too fast. Coming down off some uppers. Up around the corner we go and…."

Allie's heart sank. She'd seen it before, once live, and a thousand times after in her nightmares. The Dark Thing.

In the hologram, a little girl in pajamas stood by the mailbox at the side of the road. An unmailed letter glowed in her hand against the darkness. Later the investigators would find it in the canyon below, the address to *Santa, North Pole* done in crayon.

The approaching Jag cut the corner too sharp. Tires hit gravel and lost traction.

The view switched to through the windshield. Out of the blackness materialized the girl, on tiptoes, mailbox door open, letter held overhead. She turned into the headlights. She squinted and her soft face, still perfect as a porcelain doll's, registered confusion, then panic. She screamed as the Jag's bumper cut her off at the knees. The mailbox snapped off, flew over the fender, and off into the yard. The girl rolled up over the hood. Her head hit the windshield with a sickening crack before she sailed over the roof and down the car's rear.

The scene cut back to the exterior. The Jag screeched to a halt. The little girl lay on the side of the road, still as stagnant water. Oates snapped his fingers and the scene paused.

Allie's lips pursed. Her lower jaw started to tremble.

"Now, dear Allison," Oates asked, "did you help that poor girl you ran down? Did you call 911? Refresh *my* memory. Your first thought was about…let me see…."

Tears streamed from Allie's closed eyes. "How it would ruin my career," she whimpered.

Oates snapped his fingers again. In the hologram, the Jag's brake lights winked out, and the car fled the scene in a cloud of dust. The hologram vanished.

"Yes, of course," Oates said, affecting enlightenment. "You asked that you not be caught, I made your wish come true, and so we made our little deal. Ah, Los Angeles. Always easy pickings. So you've already signed your soul away to me." The red flicker in Oates' eyes danced brighter. "True nature shows itself under stress, and yours is selfishness. Don't deny it, don't be ashamed. I applaud it. Humans reject their nature and miss all the fun."

Allie's eyes focused on Oates like a laser. Despite the pain in her arm, the tears stopped.

"That's not who I am anymore, you bastard," she said. "That was a mistake. I snorted my way into rehab trying to forget that moment, that weakness. It cost me my career and nearly my life. I'm sorry and I've suffered for that sin."

Oates laughed.

"Sorrow and penance?" he said. "Two separate things. Only one delivers forgiveness. You have only sorrow. Your soul is still firmly mine. And you have a role to play in opening the Portal."

Allie answered without hesitation. "Not in a million years."

Oates grasped the air and twisted it. A horrible snapping and tearing sound came from Allie's good arm. The jagged white bone of her ulna tore through her skin in a compound fracture. Pain ripped through her like a lightning bolt. She collapsed into the pew with a piercing scream.

Oates stepped over next to her and bent down, his face inches from Allie's. His breath smelled of decay and blew hot as the air from an open oven door.

"I can take you anytime, any way that I choose," he said. "Sure you want to do this the hard way, one bone at a time?"

The excruciating pain nearly blotted her senses. She gritted her teeth. Better to die, no matter how horribly. "Do it."

"Your call," Oates said. "But first I'm gonna raise the stakes. The guy who did his handiwork on your pal the rev? He's itching to get started on your boyfriend, little Scottie. And Scott'll last much longer than that old man did. He'll be a lot more fun."

A vision of Scott peeled alive like the reverend flashed through her mind. She couldn't let that happen. And if she agreed, he'd still be free, free to try and stop what Oates had in motion.

"I'll do it," she managed to whisper.

"Wonderful."

Oates waved a hand over her. Her right arm returned to normal. Then from underneath her makeshift bandage, her left repaired itself as well.

"What black magic does, black magic can undo. Opening the Portal requires all volunteers, though I don't lose points for coercion." Oates reached down and touched her forehead. His fingers felt reptilian-cold. "And off we go."

They both disappeared and left the church empty.

CHAPTER FIFTY-FOUR

They reappeared in the bedroom of a house. Oates stood next to her. It took a second for Allie to orient herself. She looked at the floor, gasped and stepped back.

Ben and Carole O'Reilly were sprawled on the floor. The woman had two gaping holes in her chest and lay in a puddle of dried blood. Beside her, her husband's dead face was frozen in a rictus of agony. His glasses sat on the floor, lenses down and arms up like a dead insect. In one hand, he held an open amber pill bottle. Little blue capsules lay scattered on the carpet by the white lid.

"She's the one?" someone said behind her.

Allie spun around. A lean, scary man stood tall against the closed bedroom door. He gripped an automatic rifle in one hand. He looked utterly cold, like a statue, unfazed by two corpses at his feet or by the instant appearance of Satan and a stranger.

"Poetic justice," Oates said. "You'd be surprised how few of the truly damned I have to pick from in this town. Kyler, you keep her here, alive and unharmed, 'til I call."

"Yes, sir."

Oates disappeared. Allie backed away from Kyler and the dead. Kyler studied the fear and revulsion on her face and cracked a small smile. He pointed at Ben's corpse.

"He saved me two rounds," Kyler said. "Funny as hell, really. I shot the wife, and before I could finish him, he grabbed his heart and dropped to his knees." Kyler laughed. "He goes fiddling for his pills to save his life, like I'm not about to kill him anyway."

Allie backed against the window and averted her eyes from the O'Reillys. She sized up Kyler. He looked all business and all psycho. A bad combination. She glanced out the bedroom window. The old Rogers farmhouse stood in the distance. She'd been away awhile, but she knew where she was. Right near where all this started in 1720.

"It's going to happen here, isn't it?" she asked.

"And you'll have a front-row seat. Won't miss a thing."

"Why does he need me here? He has his coven complete."

"He didn't tell you? You volunteered without knowing? Wow. Well, it takes more than just the witches. They open the Portal, but he's got to wedge something in there to keep it open."

"Which is?"

"A little human sacrifice. One beating heart of the damned." He pointed his rifle at her chest. "Like that blackened one in there. He'll rip it from your chest and then he can keep you living and it beating as long as he wants. I've seen him do it."

"No, that can't be. The witches before—"

"Never got that far. And five little girls, naïve as they were, wouldn't accept the human sacrifice of one of the townspeople as part of the deal. It was going to be Oates' surprise."

And now it's mine, Allie thought.

How few of the damned I have to choose from. That's what Oates had said. Probably true. People here weren't perfect but she doubted that many of them rated eternal damnation. She could be the only one, or at least the only one Oates could get in time. Without her, the Portal would slam shut again. She could end this. She just needed to be dead.

The guy with the rifle hit every note on the sociopath scale, but no matter what she did to provoke him, he wouldn't kill her. Oates had specifically denied him the pleasure, and he hadn't gained so much of Oates' trust by marching to the beat of his own drummer. Dying would have to be her do-it-herself project.

Her eyes darted around the bedroom. There wasn't so much as a pair of scissors. Her mind raced through options. A leap out the first-story window wouldn't even sprain an ankle. There might be razor blades in the attached bathroom. Kyler would let her pee herself before he left her alone in there. Electrical outlets along the wall. No power. And besides, she'd been shocked by those before and they barely made her heart flutter.

Heart flutter! She looked at the blue capsules on the floor, then sharply away so she didn't telegraph her thoughts. She knew one of those was dangerous to take with a healthy heart. A handful ought to be damn near fatal. And that was the organ Oates needed. If she could get a few of those down, she'd be dead before the ceremony even began.

Kyler cocked his head, as if hearing something far away. He nodded. "Let's go. Showtime."

Dammit. Just when I had a plan... she thought.

He stepped aside and opened the bedroom door. He motioned her out with the rifle barrel.

One last chance came to her. She'd been nominated for a Daytime Emmy once. Time to see if she still had it. She blocked the scene in her head. She sketched her character, terrified bimbo actress. Action!

She stepped toward him, across the corpses on the floor. She dug the toe of her shoe under the woman's wrist. She feigned alarm and fell forward, across the pills on the floor. One hand skated across the pool of dried blood. She shrieked like a little girl.

"Get the hell up!" Kyler said. "Now."

She raised herself up with one hand and scooped up a handful of pills with her other. Kyler tugged at her shoulder and pushed her down the hallway.

He hadn't noticed a thing. All those acting classes finally did something good.

She couldn't just shove the pills in her mouth and swallow. Kyler struck her as the type who had tricks to get her vomiting in a hurry. She'd have to wait, find a time when no one was looking. She'd make sure the heart Oates prized so much became worthless.

CHAPTER FIFTY-FIVE

Scott raced his truck through the deserted downtown streets. He blew through the stop sign on Main, spun the wheel and jerked his truck to a stop on the sidewalk right in front of his store. Out of the truck and halfway to the door, he realized he didn't have the keys.

He whirled around and pulled the heavy, pagoda-like metal top off the town litter can by the curb, one of the civic projects he'd voted *yea* on what seemed like a century ago. He hauled back and launched it at the hardware store's front door. It crashed through the glass and sailed into a display case, providing a little more collateral damage.

Scott dashed through the broken door. His feet slipped on the nuggets of broken glass that carpeted the polished wood floor. He skidded around to the back of the counter, and down to his knees. He slid the Summoner out from underneath, then fished around for the notes on satanic lore. He put both on the counter.

This is my father's plan, he thought. *I'm still following in his footsteps.*

But his father had never thought Scott would track these particular footprints, since he'd never shared his supernatural knowledge with his son. Gary Tackett hoped his secret sin and all its aftermath would die with him. No such luck.

Scott ran down the paint aisle and returned shaking a clattering spray can of red. He grabbed the diagram of the demon's trap and began to spray a copy of it onto the floor. The can kept clogging and Scott performed a mad combination of shaking and spraying to finish the circle and the collection of odd symbols around it. When he was done, he tossed the can down an aisle.

He turned to the counter and placed his hands in the handprint indentations. To his surprise, the disk stuck to his palms, and became feather-light. He stepped around so his back faced the shattered door and held the disk before him like a book. He read the inscription along the edge three times.

A swirling hologram appeared before him, just like the one Oates cast on the dock that night before. But this one had Oates center stage. Scott recognized the old Rogers farmhouse in the background and knew where Oates was. Oates looked confused at first. Then he looked straight at Scott through whatever wormhole this thing created.

"Looks like you found Daddy's toy," Oates said. "Gotta be careful. That's for ages eight and up."

Scott worked to tamp down the terror he felt. Even with Oates miles away, just talking with him made his skin crawl. "I'm doing okay so far."

Oates stepped closer. His face filled the hologram, which made his head about five feet tall. His eyes flickered red. "Put that down before you hurt someone. Or someone hurts you."

"Am I interrupting something? You look upset."

"You haven't seen me upset. Yet. Put that thing away."

"Why don't you make me?"

That little barb slipped out before he knew it. Oates' eyes narrowed. He'd just seriously poked the caged tiger with a stick. Scott bit the inside of his cheek to keep from looking terrified.

Oates disappeared.

The air suddenly felt supercharged with electricity. Scott's stomach fell. It was about to hit the fan.

Oates appeared in front of him. Evil oozed from him like weeping pus. Scott fought the rising fright within him. He held the Summoner in front of him like a shield, though he was certain it had no such function.

"You wanted a conversation?" Oates demanded.

Scott checked the floor. Oates stood dead center of the demon's trap. He breathed a sigh of relief and managed a tiny smile.

"We'll have plenty of time for one now," Scott said.

Oates raised an eyebrow, then looked around the floor at the fuzzy red circle and runes that surrounded him. The fury in his face turned to fear.

"A demon's trap?"

"Just for you. Get comfy."

"Where'd you come up with this idea so quick?"

"Thank my father. He liked to plan ahead."

"So he was plotting a double cross all along. What a world when the Devil can't trust a murderer."

The descriptor rankled Scott. "The two of us still managed to ruin your ceremony. You're not leaving here."

Oates raised his palms to his cheeks. His look shifted to mock terror. "Trapped forever. What ever will I do?" He took two sidesteps to his left, and out of the red painted circle. "Hmm, maybe I'll do that."

Scott's jaw fell open as he went from supreme to screwed in a split second.

"Demon's trap," Oates said. "Little disinformation campaign I dreamed up. Why would you think some squiggly lines would best the power of Lucifer?"

Oates reached for the Summoner. Sparks flew around his fingertips. He recoiled in pain.

"My father added a little something to your design," Scott said. "It's off-limits to you." Desperate, Scott bet the long shot, and raised the Summoner. "I'll still use this to keep you here, all day and night. I made no deal with you. You can't do anything to stop me."

"Well, you're right there," Oates said. He pointed behind Scott. "But he can."

Scott turned in time to see a mottled gray dog, white teeth bared, in mid-leap for his throat. He raised the Summoner in defense, but too late. It only deflected the dog. The bite that targeted Scott's neck hit his shoulder. Teeth sank into his flesh like a set of steel spikes. He howled. The Summoner rolled away as he whirled under the dog's impact. He grabbed the dog by the neck with one hand and squeezed. Its jaws released. The dog dropped to the ground on its side.

Blood poured from his shoulder. He pressed a hand against it to stanch the flow.

The dog rolled to its feet and sprang at him again, this time lower. Head lowered, it rammed Scott in the stomach. He wheezed, fell backward, and slammed onto the floor. The back of his head hit the sales counter. He saw stars. The dog snarled and pounced on his chest to deliver the killing bite it had intended from the start.

"No, no," Oates said.

The dog paused. It rumbled a low, frustrated growl.

"Now he's earned something special," Oates said. "He gets to live and watch the world go up in flames." He pointed at the Summoner. "Throw that thing in the harbor."

The dog looked genuinely disappointed. It jumped off Scott's chest, grabbed the Summoner between its teeth, and trotted out through the front door's empty frame.

"I'll find another way to stop you," Scott said.

"Little Scottie," Oates said, laughing. "You don't even know what you don't know. You got no cards in this game. I've had a full house all along, while you got a pair of twos. Your team is really my team. Your supposed-saintly father's soul was mine, and you never knew it. So's dear Allison's, and she's waiting to help me open the Portal wide."

Scott's blood chilled at the thought of Allie being enslaved to Oates. It couldn't be. Not his Allie Cat.

"You're lying," Scott said.

"You know by now, I never lie." Oates laughed. "You still think she's some innocent high school girl? She spent years in Hollywood. I own that town. She got into dirt that never made the news, dirt you'd never forgive. My kind of dirt. Between her and your father, you got a knack for loving the damned. That's why before this day ends, you'll become one as well."

Oates disappeared.

At the mention of Allie, Scott's adrenaline had surged. He grabbed the edge of the counter and pulled himself up. His plan had been a colossal failure, and Oates had somehow dragged Allie deeper into this nightmare.

Could what he had said be true? Could Allie have somehow made a deal with the Devil? He couldn't imagine it. Then, he couldn't imagine his father doing it, either, and every bit of evidence said he had. And he sure didn't like Oates' certainty that Scott would do the same thing himself.

He didn't have time to sort all that out. In the image he'd seen through the Summoner, he did confirm that the Portal was near the Rogers farmhouse, which made sense since that was where the 1720 witches had tried to open it before. Milo was dead, and that left no one else in the know about the situation, no one else to help shut it down, and if Oates wasn't lying, no one to get Allie out of harm's way. No one but Scott.

He rose and went to the first aid kit he kept behind the counter. He slapped a big bandage over the dog bite to slow the bleeding. The pain added another voice to the chorus that already sang from the punctures in his back.

He staggered down the tools aisle. At the garden section, he tucked a bush machete into his belt and picked up a hatchet. He'd literally be taking a knife to a gunfight going up there. Maybe if he could catch Oates' men off guard....

He knew he was kidding himself. He felt like some foolish Rambo-wannabe with his semi-deadly lawn tools. He didn't stand a chance.

He also didn't have a choice.

He looked out the front window. The street was empty. Even the dog was gone. Scott made his way to his truck, fired it up, and headed for the Rogers' farmhouse.

CHAPTER FIFTY-SIX

To Camille's relief, Oates reappeared in the backyard. His odd discussion with someone in a hologram, and then his abrupt departure, had made her very nervous. Their window for success was so narrow. If the witches didn't get started soon…but she certainly wasn't about to question Oates about his planning.

Oates entered the house and returned with a thin dark-haired woman in tow by the elbow. The woman reminded her of one of the characters from the *Malibu Beach* TV show. Blood coated both arms, but she did not appear to be injured. She looked like she'd been through the wringer, and much worse for the wear. Oates yanked her to a stop a few yards from the inverted cross and forced her down on her knees.

Kyler stepped out of the house and stood beside Camille.

"What is she here for?" Camille whispered.

"Another part of the ceremony," Kyler said.

"What other part?" A sense of unease seeped into her.

"Kyler," Oates called. "Tackett's a busted-up mess over in the hardware store. Get him. Bring him here to watch the show."

Kyler nodded and left.

"Begin," Oates said to Camille.

She'd expected something a bit more dramatic to start the ceremony she'd awaited for almost a decade. Camille took a deep breath and set out alone for the inverted cross. She carried the goat's head walking stick in one hand. The rest of the coven stayed back. Once there, she paced out six and a half feet into the backyard's scorched grass, the distance she'd practiced for the last eight years. With the cross as a center point, she scraped a circle into the ground with the walking stick. Half of it traced across the burned house's charred concrete pad. Only with the Greenes' house leveled could the circle be completed. She added the familiar twin triangles inside the circle.

Oates joined her at the inverted cross. Camille picked up the Portal. When it touched her hands, the inlaid gold acquired a soft glow, as if backlit by a bright light. The carvings of each creature in the corner gained detail. Oates extended a hand and the inverted cross began to hum. Camille hoisted up the Portal and placed it on the vertical tip of the inverted cross. It defied physics and balanced perfectly. Oates retreated well outside the circle and watched the coven proceed.

Each of the other witches took their practiced places on the diagram and faced the inverted cross. Camille took her position and completed the circle. They all closed their eyes and extended their hands out to their sides. The width of the circle left a foot-wide gap between their fingertips.

Camille watched the always-impassive Oates transform into a man consumed by emotion. A maniacal grin stretched across his round face and his eyes danced like twin wildfires. Camille had waited eight long years for today. Oates had waited three hundred and, even to an immortal, that had to be a long time. Camille swelled with pride, ready to unlock the door for the rest of his followers.

Camille began the memorized incantation. In a deep bass Latin, she called on the powers of darkness to work through her and deliver the Earth to its rightful ruler, the angel Lucifer.

On cue, all four others joined in her chant. With each repetition their voices grew louder, stronger. The Portal glowed brighter. The carvings of the demons in each corner, the guardians that would rise to protect the open portal, began to move, swinging heads and tails in time with the rhythmic incantation. Storm clouds blossomed in the blue sky, black roses that spread until they grew together into a cobalt and charcoal mass. Sunlight died, and dusk enveloped the island. The clouds began to spin counterclockwise, like a windless hurricane, with the eye centered over the chanting witches.

Camille writhed in ecstasy, consumed with an electric joy. Her black hair swayed across her back. Her visions of a future ruling the underworld with Lucifer were coming true. She would finally be complete. She would love and be loved as never before with a penitent world at her feet to serve her. She began the second spell.

Her second invocation described her pure, inviolate body as a worthy vessel of the true offering, her soul. That soul that could power the conduit between the worlds that God had so wrongly separated.

The other four began to repeat the new incantation. Wisps of swirling light emanated from each witch. From fingertip to fingertip, the light stretched out until it joined the five in a complete circle of power and flesh.

A swaying strand of light emerged from each witch's chest like a charmed snake. It slithered out through the air toward the inverted cross at the circle's center. In sync, all five beams reached the glowing Portal. The women's heads jerked back hard, widened eyes trained up at the churning charcoal sky, but their chanting continued uninterrupted. Camille felt her mind float free while her body continued the ritual.

The Portal flared brighter, and lit the witches' faces like a spotlight. The heads of each demon rose out of the Portal's face, now three-dimensional and in full color. Each grew as it swayed in beat with the rhythmic prayers. The heads grew closer to full size as the beasts readied to cross over into the mortal world.

Blood gushed from between the witches' legs, five torrents that soaked the ground around their feet. But the puddles retracted into the design Camille had etched on the ground, lines that absorbed the blood and turned cardinal red, a red that then crept out around the circle and across the triangles, until the entire symbol glowed.

The witches' skin went gray and shriveled tight to their bones. Camille felt no pain and did not despair over the withering husk. Joined with her master, Lucifer, she'd need no such thing in their new kingdom.

A sudden, disorienting ripple passed through Camille's consciousness. Then followed a crushing wave of weakness. Her dying body continued the ritual, but her soul was draining away like an unclogged sink, swirling down into the Portal.

Confusion rose within her. This wasn't what Oates had promised. He'd pledged that they would be together forever, that opening the Portal would join them as one. But she and the other girls weren't opening the Portal at all. The Portal was drawing their souls from them, and opening itself. They were not the Portal's masters. They were its slaves. When the process was complete, her body would be dust, her soul consumed. There'd be nothing left of her at all.

Camille went blind with rage. Oates had used and deceived her, no different from all the others before him, another lying foster parent. She struggled to stay in this world, to hold on to all that moments ago she was so eager to abandon.

But the Portal's riptide was too strong. The rest of her was pulled away in the slipstream of her departing soul. The Portal pulled Camille farther and farther away from the shore of consciousness. The Portal drew her deeper into its abyss, and the light of the rest of existence shrank to a dimming sliver on the retreating horizon.

CHAPTER FIFTY-SEVEN

Kyler braked his truck to a stop across the street from the hardware store. Oates had really done a number on the place. The shattered front door hung loose on one hinge. The interior was dark. He didn't like that much, but the chickenshit civilian he was hunting would use the darkness to hide long before he'd use it to ambush.

Kyler slid out of his truck with his rifle aimed at the hardware store. A show of force would be plenty to get Tackett to move. Instructions were to bring Tackett back alive. Not that the use of a little force was completely ruled out. How much force kind of depended on Tackett's attitude. Kyler rooted for Tackett to have a bad one. Alive and unharmed were two radically different things.

Kyler walked across the street and onto the sidewalk. Nuggets of glass crunched under his feet as he made a slow approach to the store. He led with the barrel of his rifle and stepped through the empty doorframe.

Displays lay in a jumbled pile to one side and a spray-painted red circle surrounded by runes covered the resultant open floor. It looked like some version of the usual hocus pocus bullshit most of Oates' followers messed around with. Whatever it was, it meant nothing to him. He stepped over one of the runes and into the store. His foot stopped just short of a puddle of blood. He smiled. Wounded prey.

"Tackett!" he shouted. "You've got an audience with Oates. Get your ass out here."

Silence.

"You do not want me to come and get you. I can bring you to him whole or damaged, he doesn't care."

Kyler ripped a burst of bullets into the ceiling and down the main aisle. Acoustic tiles disintegrated into snowy dust. "Get the hell out here!"

Nothing. A few firecrackers like that generally got a scream or a whimper from the future victim. He second-guessed if Tackett was here. But Oates said he was, and Oates had never been wrong.

Kyler's weapons-grade senses, honed by combat, kicked into high gear. Maybe the little jackass *had* set up an ambush, ready to attack him with a trowel or a paint roller. *Bring it on, little man.* He made a wary advance down the aisle, scanning the area over the sights of his rifle.

At the rear of the store, he assessed the stacks of trash cans and snow shovels. Nowhere to hide there. He sidled over to the rear door and threw the deadbolt. No one was going to burst through there once he turned his back. He headed back up another aisle.

This one was empty as well, and as he reentered the foyer, he began to doubt Tackett was here. The Portal had Oates distracted. Oates could be slipping. Kyler swept the remaining aisles, silently, efficiently. He finished, convinced he was alone.

He pointed his rifle down and headed back to his truck. Maybe Tackett had gone home, or to the church. He figured he'd better check somewhere else instead of returning to Oates empty-handed.

He jogged back across the street. He tossed his rifle into the truck's passenger seat and climbed in. He slammed the door. The cold barrel of a pistol jabbed him hard in the back of the head.

"Good to see you, buddy," Milo mimicked. "I was afraid I'd miss seeing you."

Kyler's eyes flicked to the rearview mirror. That stupid kid cop was resurrected and in the back seat. Kyler wasn't as shocked as he was angry. When he left someone for dead, they needed to damn well stay dead. Why did Oates have to interrupt his insurance shot?

"If it isn't the town rent-a-cop," Kyler said. "Somehow back from the beyond. I knew I should have put one in your head for good measure."

"Make a stupid move and you'll know exactly what that feels like." A pair of handcuffs landed on the console beside him. "Put those on, around the steering wheel. You're under arrest."

"That's not going to happen."

"Yeah, a big part of me was hoping it wouldn't."

Kyler cycled through his options. Rifle too bulky and far away. Pistol at an awkward angle in his holster, ditto the knife in his boot. He could jerk left, deflect the gun up with his shoulder. Dudley Do-

Right would shoot and miss. Kyler would have both hands on the gun in a flash, and a split second later he'd have it crammed down the stupid cop's throat.

He barely executed a flinch to the left before a bullet tore through his brain.

* * *

Milo's ears rang from the gunshot in the enclosed truck. What was left of Kyler lay against the steering wheel, a small hole in the back of the head, and a gaping, bloody maw where he used to have eyes and a forehead. He'd always imagined he'd feel awful if he ever took a human life. All he felt was relief. Kyler wasn't quite human.

Milo climbed out of the back seat. His dark blue Kevlar vest showed through the two holes in the back of his shirt. The shooting in the cruiser had thrown Milo against the steering wheel and knocked him unconscious, but his composite savior had kept him very much alive.

He'd revived to find that the Portal, Oates, and Kyler were gone. He returned to the church to warn Scott and Allie but the place was empty. He'd guessed maybe they went to the hardware store. When he hit Main and spied Kyler's truck two blocks up, he took the opportunity to chalk one up for the good guys.

He could only think of one place Scott and Allie might be, the one place he most certainly wished they weren't. The area around the old Rogers farmhouse. Whatever was going to happen with the Portal would be happening near there. He holstered his pistol and jogged down an alley to his parked cruiser.

He paused at the door and took a deep breath. Minutes ago, a roiling mass of threatening dark clouds had replaced the blue afternoon sky, the accretion so thick it blocked the sun. The clouds spun in the shape of a huge evil eye. The eye looked centered right over the Greenes' burned-out house.

The Portal must be opening, Milo thought.

He had to get there fast.

CHAPTER FIFTY-EIGHT

A red beam of light blasted up from the Portal and set the clouds in the sky boiling. Allie had to close her eyes to slits against the bright light only feet away. A force locked her knees in place on the ground, just a foot from the circle the coven formed.

Oates stood in the grass outside the witches' chain. He gazed upon the glowing circle with a look of reverie. The glow of the Portal's beam bathed him in ocher. He stretched out his arms and began to transform. His pudgy body contracted and elongated as his skin darkened to an unnatural crimson. His fingers stretched and narrowed and his fingernails blackened into the sharp claws Allie remembered from her nightmare. His eyes danced in anticipation and he smiled to reveal a mouth full of teeth, tips sharpened like a shark's. Points sprouted from his ears as the lower lobes stretched down and curled, like melting wax. A bony crest swelled on his forehead.

Was he knowingly shedding the Oates persona as no longer necessary? It seemed more like his focus on the ritual consumed him and he simply lost control of the illusion of Oates with which he had been masking himself. Either way, he would open the door to his realm in his true form.

Allie shoved the handful of stolen pills into her mouth. She was about to swallow, and paused.

Scottie would come. White knight rescues were what he did. He wouldn't let this happen. He'd find a way. She had to give him that chance before she killed herself.

She tongued the pills down into her cheeks.

Horrific creatures in the Portal's corners snarled and snapped as they struggled to pull themselves free from its face. The shriveled husks of the witches still stood, their empty skins like dirty clothes pinned to a circular clothesline of blazing alabaster light. They had to be dead, but in some way she could sense they weren't.

Satan turned to face her. "Your time to shine, dear Allison. Greed is a terrible thing to waste. The Portal's open for me to enter, but I need it open long enough for those beneath to escape. Cue your sacrifice."

Satan stepped forward and spoke a short, unintelligible incantation. Then he plunged his red, clawed hand into Allie's chest. She felt like she swallowed the sun. The inside of her chest seared like a steak on a grill. The pain turned the world white. She closed her eyes and screamed in a voice so high it sounded alien.

Satan pulled her heart from her chest. The pain stopped. She waited for death, but it didn't come. She opened her eyes. Satan held her bloody, beating heart in his hand. She could still feel her pulse hammer in her neck, but her heart wasn't there to pump that blood. Satan gave it a squeeze. Allie's chest constricted and she gagged.

"A beating heart of the damned will keep this open forever. Why go down for the party, when I can invite everyone up here? There's a reason God separated your world and the demonic. You're all easy prey."

Satan laughed and faced the Portal. He passed his free hand over her heart and began a second incantation.

Scottie isn't coming to the rescue, she thought. She wasn't some kid in a crappy Mustang on the side of the road. She was an adult on the brink of the end of the world.

Allie tongued the pills she'd stuffed in her cheeks up into her mouth. There had to be over twenty of them. She chewed until she'd pulverized them, then swallowed.

Whatever damage these things were going to do, they'd better do it fast.

★ ★ ★

The closer Scott got to the Greenes' house, the more certain he was that his hunch was correct. The red beam that had started sending the sky into apocalyptic convulsions had to be coming from there. He pulled in behind the house next door, jumped from his truck, and stopped at the edge of the O'Reillys'. He crouched and peered around the corner.

The Greenes' yard glowed like some landing alien spacecraft. Five women he assumed were Oates' witches, or what remained of them, stood in a circle around the glowing Portal. The Portal seemed to hover a few feet off the ground and the wide pulsing red beam at its center was the one lighting the sky afire. Bizarre, radiant creatures, like hideous gargoyles, pulled themselves free from the Portal's corners.

Just inside the circle stood Satan, scaly, sinewy and bright red, hands studded with long black claws, knife-edge teeth pointing from his grinning mouth. In one hand he held what looked like a bloody, beating human heart. His Oates persona must not have been needed anymore. Perhaps he wanted to experience his triumph in his natural form. The sight of the true Devil brought up in him a deep, inner terror, worse than seeing Oates, a universal fear implanted in mankind's subconscious at the dawn of time.

Any fright this scene engendered disappeared when he saw Allie. His hope that Oates had been lying about her having a role to play in this evaporated. Just outside the circle, practically facing him from behind Oates, she knelt in a position so awkward it had to be forced. Blood coated both of her arms and a red circular spot stained her upper left chest. He had to get her out of there.

The weapons he'd brought were useless, even ridiculous. What could he do in the face of this much pure, evil power?

On the ground ahead of him, he saw the bloodstained linen he had used to wrap the Portal. A stanza from the scroll popped into his head:

The Portal's opening can only be blocked
Sealed closed by the blood of descendants of Snow.

Reverend Snow's blood soaked the altar cloth. A million-to-one-shot interpretation of how to shut the Portal sprang into his head. But it was the only shot he had.

Satan thrust the heart into the center of the beam from the open Portal. The beam brightened. The opening spread all the way to the portal's outer edge. The glowing creatures expanded.

The beating heart in Satan's hand slowed. The beam dulled. It retreated from the Portal's edges.

Satan pulled the heart from the stream. It managed a few irregular, feeble beats. He placed his other hand over it. Red light flared from between his cupped palms. He pulled his hand away. The heart beat even slower. He spun around and stomped over to Allie at the circle's edge. He stared down at her in a towering rage.

"What are you doing to this?"

The realization that the heart in Satan's hands was Allie's made Scott's stomach clench.

Allie forced a weak smile to her lips. "Everything I can."

In fury, Satan curled his fingers around her heart and tried to crush it. It stayed solid as stone. He squeezed with both hands. No effect.

"You whore!" he screamed at Allie. "Redemption through the selfless sacrifice."

He snarled in frustration and threw down the heart. Allie collapsed on her back.

Scott saw his chance. He ran for the Portal. He scooped up the bloodstained altar cloth on the run. He passed through the surging white band of power between two of the witches. The charge blasted through his chest like high voltage. His legs went weak. His head reeled. He staggered forward the last two steps. Satan whirled around.

"You?" Satan shouted at Scott. "You'll burn in Hell with me forever!"

Scott squinted against the blinding glare of the beam from the Portal. The ground below and the sky above pulsed a deep red. Contorted arms pulled the misshapen, repulsive creatures from the Portal's face. A gryphon head to his right swiped at him and missed by inches. Scott grabbed an edge of the altar cloth and flapped it out over the Portal.

The blast from the beam should have brushed the altar cloth aside, or the energy set the linen ablaze. But the cloth snapped into a rigid plane, cut the beam like an axe blade, and hovered over the Portal. Above the cloth, the beam disappeared, as if absorbed by the linen. The cloth's dark, splatted bloodstains flashed bright yellow. The swirling magenta clouds above froze in place.

The altar cloth turned flaccid and settled over the underworld creatures like a collapsing parachute. As the cloth touched each one, it howled in pain. Claws made sharp jabs against the linen, pop-up pointed tents that should have rent the cloth to shreds. But the cloth merely stretched like an opaque shrink wrap, then contracted and forced the demon underneath back. The bloodstains flashed again. The four demons went still, and shrank back into the disk. The altar cloth settled over the Portal. The surging beam beneath the Portal cut off. The white energy beams from the witches stopped flowing, and the Portal dropped off the inverted cross. The satanic diagram on the ground went dark.

The five witches collapsed like marionettes with cut strings. Their bodies lay lifeless around the dead circle.

Satan roared and reached for the Portal. His black, clawed fingers touched the altar cloth and blue fire enveloped his hands. He yanked them back. He reached again for the Portal. This time, the flames met him halfway. He recoiled, face twisted in pain. He stared in frustrated fury at the Portal, then down at Scott. He transformed back into Oates, but his pupils stayed red flames.

"This ain't over, not even close," Oates snarled. "The rest of your life? Gonna be nothing but pain."

Oates disappeared.

Scott staggered over to Allie. Her heart lay at her feet, still managing one slow, labored beat each second. Her chest rose and fell in shallow, hitching breaths. Scott knelt beside her. He slipped his hand around to cradle her head. Her hair still felt like silk. Her eyes fluttered open.

"Scottie." She barely managed the whisper. "Did we win?"

"Hands down. Hang on for me, Allie Cat."

He wondered how she could. Her heart lay outside her body. The beats were two seconds apart. Her eyes rolled up into her head. Her skin went from pale to ashy.

A hologram window like the one the Summoner created opened up beside him. Oates' face leered at him from the cockpit of the *Killin' Time* as the boat cut past the breakwater at the harbor entrance. The wheel spun itself a course correction at the empty helm.

"Trouble, little Scottie?"

Scott wished he could reach through the window and strangle the bastard.

"Kind of looks like dear Allison's a goner, huh?"

Scott touched her neck. Rage mixed with sorrow as Allie's pulse faded against his fingertips. He gritted his teeth in frustration.

"I *could* save her," Oates said in an offhand way.

"As if you're God," Scott said. Tears welled in his eyes.

Oates' face darkened. "As if I'd want to be, jackass."

Allie's heart disappeared from the ground and reappeared on her chest, over the red blotch on her left rib cage. Scott pulled his hand from her neck in shock. The heart beat twice.

"Dark magic pulled it out," Oates said, "and dark magic can put it back. It's up to her to keep it beating after that. Or let God intervene. She's his again now, anyway."

The question was out of Scott's mouth before he'd formed the thought. "Your price?" The panicked tone of his voice betrayed that the cost was immaterial.

"Your soul for her life. And you better deal fast, while she's still got one."

Allie's skin lay flaccid and gray. Scott remembered her vibrancy, her warmth, her happiness at finally turning her life around. He felt the ache in his heart and the impending emptiness if he let her, again, leave his life, this time forever.

"You know you're gonna do it." Oates said. "It's in your genes, little Scottie. Like father, like son. Just say we have a deal. Close the inevitable circle. In another second, it'll be too late."

Scott caught his breath at the horrific realization that Oates was indeed right. Whatever dark reason his father had for murder, he'd stood on the edge of this same abyss Oates now offered, and jumped. Scott could do no less for Allie. He looked Oates in his malignant eyes. A *yes* formed on his lips.

"No deal," croaked a voice to his right.

Camille raised herself off the ground. She looked at Allie with eyes shriveled as raisins, suspended in blackened eye sockets. Her once-thick raven hair now framed her face as wispy, frazzled gray curtains. Leaden skin stretched over her bones like desiccated parchment. Not an ounce of muscle or fat remained, yet somehow she crawled across the ground to Allie's side, goat's head staff in her right hand. Each twist of her joints sounded like sandpaper on stone. She touched the staff to the now-dark circle on the ground.

Oates' face screwed up in anger. "Don't cross me, witch. I'll break you in two. I own your soul."

"Your hold is gone." She wheezed gray dust. "Your contract is broken. You lied to us."

Around the Portal, the four wasted witches each reached out a shriveled hand and touched the edge of the circle on the ground. From each, a faint rose-colored pulse cut around the curve. They raced around and simultaneously met where Camille's staff touched the arc. The goat's head glowed. She moved her left hand over Allie's heart.

"You bitch!" Oates screamed.

"What black magic does, only black magic can undo." Camille mumbled an incomprehensible incantation. Red light flashed under Camille's palm and she pushed Allie's heart through her chest. Camille's head sagged, and she rolled to the ground on her back.

The five spurned witches transformed into solid black statues, then collapsed into piles of dust.

Scott scooped Allie up with both arms. He buried his head against her cold, still neck.

"You come back to me, Allie Cat," he whispered. "Losing you once was more than enough."

Her pulse bumped back to life and did a slow beat against his cheek. Her skin warmed. She took a jagged breath so deep she nearly burst from his arms. Scott practically exploded with relief. He checked Allie's arms, her chest. No trace of all the damage she'd been through. He looked up. The vision of Oates was gone.

The clouds above shrank, first in on themselves like tumors in the sky, then contracted to black pinpricks. When they vanished, only a clear cobalt-blue sky remained.

Allie's eyes opened, washed out, weak. A hint of color returned to her face. She raised one hand and patted around her chest. Her brow furrowed in confusion.

"All back in one piece?" she said. "How…?"

"You'll really be happier if I tell you about that later."

A police cruiser came screaming up the road, lights ablaze, Milo at the wheel. Scott's heart skipped a beat at the deputy's apparent resurrection. The car hopped the curb and flew across the Greenes' front yard. It skidded to a stop a few feet from Scott in a spray of grass and earth. Milo jumped out and ran to Scott and Allie's side. He looked down at Allie and grimaced.

"Is she okay?" Milo asked.

"She's alive," Scott said. "And apparently so are you. I saw Kyler shoot you."

"I'm sending Kevlar an endorsement about that." Milo knelt beside Allie. "Let's get you to the clinic."

"The roads?" Scott said.

"Clear. Oates' men are dead. Bewildered dogs are slinking back home. I saw that black speedboat tear-assing out of the harbor so I'm guessing Oates escaped."

"Like cowards always do."

"The coven?" Milo said.

"Uh, gone. I'll explain that one later, if I can. Kyler?"

"Face-down outside your hardware store, I'm afraid."

"Face-down is perfect." Scott turned to Allie. "Let's get you checked out."

Scott helped her over to the cruiser and into the back seat. He sat down beside her and pulled the door shut. Milo climbed into the driver's seat. Allie lay down and rested her head on Scott's thigh. Milo gunned the engine and rocketed them out into the street.

"Whoa!" Scott said. "Slow it down! Don't get us killed now."

Milo flashed a sheepish grin in the mirror and eased off the accelerator. Allie touched Scott's knee.

"I was dead," she whispered. "Really dead. I did it all. The floating out of my body. The bright light. Everything."

Scott had heard the scientific explanations for that kind of experience. Something about oxygen deprivation to the brain and triggered memories. He reached down and massaged her shoulder. "I'm glad it didn't take. Did St. Peter meet you at the gates?"

"No. It was your father."

Scott stopped rubbing her shoulder. "What?"

"He told me it wasn't my time. That I had to return. Then I was back in my body." She paused. "He had a message for you. He said someday you'd understand the deal. That was it. What deal?"

Scott stared out the window as Milo stopped in front of the clinic. The backup generator had kept the lights on inside. A nurse cautiously stuck her head out of the front door. Milo got out.

"Scottie?" Allie said.

"I don't know what he meant," Scott said. He so wished that statement was true.

CHAPTER FIFTY-NINE

Captain Montgomery looked out the front window of the state police cabin cruiser at Stone Harbor as the boat entered the harbor channel. He wasn't sure what to expect.

Since Friday morning, when the returning ferry had delivered a .38 pistol murder weapon from the island for analysis, Montgomery had been trying to raise Scaravelli with disturbing results. All day Saturday, there was no radio or telephone communication with the island, and according to the power company, the island wasn't pulling one volt of juice through the cables under the Sound. He had decided to gather a few troopers, take the police boat over to the island, and see what the hell was going on.

His first view of the town exceeded his worst fears. Several vessels in the harbor looked like victims of explosions, their charred hulls resting in the shallow water near the marina. Smoke rose from the town near the top of the hill. No vehicles moved in the streets.

He raised a pair of binoculars to his eyes and scanned the dock. A beheaded corpse lay across the planks near the end. He made out the unmistakable outline of an M4 on the planks by the body.

He turned on the boat's flashing blue lights, and through the PA told the officers onboard to stand ready for action. He didn't have any idea what they'd be stepping into.

He couldn't know that it was already over.

CHAPTER SIXTY

When Scott brought Allie into the clinic, they were the only people there except an LPN and one of the island EMTs. The combination of armed gunmen, wild dogs, and a pillar of light turning the sky purple was more than enough to keep the rest of the town inside in safety.

Scott shortened the nurse's line of questions and avoided having to explain the inexplicable by just saying Allie was having chest pains. The nurse led them to a corner bed, pulled the fabric divider around them, and after a quick check, said her heart sounded normal. She left to get an EKG for a more detailed diagnosis.

Scott stood by the bed and held Allie's hand, still too cool to the touch for his comfort. "Everything's going to be all right."

"But it shouldn't be," she whispered. "I had my heart ripped out of my chest. I saw it happen."

The clinic outside their little curtained room went berserk. Scott glanced through a slit between the curtains. The casualties of Oates' three-day visit began to arrive. Dog bites. Gunshot wounds. The nurse and EMT went into triage mode.

Allie squeezed Scott's hand. "Whatever you did worked. I knew I could count on my white knight to come through."

Guilt bubbled up inside him. He hadn't saved her at all, and on top of that, he'd been seconds from selling his soul to Satan.

"It wasn't me," Scott said. "The witches did it. At the last second, they double-crossed Oates and used what little power they had left to put your heart back."

"I should be dead anyway. I took enough pills to kill us both, and I saw my heart stop beating in Oates' hands."

"I guess we'll chalk that up to a power higher than the witches'."

She squeezed his hand again and managed a weak smile. "Still, you were there to save me."

And almost threw everything away to do it, he thought, *just like my father.* He couldn't take more of this underserved praise. Their renewed relationship had to have no secrets.

"Allie," Scott said, "when you were laid out on the ground, with your dying heart on your chest, Oates appeared."

"Wait, you told me Camille returned my heart."

"She did, but before that, Oates returned. He offered me a deal. He'd heal you in return for my soul."

Allie closed her eyes. "It's a good thing you had Camille on your side."

"No," he said. "You don't understand. I didn't know she was. I was a split second from saying yes."

Allie opened her eyes again. The edges of her mouth turned down. "Why would you do that?"

Scott held her hand with both of his.

"For all of this," he said. "For the dream I'd always had of you and me and a perfect life together here in Stone Harbor. Because a wonderful lifetime with you was worth whatever miserable eternity purchased it."

"But you didn't take the deal. And you might think you were going to, but in the end you wouldn't. Giving in to evil just isn't in your nature."

His last secret boiled inside him, begging to be told, to admit to his father having killed someone in cold blood, selling out to Oates, and acting as his eyes and ears on Stone Harbor. Shattering Allie's reverential image of the man was all that kept him from blurting it out. Scott wouldn't keep anything about his life a secret from her, but his father's life could be something else. He leaned forward and kissed the top of her head. "You are amazing."

A look of shame crossed her face.

"Hardly," she said. "I was part of that ritual because I'm anything but amazing."

"You aren't responsible for what you were forced to do, especially when it would have killed you."

She looked away. "You know Satan couldn't make me to do anything, couldn't even teleport me, not without leverage."

Oates had said he owned Allie's soul. Scott had dismissed it as a lie. It had to be a lie. If it wasn't, he wasn't sure he wanted to know. He especially didn't want to hear it from her own lips.

"In LA, I was driving home late at night. I was so exhausted. The studio offered me a driver, but I turned them down, didn't want to leave my Jaguar on the lot over the weekend." Tears welled in her eyes. "There was a little girl on the side of the road outside her house. I mean, it was so dark and then all of a sudden she was there."

A tear rolled down her cheek. Scott squeezed her hand for support. She didn't squeeze back.

"I killed her. And then I drove off, praying that somehow I'd get away unseen, that my career wouldn't be ruined. And that prayer got answered by the wrong guy."

She pulled her hand away from Scott's and tucked it up to her chest. She exhaled and her body seemed to shrink inside her clothes.

"He's got my soul. I deserved to die out there."

Scott reached over, grabbed her hand in both of his, and squeezed it tight.

"But you didn't. Your sacrifice of your life to stop Satan earned it back. He said so before he disappeared. Reverend Snow used to preach that the cornerstone of Christianity was forgiveness, that it was available unconditionally. You are alive and whole. I'd say that's a sign of forgiveness."

She turned her pleading eyes to him. Brown and deep and beautiful as they had ever been.

"Do you really think so?"

"Events speak for themselves."

"I hid what I did from you. If you want to walk away now that you know...."

"Allie Cat, there's the person you were ten years ago, who is the same person you are right now. I don't know who the person was in between. But it wasn't you."

A smile flickered across her lips. Color rose in her cheeks.

Down the hall, a fresh flurry of commands echoed as a new batch of injured townspeople entered the clinic. The nurse yelled to have people who weren't bleeding wait outside.

"Let's clear this space for someone who needs it," Scott said. "Feel strong enough to move?"

"Let's find some quiet. Please."

"I know just the spot. It's got a front porch with a view of the stars."

"Does it have a swing?"

"I've been meaning to get one."

"Let's go."

Scott helped Allie up, and led her out the clinic's back door.

CHAPTER SIXTY-ONE

It took two weeks and a rail crash in downtown Baltimore for the media to finally let go of the story of Stone Harbor. The normally reticent townspeople redoubled their efforts to avoid discussing anything with outsiders. The collective duty to the town that made their forefathers suppress the story of the first coven of witches on the island was still deeply ingrained, and the few who knew made no mention of Camille and her coven. The psychotic dogs event also went without acknowledgement, thought that might have been driven more by owners wanting to live in denial.

Scott, Allie, and Milo, the only three who really knew the whole story, were content to let the press create their own fictional cover story. The reporters settled on Scaravelli as the antagonist. The Dickey girl's necklace in his desk tied him to her disappearance and the supposition was that he killed Natalie Olsen as well and framed Carl Krieger for both. The pistol Krieger had supposedly used turned out to be a former NYPD revolver, signed out to and reported lost by Scaravelli years ago. They spun the story that the chief brought Kyler and the gang of thugs onto the island, where they got way out of hand. The justice system bought it. Scaravelli was arrested and sent to the mainland. That left Milo as the de facto chief of police, and no one in town said a word against it.

*　　*　　*

The second Saturday after the aborted ritual, Scott rolled over in bed and found the other half empty. He patted it twice before opening his eyes to confirm that for the first time since Allie moved in last week, she was up and awake before he was.

The clock read 9:10 a.m. That revelation sent a bolt of panic through him until he remembered he'd closed the hardware store today to pour the floor for the new detached garage. Comfortable as the bed was, he needed to get up and get that concrete poured. Sure as sunrise, everyone in town who complained that he'd closed the store on a Saturday would drop by to make sure their minor inconvenience had been for a good cause. Plus, the rented concrete mixer was ready and waiting beside the pile of formers. He rolled out of bed with a groan and headed into the kitchen.

He expected Allie to be there, coffee in hand. The kitchen was empty, the coffeepot still pristine in the machine.

"Allie Cat?"

The silence he got in response sent a sick feeling through his stomach. There were a dozen normal reasons Allie would be out early, but a black feeling of dread blotted all of them out. Something felt very wrong, very empty.

His phone rang from its charger on the kitchen counter. The number was local, but not familiar.

"Hello?"

"Hey, Scottie," said Allie.

Scott sighed with relief. "Jesus, Allie. You scared the crap out of me, waking up to an empty house. Where are you calling from?"

"My new cell phone. I bought it yesterday."

"Welcome back to the twenty-first century. What a pleasant surprise."

"I have an unpleasant one too."

The dread in his gut went back to full boil.

"I'm heading back to California," she said. "The parents of the girl I killed deserve closure. I'm turning myself in to the police."

In anyone else, Scott would have commended such a noble and selfless decision. But the first emotion to flash through him was desolation. The woman he'd lost for ten years was about to be lost again. The last week had exceeded every high school fantasy he'd had about his future life with Allie. Surviving the nightmare Oates spun out across Stone Harbor had strengthened their bond in ways the decade they'd lost never could have. The house was alive again. He felt complete.

"Allie, come home and let's talk this through a bit. That's a big decision out of nowhere."

"It's not out of nowhere. From the moment Oates made me relive that night, I knew this was what I had to do. Black magic or not, it's a miracle I didn't die when Camille plunged my near-dead heart back into my chest. My life wasn't saved just so I could do happily ever after in Stone Harbor with you. I have a debt I need to pay."

That was the Allie he fell in love with over a decade ago, the one who always did what was right, the one who put others before herself. And she was completely right.

"Well, let's spend today together, just you and me."

"I'm already on the ferry, Scottie. I had to wait until now to tell you, because we would have that one last day, and it would be enough to let the selfish part of me convince me to stay."

Scott shook his head at her being right again. "And the selfish part of me would be completely on board with it."

"It's all planned out," she said. "My old agent knows a good lawyer who'll take the case. He thinks the charge will be vehicular manslaughter."

"Damn, Allie Cat. What's the penalty?"

"As little as a year, as much as fifteen. Depends on the judge. Whatever it is, I earned it."

"All right, then we'll do this together. Last time, you were out on the West Coast going through hell by yourself. This time I'll be there to support you."

"No, you won't! You have a life here in Stone Harbor, and you are going to live it. And you need to do something with the Portal, or have you forgotten that?"

The dreaded thing was still in the basement, wrapped in the altar cloth that saved the world.

"But I don't want to live that life without you, Allie. This last week has ruined me for anything else." The next sentence came out before he realized it. "I'll be waiting here for you to come home."

"It might be a long wait."

"I think I've already proven I'm pretty good at waiting for you."

"I'll call you when I land in LA. I love you, Scottie."

"I love you, Allie Cat."

The call ended and Scott just stood there with the phone against his ear, wishing he could back up time just eight hours, and freeze it forever.

CHAPTER SIXTY-TWO

Every muscle in Scott's body ached. He'd hoped that the physical labor would help cover the pain of separation from Allie. He'd been wrong. It just made him tired as well as empty. But he had to finish today, for more reasons than one.

The sun had about an hour of life left before it would kiss the day goodbye at the horizon. He'd worked the formers for the garage's concrete pad all day, squaring and leveling them to perfection. The concrete mix in the spinning mixer was almost ready to pour.

In the dead center of the pad, he'd dug a recess a few feet around and three feet deep. A brick stood on end in the center. He stepped out of the prepared area and switched off the rumbling concrete mixer. The barrel coasted to a stop and silence filled the air. He took a deep breath and headed for the house.

Scott went down to the basement and flicked on the light. Storage boxes lined the unfinished walls. The Portal lay in the center of the concrete floor, still swaddled in the altar cloth. It was as if the evil in the Portal had terrified the boxes and sent them fleeing to the room's far edges. Even at halfway down the stairway, Scott could feel it. Not as strong as when Oates had it opened, not even as strong as when he and Allie had found it in the church crypt. But the Portal still radiated malevolence, like a subsonic thrum that threatened to ramp up to a thundering crescendo at any minute. Scott took the last few steps to the Portal's side like he was walking across late spring ice.

He knelt and grasped the Portal with both hands. The Portal shifted underneath the altar cloth, the same slight deformation he'd felt the first time he'd touched it. Although the altar cloth kept him safe from direct contact with the evil inside, and its ability to draw him in, it still felt unnerving.

He carried it upstairs, out the back door, and into the ocher light of the day's dying sun. He stepped over the formers for the concrete pad, knelt by the deeper hole in the middle, and balanced the Portal on the brick at the hole's bottom. The altar cloth lay over it like a tablecloth. Scott pulled it away like a magician's reveal.

A chill ripped up his spine at the sight of the Portal. Despite all the power that had surged through it, it appeared unchanged from when he'd first seen it in the church. The glossy finish remained unblemished, the inlays still shone, pristine and sharp. The demonic figures around the edge seemed to eye him in silent fury, awaiting the chance to exact revenge for their renewed incarceration.

Scott backpedaled out of the prepared area, eyes still locked on the Portal. Knowing it was inert for the next three hundred years did nothing to dampen the fear the thing engendered. He switched on the concrete mixer. The rolling barrel rumbled to life with a grind of aging, dusty gears. With a flip of his hand, he dropped the discharge chute and aimed it at the Portal's new grave inside the formers. A slurry of concrete rushed down the chute.

The thick gray mass pooled in the bottom of the hole, then rose until it covered the lower half of the Portal. Scott gave the mixer a bump in speed and a surge of slurry subsumed the rest of the Portal. In his mind, Scott imagined the screams of the demon figures, now twice entombed. The concrete bubbled up out of the hole and began to ooze toward the frame of formers. An hour later, by the artificial light of the house security lights, he had a full concrete slab over the Portal's new, and hopefully last, crypt.

He wiped his hands on his pants and scooped the altar cloth up from the ground. He'd decided not to bury the Portal in its power-dampening shroud. In the event it was found later, he didn't want his only defense against it found as well.

The cloth's bloodstains illuminated in the darkness, glowing in that same yellow hue they made when they covered the Portal. Energy danced across his fingertips. He'd assumed the bloodstains' glow that day had been them absorbing the power of the Portal. But now he knew it was the blood channeling the stronger power that subdued the Portal, a power as positive as Oates' was negative.

Everything around him went white. Then a scene coalesced. Scott's heart sank at the familiarity. The setting was the main counter of the hardware store. Scott's father, Gary, stood behind the counter reading an inventory list, in a time before he grew his widower's beard. Oates leaned against a display to the right, inspecting his fingernails, wearing a black turtleneck.

This was the moment his father had sold his soul, and become a murderer.

"You're having some wonderfully dark thoughts," Oates said.

Gary looked up startled. He did a double take to the front door and back. "Who the hell are you?"

"An answer, a solution, a friend. When someone contemplates murder, I like to drop by."

"How would you...." Gary came out from around the counter, baseball bat in hand. "Get out of my store."

Oates snapped his fingers. The bat disappeared. Gary stopped dead in his tracks.

"We can dispense with all the theatrics. You called me, whether you know you did or not. I chose to answer. I think you know who I am. Every living soul can feel it."

Fear crept into Gary's face. Scott knew exactly what he was feeling. He'd felt the same thing, standing in the same place, when Oates first walked into the hardware store on him.

"Mind if I call you Gary?" Oates said. "This kind of transaction does put us on a first-name basis."

"I'll call you Lucifer?" Gary said.

"Most do. I'm good with it. But let's stick with Mr. Oates. Now, you understand what you're about to do is murder," Oates said. "Murder has consequences. In prison, you'll lose all this, and your son."

Gary nodded. "I don't see any other option."

"No one ever does. I'll wipe away the consequences. You'll never be caught, never punished."

"In trade for my soul, I assume?"

Oates laughed. "No, once you kill, I've already got your soul. But while I keep you free, you work for me."

"I'm not killing anyone else."

"Nothing so active is necessary. You're just gonna watch. Something valuable of mine is on the island. If it surfaces, you'll tell me. Simple."

Gary gave Oates a wary look. "And no one, especially my son, will ever know I'm a murderer?"

"You'll die with your name untarnished. All you have you'll leave to him."

This was where Oates skipped ahead in the vision. This time there was no break.

Gary gave his head a slow shake, and bit his lower lip. "I've never supported euthanasia. The church teaches it's wrong. It's illegal. But when it's someone you love…."

"You don't need to rationalize anything to me. I'm the king of anything goes. But if you really think what you're planning to do is fine, don't be so sneaky about it. Just deliver the poison you plan on giving your wife to her doctor and have him administer it. You know he won't."

"She's suffering. The disease is killing her anyway. She'd want me to do it."

"The same way she'd want you to stay out of prison, to watch over her grandchildren when they arrive, to leave both your reputations in this town spotless. I'm here to help." His malignant smile said exactly the opposite.

"I can't bear to see her suffer so," Gary said. "You have a deal. May my son and God forgive me."

The vision disappeared.

A weight lifted from Scott's heart. His father hadn't acted out of malice, killed someone over debt or jealousy or wild rage. He'd eased his mother's suffering, delivered her from the scourge of the disease that was destined to take her anyway. If his father had told Scott, Scott would have approved. Hell, he would have helped him. He knew his mother would have begged him to do it.

And it hadn't earned his father eternal damnation. His spirit had met Allie when she died, turned her back around to come home. However redemption worked, his father had earned it. And his father had promised her that Scott would understand someday. Somehow he'd used whatever connection this altar cloth had to the afterlife to send that message through, this time without Oates' edits.

Scott clutched the cloth against his chest. Tears welled in his eyes as he felt, for the first time in weeks, at peace with his past. And for the first time since the morning, strong enough to face the future, that far distant time when his descendants would have to protect this ground from whatever Satan might send their way.

And there was only one way he wanted to have those descendants.

He knelt down beside the wet concrete. With a nail left over from building the formers, he wrote three words.

Allie and Scott.

AFTERWORD

Big thanks go out to Teresa Robeson for her usual, irreplaceable beta reading of this book. Also thanks to Don D'Auria for his faithful support and insightful editing. My whole career is entirely your fault. Thanks also to the entire Flame Tree team, who make and market some truly beautiful books.

One night in college, I was walking up the staircase to my fifth-floor dorm room. A guy I'd never seen before passed me on the way down. Well-dressed, like he was going out someplace special, he wore a camel's hair coat that had to cost hundreds. He was good-looking, and gave me a friendly smile as he passed.

I've never been so scared in all my life.

There was nothing about him that should have been scary, but his mere presence filled me with an irrational terror that makes me shiver today, decades later. And it wasn't just me. By the time we made it to the fifth floor, the girl I was with was shaking. She'd felt it too. I am firmly convinced that we met Satan in that stairwell.

So that became the core of the Satan you see on these pages, one who walks the Earth in human form, but cannot hide his true self from instant recognition, and deep fear. I gave his story a few twists, stripping him of some of the omnipotence usually attributed to Lucifer. Because seriously, what kind of punishment for an angel's rebellion is being given immense power and dominion over Hell? God has to be much more creative at doling out sentences than that. I hope that you enjoyed this different take.

I've had a lot of people ask me what happens when Allie returns from California. In my stories, time is no match for true love. What do you *think* happens?

Russell James